The caravanmaster's horn blew urgently from the head of the column. Guards pounded up toward the van. "I don't like the look of that," Mom said.

"Neither do I." Dad pulled the pistol from his belt.

A volley of musket fire came from the woods on both sides of the road. The roar was like the end of the world. Wounded men screamed. Dad cried out and stared at his hand. He was only slightly wounded—but the precious pistol went flying.

Another volley boomed. Thick smoke showed where the musketeers hid behind trees and rocks. It smelled like a Fourth of July fireworks display.

"Get the gun!" Dad said urgently. He was opening and closing his right hand, trying to make it work again, while blood dripped from the webbing between his thumb and forefinger.

Annette took two steps toward the pistol. Then a spooked horse bowled her over. She squawked and fell.

"Get the pistol!" Dad said again, and then, "Where the devil did it go?" The horse that had knocked Annette down wasn't the only one going crazy. One of the animals must have kicked it away—in the chaos, who could say where?

And Annette and her mother had no time to search for it. Armed men were running out of the woods. . . .

Tor Books by Harry Turtledove

In High Places

a novel of Crosstime Traffic

Harry Turtledove

TOR®

A Tom Doherty Associates Book

New York

This is a work of fiction. All the characters and events portrayed in this novel are either ficticious or are used fictitiously.

IN HIGH PLACES

Edited by Teresa Nielsen Hayden

A Tor Book
Published by Tom Doherty Associates, LLC
175 Fifth Avenue
New York, NY 10010

www.tor.com

Tor® is a registered trademark of Tom Doherty Associates, LLC.

ISBN-13: 978-0-765-34627-8
ISBN-10: 0-765-34627-3

First Edition: January 2006
First Mass Market Edition: February 2007

Printed in the United States of America

0   9   8   7   6   5   4   3   2   1

In
High Places

One

Wolves howled in the woods south of Paris. The wind wailed through bare-branched oaks and chestnuts and elms. That nasty northwest wind carried the threat of rain, or maybe snow. Winter didn't want to leave in the year of our Lord 2096—or, as it was more widely known in the Kingdom of Versailles, the year 715 of the New Revelation.

Jacques the tailor's son trotted through those woods. He hoped the howls would come no closer. A sheepskin jacket and baggy wool trousers held out the wind. He was bareheaded, and had to pause every few minutes to shake straw-colored hair back from his eyes. At not quite eighteen, his beard was still scanty—more orange fuzz on cheeks and chin and upper lip than a proper man's growth.

When a twig cracked not far away, as if trodden underfoot, he slipped off the track and behind the rough-barked trunk of an old oak. His right hand fell to the hilt of his sword. The leather that wrapped the hilt was smooth from much use. The weapon had belonged to Jacques' father, but he'd been using it for the past three years and more.

Worse things than wolves were liable to lurk in the woods. Scouts from the Berber Kingdom of Berry might be spying out Versailles' defenses. Muslim slave raiders might be on the prowl, too. When they could, they seized believers in the Second Son and sold them in the great markets of Marseille and Madrid and Naples.

A doe stepped out onto the track, not fifty feet upwind of Jacques. He could see her nose twitch as she tested the air. Then a swirl of the breeze must have brought his scent to her. She snorted. Her liquid black eyes widened. With a flirt of the tail, she bounded away.

He didn't break cover. He thought she'd stepped on the twig, but didn't want to take the chance of being wrong. Patience paid. The priests always preached that, and Jacques believed it. People had been patient when God sent the Great Black Deaths, hadn't they? Of course they had, and their patience had been rewarded. After a generation and more of unending disaster, God sent Henri, His Second Son. And, thanks to Henri's prayers, the plagues finally stopped. He'd died a martyr like His older brother Jesus, but He'd saved the world.

At last, Jacques decided no scouts or raiders hunted anywhere close by. "Thank you, Henri," he murmured, and sketched the sign of the wheel on which the Second Son had been broken all those years ago. They followed the New Revelation over in the Germanies, too, but they spun the wheel backwards. Even stupid foreigners like the Germans should have known better than that.

Down the track Jacques went. His rawhide boots thudded on the hard ground. It was packed hard now, anyway. If the wind brought rain instead of snow, everything would turn to mud. Some of the streets in Paris and Versailles were cobblestoned like the ones in the big Berber towns farther south. That showed how modern and up-to-date the Kingdom of Versailles was. The idea of paving a forest track, though, had never crossed Jacques' mind, or anyone else's in the kingdom.

How much farther to the fort? The thought had hardly

crossed his mind before the forest thinned out ahead of him. There it was, on a swell of ground that dominated the view to the south. Like other forts on both sides of the border, it looked like a many-pointed star. The thick earthen ramparts soaked up cannon balls that would have smashed stone or brickwork.

A sentry on the ramparts spotted him. The sun flashed off the man's helmet and back-and-breast as he turned. He shouted out a challenge: "Who comes?"

"I'm Jacques. I'm down from Versailles with a message for Count Guillaume," Jacques shouted back.

"How do I know you're not one of King Abdallah's spies?" the sentry said.

He couldn't have been any older than Jacques. He took his duties very seriously—too seriously, as far as the messenger was concerned. "I've been here before," Jacques answered, as patiently as he could. "Plenty of men in there will know me. The seal on the letter I carry will show I am what I say I am. And if the count decides I'm a spy, he won't let me go. He'll bash in my head."

The sentry chewed on that. After a moment, he shouted to the gate crew. A drawbridge thumped down over the moat that kept attackers from getting too close. Jacques hurried across it. His boots thudded and boomed on the timbers. As soon as he'd crossed, it rose again. Heavy iron chains creaked as it went up.

Stone- and brickwork lined the inside of the passage through the rampart. Heavy iron grates could thud down to block the way. A man at a murder hole set into the roof leered at Jacques. He could pour boiling water or red-hot sand on invaders, and they would have a hard time hurting him. Every other way in was just as strongly warded. Jacques wouldn't have wanted to try to take a place like this.

But he knew why the sentry had sounded nervous. Treachery could do what strength of arms couldn't. Up till a few years ago, the frontier had lain on the Loire. Then two of Versailles' fortresses there fell within days of each other. Nobody fired a shot at or from either place. Now the kingdom had to scramble to find a new southern frontier it could defend.

When Jacques came out of the tunnel through the rampart, he blinked against the bright sunshine—his eyes had had time to get used to the gloom. He waved to an underofficer he knew. "Hello, Pierre," he called. "You can tell anyone who doubts me that I'm a regular messenger, right?"

"Who, me?" the gray-bearded sergeant said. "How can I do that when I never saw you before in my life?" Jacques' jaw dropped. Pierre pointed at him and laughed till tears ran down the gullies of his weathered cheeks. "Sweet Jesus and Henri, the look on your face was worth twenty francs—maybe fifty." He'd never seen fifty francs together in his whole life, any more than Jacques had.

"Funny. Very funny." Jacques tried to stand on his dignity. Sergeant Pierre thought that was funnier yet. Sometimes Jacques thought the best thing old people could do was dry up and blow away. This was one of those times. "Can you take me to Count Guillaume, *please*?" He made the last word as sarcastic as he dared.

He could have done worse, because Pierre went right on laughing. But the sergeant nodded and said, "Come on, then."

The keep at the center of the fortress lay behind a ditch. It was of stone, and looked more old-fashioned and more impressive than the rest of the work. When Pierre led Jacques to Count Guillaume's office, the commander was writing something. He set down his quill pen. "What's this?"

"Messenger, your Grace," the sergeant answered.

"All right." Guillaume was younger than the underofficer. He had a clever, foxy face made foxier by green eyes and red side whiskers. "What is it, young fellow?" he asked Jacques.

"I bring a letter, your Grace, from the Duke of Paris," Jacques said.

Duke Raoul was an important power in the Kingdom of Versailles. Some people said he was *the* power behind King Charles' throne. Even so, the fortress commander looked unimpressed. He also looked to have practiced the expression, perhaps in front of a mirror imported from the south. After a small yawn that also seemed practiced, Guillaume said, "Well, let me have a look at it."

"Here you are, sir." Jacques handed him the rolled-up parchment.

Guillaume did carefully inspect the seal pressed into the wax. He nodded. "Yes, that swan's Raoul's, all right." He used a pen knife to flick off the wax and cut the ribbon that held the letter closed. Unrolling it, he held it out at arm's length to read.

"Anything the men ought to know about, your Grace?" Sergeant Pierre asked.

"Well, Raoul says he's got word some kind of way about a Berber plot to take this place." One of Guillaume's carroty eyebrows quirked upward. "I don't know what he was drinking when he got that word, but it must have been plenty strong. Or do you think Abdallah's getting ready to try to bite us again, Sergeant?"

"I'd say the odds are against it, sir," Pierre replied. "Things have been pretty quiet lately." He paused and tugged at his beard. "*Too* quiet? I didn't think so, not till now."

"I didn't, either." Guillaume's gaze swung to Jacques. "What about you, son? See anything strange on the way down from Paris?"

Jacques needed less than a heartbeat to decide he wouldn't

want to be Count Guillaume's son. He would be richer than he was now—which wouldn't take much—but a lot less comfortable. To have Guillaume always looking over his shoulder, never happy with anything he did . . . He shivered, down inside where it didn't show.

But the count had asked a good question. "Sir, everything was fine till I got close to this place," Jacques said. "Then I heard a stick break. I ducked behind a tree and saw a deer. No real sign of anything else. The deer spooked when it took my scent. I guess it was my scent, anyway."

"How far north of here?" Guillaume rapped out.

"Maybe two miles," Jacques said after thinking about how long he'd needed to get to the fort. "Yes, that's about right."

"Send out a patrol, Sergeant," the count told Pierre. "We don't want those people sniffing around this place. Tell our boys not just to look for men, but for tracks and any other signs we've had visitors we don't want."

The underofficer saluted. "I'll take care of it right now, your Grace." He hurried away, shouting for men as he went.

Guillaume gave his attention back to Jacques. "I don't want you heading back till the patrol comes in. If Berbers are prowling around, they might grab you. Or you might scare them off, and that wouldn't be good, either. Why don't you go over to the buttery and get some bread and sausage and a mug of wine or beer or whatever suits you? If the cook squawks, tell him to talk to me. That should take care of it."

"Thanks, your Grace. I will." Jacques didn't think the cook would bother the count. He could no more imagine taking Guillaume's name in vain than he could taking the Lord's.

As it happened, the cook recognized him from earlier visits. Jacques drank sparkling cider with his food. It wasn't as strong

as wine or as heavy as beer. He didn't want to curl up and fall
asleep under a tree before he'd gone very far. When the cook offered to fill his mug again, Jacques turned him down.

The cook clucked in reproach. "Never say no to anything
free," he advised. "It may not come your way twice." When
Jacques explained why he didn't want more cider, the cook sent
him a sly look. "I'll give you a mug of water instead, then."

"Henri on the wheel, no!" Jacques said. The cook laughed—
he'd been joking. Oh, you *could* drink water. People did it all the
time. But nobody with any sense did it by choice. Nothing was
more likely to give you a flux of the bowels than bad water—and
you couldn't always tell whether water was good by looking or
even by smelling. People went around in misery for weeks at a
time with an illness like that. Or they died of it—it happened all
the time. Little children suffered most, but anybody could come
down with a bloody flux. Whole armies had broken up when half
the men in them or more got sick.

Pierre's patrol didn't come back till late afternoon. They
hadn't found anything out of the ordinary. "Must have just been
that deer," the sergeant told Jacques. "But you made out all
right, didn't you?" He winked. "You won't want to head north
now—too late. So you'll get supper here, and a bed tonight, and
then breakfast in the morning. Not bad, eh?"

"Could be worse," Jacques allowed. Sergeant Pierre laughed
and clapped him on the back. That must have been the right answer. Adults often used a language of understatement and saying
the opposite of what they meant. It had baffled Jacques when he
was younger—and, no doubt, it was meant to baffle him. Now he
was learning it himself. Whether he'd wanted to join or not, he
was turning into a member of the club.

———

In the Paris in this alternate, Annette Klein was known as Khadija the oil merchant's daughter. She was slim and dark, well suited to play the role of someone up from the south. In the home timeline, she was on the short side. People weren't so well nourished here—163 centimeters made her taller than average.

In the home timeline, she was Jewish. Here, she played a Muslim. Christianity here was vastly different from what it was in the world where she'd grown up. Even so, the people of the Kingdom of Versailles hated and feared and persecuted the handful of Jews who lived among them. They hated and feared Muslims, too. They didn't persecute them, though—their Muslim neighbors were too strong to let them get away with it. Islam here wasn't the same as it was back home, either, but it was less different than Christianity.

And Paris . . . The Paris she saw from above her veil only made her sad. In the home timeline, Paris was one of the great cities of the world, and had been for hundreds of years. In this alternate, it was the most important town in the Kingdom of Versailles—which wasn't saying much.

Horses clopped on cobbles or splashed through nasty-smelling mud. Knights in shining—or, more often, rusty—armor rode them. A good back-and-breast would stop a pistol shot, and even a ball from a matchlock musket if it wasn't fired at close range. Pigs and chickens and stray dogs ate garbage in the gutters. So did rats, some of them almost as big and sleek as the local cats.

Rats . . . Annette couldn't look at them without wanting to shudder. Rats had made this alternate's history split away from the home timeline's almost 750 years earlier. In the home timeline, bubonic plague—the Black Death—had killed about a third of the people in Europe, starting in 1348.

Here, the plague went on and on and on. By the time it petered out at last, four out of five Europeans were dead. What had been a thriving civilization was mostly dead, too. Not enough people were left to keep the Muslims, who'd almost been pushed out of Spain, from retaking it. They'd eventually conquered southern France, too, and Italy, and the Balkans. The Turks had also conquered the Balkans in the home timeline, but they did a more thorough job of it in this alternate.

No wonder the European Christians, or what was left of them, thought the end of the world was at hand. No wonder God acquired a Second Son here. Henri preached patience in the face of suffering. He promised a better life to come, and gathered a large following. When he said he was God's Son, the King of France and the Pope—who was living at Avignon, inside the country—ordered him put to death. And so he was broken in front of a large and sorrowful crowd, broken and then burned.

The very next day, the King of France and the Pope went into a church to thank God for being delivered from the sinner. For no reason anyone could see—an earthquake? a crucial beam breaking?—the church collapsed. Both men died in the ruins. So did most of their chief followers. After that, the Kingdom of France was never the same again. Neither was the Papacy.

And the miracle—who then could have believed it was anything else?—made the cult of Henri spread like wildfire across almost all the lands where Christianity still held sway. The Bible here had a Final Testament that spoke of the Second Son's life and deeds. Churches in this alternate had two steeples, a shorter one in front topped by a cross and a taller one in back topped by a wheel.

Even Notre-Dame de Paris, begun long before the plague broke out, was finally finished in the new style. Above the veil, Annette's brown eyes swung toward the great cathedral. As far as she knew, it was the only building her Paris and this one had in common, and even it wasn't identical in the two different worlds. Without the Eiffel Tower, without twentieth- and twenty-first-century highrises in this alternate, the cathedral's great and soaring bulk dominated the skyline here in a way its sister couldn't in the home timeline.

"What is it, my sweet?" Annette's mother asked. Tiffany Klein—here called Aisha—was only a centimeter taller than her daughter. Her eyes were the same warm brown as Annette's, and full of sympathy now. "Does the veil trouble you?"

"Huh? Oh." Annette managed to sound as foolish in the Berber-flavored Arabic they were using as she would have in her own English. "No, truly, that was not what was in my thoughts."

When she first came to this alternate, she'd kicked up a big fuss about going veiled. In the home timeline, the veil was still the symbol of the most backward and sexist parts of the Muslim world. Here, *everybody* was sexist, Muslims and Christians and Jews and Hindus and Buddhists and the Native Americans on the continents people from the Old World were just now discovering. The Industrial Revolution hadn't come to this alternate. Women really were the weaker sex here, and they paid for it.

And the veil here was just something to mark Khadija as a Muslim girl, not a Christian one. She'd needed a while to see that, but now she knew it was true. She'd needed even longer to see there might be a blessing in disguise. People didn't stare at her. What was there to stare at? Eyes, hands, and feet? They weren't worth the bother. The veil could be shield as well as prison.

Annette could see only her mother's eyes. They still looked worried. "Something bothers you," her mother said. "You will not tell me this is not so." They'd both learned this alternate's version of Arabic (and French) through the implants behind their left ears. They spoke without a foreign accent that could have raised eyebrows. Because Annette had learned it that way, it felt as natural as English to her unless she thought about it. Then—but only then—she noticed how much more formal the phrasing was.

She had to nod now, because her mother wasn't wrong. Her wave took in the whole city, especially the great cathedral that wasn't quite like the one in the home timeline. Her wide, flapping sleeve startled a couple of pigeons that were pecking at something in the muddy street. They fluttered off. When they landed three meters farther away, they cocked their heads and sent her reproachful stares.

"This poor, sorry world," she said. "It isn't everything it might have been." Most people who went out to the alternates on Crosstime Traffic business ended up saying that in one language or another. The home timeline wasn't everything it might have been, either, but the people born there lived far richer, more comfortable lives than those on most of the alternates. They weren't always happier—that wasn't the same thing. But good health, a full belly, and high technology did make happiness easier to come by.

"You speak truth—it isn't," her mother agreed. "Still, you should not speak this truth in the streets. More than a few Franks"—the usual Arabic name for any Western European—"know this tongue, and would wonder why you grieve for the world."

"You are right, and I am sorry," Annette said. "But the thought comes, and it does not want to go again."

"Thoughts come as they will. There are times and places to let them free and times and places to hold them in," her mother said.

Since that was plainly true, Annette nodded again. A local woman came by. She wore a long wool skirt that she held up with one hand to keep it out of puddles, a linsey-woolsey blouse, and a white lace cap whose pattern said what part of the kingdom she came from. She was, in other words, almost as covered up as Annette and her mother. But her face was bare to the world. Like about one face in three in this alternate, it showed smallpox scars. Seeing them made Annette want to shiver again. Except as a bioweapon, smallpox was long extinct in the home timeline.

The hand that didn't hold up the Frenchwoman's skirt held on to a three-year-old. The toddler didn't mind mud. He jumped into every puddle between the cobblestones he found. "Henri on the wheel, don't do that!" his mother said. When the mud he splashed up splattered her once too often, she let go of his wrist and whacked his bottom. He howled. She wagged a finger in his face. "I told you not to do that. See what you get when you don't mind?"

Annette had to work hard not to stare. In the home timeline, nobody would spank a child in public. Hardly anyone would spank a child in private. She wondered if this little boy would be warped for life. He hadn't gone ten meters before he was singing and looking for more mud puddles to jump into.

"Children are tougher than you think," Annette's mother said, her voice dry.

"They must be," Annette answered.

"They are. Our ancestors got spanked, too, remember. They lived. He will, too—or he won't die from that, anyhow."

"No." Annette let it go at that. Somewhere between a third and half of the children in this Paris died before they got to be five years old. Smallpox took some. So did measles and whooping cough and diphtheria. All of those had vaccines in the home timeline. But diarrhea, from one germ or another, was the biggest baby-killer here. Clean water and clean food made those kinds of illnesses almost unknown in the world where Annette grew up.

Nothing was clean here. This Paris had no sewers. It dumped slops in the streets. The stink was everywhere. So were the flies. Not uncovering much of yourself had one more advantage here—you didn't get bitten so much.

Annette and her mother walked past a butcher's shop. The meat was out there in the open. It wasn't refrigerated. No one knew about refrigeration in this alternate. If they wanted to preserve meat here, they dried it in the sun or salted it or smoked it. More flies crawled over the fresh meat on display. The butcher, his hands filthy and his leather apron bloody, brushed them away from a beef tongue as he haggled with a woman who wanted to buy it. When they settled on a price, he picked it up and gave it to her. She put it in a grimy canvas sack along with whatever else she'd already bought.

A shop right next to the butcher's sold spices. Many of those came up from the Muslim kingdoms. Without refrigeration, meat went bad fast. If you used lots of pepper and cinnamon and nutmeg and ginger, you could keep on eating it for a while even after it started to go off. Of course, you might get sick if you did. But if the choice was between maybe getting sick and going hungry for sure, what would you do? You'd eat, and you'd hope.

And you'd pray. A monk in a black robe sent Annette and her mother a sour stare as he walked past them. He was a Ladnerian friar, an order that didn't exist in the home timeline. He wore both a wheel and a crucifix on a rawhide thong around his neck. The Ladnerians were reformers. They wanted to keep money out of the churches. That battle went on, and was usually lost, in one alternate after another.

They turned a corner. "There." Annette's mother pointed ahead, to a market square next to the Seine. "There is your father's stall."

"I see it," Annette answered. Beyond the merchants' stalls, men were fishing in the river. They did that in Paris in the home timeline, too. There, as far as Annette knew, nobody ever caught anything. Here, a man drew a trout out of the river. Several more lay at his feet. This Seine was less polluted than that one.

That didn't mean it was clean. Annette's stomach did a slow flipflop as she watched a woman dip a bucket into the water and carry it away. Whenever it rained, it washed the filth from the streets into the river. Nobody here had ever thought of boiling water before using it, either, and bad water was at least as big a killer as bad food.

Annette's father waved to her and her mother. His real name was Jacob. In this world, he went as Muhammad al-Marsawi—Muhammad, the man from Marseille. Here as in the home timeline, Muhammad was the most common men's first name.

"Fine olive oil!" her father called. "The first pressing! Fine olive oil!" Olives didn't grow as far north as Paris. Olive oil was an expensive luxury here. People mostly used butter or lard instead. Nobody in this alternate had ever heard of cholesterol, either. It probably didn't matter. Disease killed most people here before heart attacks or strokes could.

A merchant came up to her father's stand. Dad had a loaf of bread handy. He dipped it in the oil and offered it to the local. The man chewed thoughtfully. "It's not butter," he said.

"No, it's not," Dad agreed. They were speaking French. The language was less perfectly polished here than in the home timeline. It also had what would have been a northern accent in Annette's world. The plagues hadn't hit so hard there, while they'd almost emptied Paris. Even all these centuries later, you could still hear that in the way people talked. This French had also borrowed many more words from Arabic than French had in the home timeline. Annette's father went on, "Where I come from, people would say it's better than butter."

The merchant bowed. "You will forgive me for saying so, *m'sieu*, but you are not where you came from."

"Really?" Dad raised an eyebrow and bowed back. "I never would have noticed." He and the merchant both laughed. The Klein family was based in Marseille. The transposition chamber that took them back and forth between worlds was there, too. One day soon, there was supposed to be a chamber in Paris. Annette would believe that when she saw it. Crosstime Traffic worked in so many alternates, no one of them got all the attention it should have.

She liked this Marseille better than this Paris. The weather was nicer—warmer and drier. The city was cleaner. The streets there were all cobbled, and had real gutters to get rid of some of the garbage. Marseille didn't stink as badly. And the people who lived there were a little less backward, or at least more polite about it.

This merchant seemed intent on sneering at the olive oil. "But since this is not butter, my friend, who will want to buy it? Who will want to use it?"

"More people than you can imagine, m'sieu," Annette's father said. That was truer than the merchant could imagine. Olive oil from this alternate's southern France went back to the home timeline. So did olives pickled in vinegar and brine. The locals made them just fine, and had varieties different from the ones in the world where Annette grew up. The oil and the olives both brought Crosstime Traffic good money.

The local merchant was a tougher customer. "If I buy it from you, who will buy it from me?" he asked. "It's not what people here are used to."

"Paris has some cobblestones these days," Dad remarked, seemingly out of the blue. "It didn't used to."

"Forgive me, m'sieu, but I do not see how this answers me." The merchant scratched his head. Annette was tempted to do the same thing.

Dad only smiled. "One of the reasons Paris has some cobbles is that Marseille and other cities farther south have cobbles. Is it not so?" He waited for the local trader to nod, then went on, "The Kings of Versailles want to keep up with what their neighbors do. So do the people here. One thing their neighbors do is use more olive oil than they do. A clever man, as I'm sure you are, would see that his customers remembered it while he was selling them the oil."

"It could be." The merchant, being a merchant, tried not to show he was impressed. But he was; even Annette could see as much. Nobody here thought about advertising, not on purpose. You had a product and you cried it through the streets—that was as far as things went. The local added, "*You* are a clever man. No wonder you are rich."

"I wish I were," Annette's father said. By this alternate's standards, anyone from the home timeline was richer than a king. Talking about that not only broke all the rules but was really stupid besides.

Laughing, the merchant said, "However you please." No one in this timeline would ever admit to being rich. Nothing else could do a better job of attracting tax collectors. Rumors of money drew them the way dead meat drew vultures. The merchant went on, "I will buy five jars from you—no more. I'll see if I can move them the way you suggest. If they do well, I'll buy more when I see you again."

He's going to try to create demand, Annette thought. The local probably didn't look at it in those terms, but that was what it amounted to. Annette's father bowed. He and the merchant haggled. When they reached a price they could both live with, they clasped hands. The merchant went off to get the money and to bring back workers to carry away the jars. Down farther south, the workers would have been slaves. Here, he probably paid them a little something. Slavery wasn't illegal in the Kingdom of Versailles, but it was uncommon.

After the merchant paid and took his olive oil, Dad let out a sigh of relief. "We'll be going home soon now," he said. Anyone who understood Arabic would think he meant going back to Marseille. They would be going back there, all right. But after that, they'd be going back to the home timeline. Before long, Annette would start her freshman year at Ohio State. Along with her high-school diploma, she'd have a year of fieldwork to her credit. She could hardly wait.

Jacques' feet hurt when he got back to Paris. He could feel every pebble in the roadway through the sole of his left boot. When he found the chance, he would have to see a cobbler and get thicker leather put on there. First things first, though. He needed to get back to Duke Raoul and let him know Count Guillaume had the message.

He paid a boatman a couple of coppers to carry him over the Seine to the right bank. The duke's castle stood there, not far from the great cathedral. Raoul—or, more likely, one of his clerks—would repay him the boatman's fee. A lot of boats went back and forth on the Seine. A good many went up and down the river, too. Moving anything heavy was much cheaper by water than by land.

The boatmen shouted and cursed at one another. None of them wanted to give way. They felt less manly when they had to. "Where will you find a cavern dark enough to hide your ugly face?" the man rowing Jacques screamed at a fellow on a barge that threatened to cut him off.

"I would rather be a dog and bay at the moon than a wretch like you," the bargeman retorted. They paid each other more compliments till the rowboat slipped past. If they'd said things like that on dry land, they both probably would have gone for their knives. On the river, they took insults for granted. If Jacques' boatman and the other fellow met in a tavern, they were more likely to laugh and to buy each other wine than to brawl.

Boats hardly ever smashed together, either. The system looked—and sounded—odd to somebody who wasn't part of it, but it worked.

"Here you are, friend," Jacques' boatman said as the boat went aground near the riverside market.

"Thanks." Jacques hopped out. Mud squelched under his feet. The boatman started waving his arms and shouting for a passenger so he could go back across the Seine. For the small fees he got, he worked hard.

People in the market were waving their arms and shouting, too. Nobody ever bought at the first price. You had to pretend you were having a fit to get the seller to lower it. Then he would pretend to have a fit so he didn't have to lower it too much.

Somebody from the south had just finished making a deal with a local merchant. Jacques knew of the merchant, but wasn't rich enough to buy from him. The local man looked pleased with himself as his followers carried off five big pottery jugs. The Arab looked pleased with himself, too. That usually meant a good bargain.

Jacques sent the Arab a suspicious stare. Any trader up from the south might be a spy. The traders who went into Muslim countries from the Kingdom of Versailles always kept their eyes and ears open. Why wouldn't southerners do the same here?

The Muslim merchant had two women with him. Were they wives? Were they daughters? Were they one of each? All Jacques could see of them were their hands and their eyes. He thought one of them couldn't be much if any older than he was, but he couldn't be sure. At least with girls from his own kingdom, you could see what they looked like. With these women, everything was a mystery. Did that make them less interesting or more? Again, he couldn't be sure.

He spoke some Arabic and followed more. He wasn't fluent, but he could make himself understood. Anyone who spent a lot of time along the border picked up bits and pieces of the language they used on the other side. Plenty of King Abdallah's men knew fragments of French. The merchant was as smooth in it as if it were his birthspeech. For all Jacques knew, it was. Some who'd been born Christian followed Islam now. Some who'd been born Muslim now reverenced Jesus and Henri, too, but not so many.

"We'll be going home soon," the trader said in Arabic. The younger woman and the older one both exclaimed in pleasure. They didn't want to stay here, any more than Jacques would have wanted to live in their country.

Bowing to them, Jacques said, "May God give you a safe journey," in their language.

They all exclaimed. Jacques couldn't hide his smile. Muslims were often surprised when they ran into a Christian who knew Arabic. Some of them couldn't have been more surprised if their horses had started talking. To be fair, this fellow didn't seem like that. "The Prophet's peace upon you," he said, and then, "Unless I am mistaken, you will be coming home from a journey."

How did he know that? Jacques looked down at himself. It probably wasn't hard to figure out. He was splashed with mud up past his knees. His boots were wet—he'd had to ford a creek. His clothes were grimy. His hair probably stuck out in all directions, too. He ran his fingers through it, not that that would do much good. "Yes, you're right," he said—why not admit it?

"Where have you come from, and what is the news?" the merchant asked, switching from Arabic to his flawless French.

And Jacques started to tell him. Doing it would have been easier and more natural in his own language. But then he remembered the thought he'd had before. A merchant who was only a merchant might ask a question like that. So might a merchant who was also a spy. Sticking to Arabic—he wanted to practice—Jacques answered, "Not much news, I fear—not for a great lord like yourself. A long, dull way here." He pretended to yawn. Then he yawned for real—he truly *was* tired.

"He speaks very well," the younger (he thought) veiled woman said to the older.

Jacques knew better than to come right out and say something to her. He would have been too familiar if he had. He spoke to the merchant instead: "Your . . . daughter gives me too much credit." He put a question in his voice, since he wasn't sure the woman was a daughter.

But the Arab merchant smiled and nodded, so he'd guessed right. The man said, "No, Khadija is always pleased to hear our speech. And she does not praise beyond what you deserve, for you speak very clearly. You are easy to understand." He bowed.

So did Jacques. He knew Arabs praised more freely than people from his own kingdom. That was one of the things that made them hard to trust. Even more than Jesus, Henri taught that men should be modest, because most of them had plenty to be modest about. Jacques said, "Tell your daughter I thank her for troubling to understand my words."

The older woman—Khadija's mother?—started to laugh. "We had better watch this one," she said. "He has a flatterer's tongue."

If she hadn't laughed, Jacques would have thought she was angry. As things were, he took a chance and bowed to her, more deeply than he had to the merchant. "How can the truth be flattery?" he asked.

All three Arabs laughed then. Khadija said, "You were right, Father. He is as smooth and slick as the oil you sell." In a different tone of voice, that would have been an insult. The way she said it, it sounded more like one friend teasing another.

He went on chatting with them, not about things that could matter to a spy, just passing the time of day the way he would have with friends. He had to remind himself he needed to report to Duke Raoul. He wasn't late enough to make the duke wonder where he'd been, but he would be if he hung around the market square much longer.

All the way to the castle, he wondered what Khadija looked like. Was she pretty? He had no way to know. He'd just seen her eyes and her hands. But he liked her, and so he thought she was.

Two

The innkeeper thought Annette and her family were odd because they had no servants or slaves. They couldn't hire locals, not without showing them things they shouldn't see. And there weren't enough people from Crosstime Traffic here to play the role. This alternate hadn't been opened for long. People from the home timeline still had a lot to learn here.

Back home, people said Crosstime Traffic was spread too thin. When Annette was in the home timeline, she'd said the same thing. People had known how to travel from one alternate world to another for only about fifty years. They had so many to explore, so many to examine, so many to exploit. Without food and energy from the alternates, the home timeline probably would have collapsed by now. But there was so much to do. And even though Crosstime Traffic had become far and away the biggest corporation in the world, there weren't enough people to do it all in a hurry.

So if the innkeeper scratched his head and muttered to himself . . . then he did, that was all. It didn't matter if he thought the Kleins were peculiar. If he thought they were peculiar because they didn't belong to this alternate . . . that would matter. But he didn't. He had no reason to. Some people drank only water. Some people fed their dogs better than they fed themselves. He thought they were peculiar like that—strange, yes, but harmless.

Dad took a big brass key off his belt to open their room. The big brass lock on the door looked just like the ones they made here. No local burglar could hope to beat it, though. It was brass only on the outside, case-hardened twenty-first century steel within. Dad's key had a microchip that shook hands with one inside the lock. Without that handshake, the lock wouldn't open, period—exclamation point, even. The same kind of lock secured the shutters over the windows.

After they went inside, Dad used another lock and a stout wooden bar to make sure the door stayed closed. He plopped himself down on one of the stools in the room—only nobles here sat on chairs with backs. "Whew! It will be so good to head for home," he said in Arabic.

"*Oh*, yes," Annette held her nose. "I can't wait to get back to air that doesn't stink."

"People back there complain about pollution." Her mother had to use the Arabic word that usually meant a religious offense. No one here worried about polluting the environment, or even knew such a thing was possible. People just wanted to take what was there to be taken. Mom went on, "The home timeline has to be careful, too. I understand that. But anybody who's ever smelled a low-tech alternate will tell you there's pollution, and then there's pollution." As Annette had, she held her nose.

"Even getting back to Marseille will be good," Dad said. "I didn't think we'd land in any trouble up here, and we haven't, but it could have been bad trouble if we did. We're a long way from anybody who could give us a hand."

Staying inconspicuous made things harder. They couldn't carry assault rifles here. They couldn't drive an SUV between Marseille and Paris. Actually, that might have been just as well. What passed for roads here would have murdered any car's shocks in nothing flat. They traveled on foot, on horseback, and by boat. Dad had an automatic pistol, but it was disguised like the locks. It looked like one of the big, clumsy weapons the locals used. And it was for the worst emergencies only.

Mom sighed. "This poor alternate. Since the plagues, it's had nothing but bad luck."

"As long as we don't catch it," Annette said.

"You can say that again." Dad bent and knocked on the leg of his stool. They knocked on wood for luck here, the same as they did in the home timeline. A surprising number of small things were the same. All the big things were different.

Annette felt like sighing, too. "Europe was all set to take off. It did in the home timeline—all the explorations, and the Scientific Revolution, and the Industrial Revolution. Here—"

"Everybody died," Mom said. That wasn't how Annette had intended to go on, which didn't mean it wasn't true.

"No Scientific Revolution anywhere but in Europe in this alternate, either," Dad said. "The Muslim world knows some things the Europeans—what's left of them—don't, but the Muslims don't know how much they didn't know before the plagues."

"Thomas Aquinas and al-Ghazzali," Annette said. Her father nodded. They'd drilled that one into the Kleins in their briefings. In the home timeline and here, the Christian saint and the Muslim holy man had asked the same question—was scientific research compatible with religion?

Aquinas had said yes. He said there could be no conflict between religion and science. All knowledge, to him, was one. He made Aristotle's logic fit inside the Christian faith. In the home timeline, that helped pave the way for the Scientific Revolution.

Al-Ghazzali had believed just the opposite. He thought scientific research undermined faith, and he thought faith was more important. In the home timeline, Aquinas' view dominated western Christianity. Al-Ghazzali's prevailed in Islam.

Al-Ghazzali's ideas prevailed in Islam in this alternate, too. If anything, the Great Black Deaths here had only made those ideas stronger. If God could do such a thing, how could any man hope to understand Him or His works? Muslims in this alternate feared and distrusted science. They clung to religion, and they clung to it hard.

The irony was, al-Ghazzali was right about whether science undermined faith. St. Thomas Aquinas was wrong. Studying science *did* weaken belief in God and in traditional religion. A lot of experience in the home timeline and in alternates with breakpoints more recent than this one's showed as much.

That studying science could also lead to a richer, healthier, more comfortable and more knowledgeable life on earth . . . was beside the point if you thought religion the be-all and end-all. Just about everyone in this alternate felt that way. Some people in the home timeline still did, too. Every so often, they used the products of science—explosives, radioactives, tailored viruses— to try to make their point.

"By the time Western Europe got its people back, it wasn't the same kind of place any more," Mother said.

Europe had needed more than two hundred years to get back to where it had been before the plagues came. It never took off, the way it had in the home timeline. That was partly because Muslims had reconquered Spain and Portugal and reoccupied Italy. It was also partly because of the Second Son and the Final Testament. Henri's take on Christianity wasn't as hostile to science as Islam was. But Aquinas' certainty that science and God went hand in hand was one more plague victim in this alternate.

"I wonder why China didn't do it," Annette mused.

In this alternate, the Manchus still ruled China. No pressure from Europe had weakened their dynasty there. China was the biggest, strongest, richest country in the world. But it wasn't much further along than it had been at the breakpoint, either. Some Emperors favored scholarship, some didn't. The ones who didn't tore down what the ones who did had built. In this alternate as in the home timeline, great Chinese junks under Zheng He had visited Arabia and East Africa in the 1410s. They'd taken Chinese porcelain to Africa and a giraffe back to China. But no Chinese ships had made the journey again in all the centuries since. Trade stayed in the hands of Arab and Indian and Malay middlemen.

Scholars in the home timeline still argued about why things turned out this way. They would go on arguing, too, till they knew a lot more—and probably even after they knew more. Arguing, testing ideas against evidence, moved scholarship ahead.

"China has always been very good at *how*," Dad said. "It hasn't been so good at *why*. Being good at how will make you more comfortable in the short run. In the long run, finding out why things work the way they do makes for bigger changes."

"Some people say you need to believe in one god first, before you can believe there's one *why* behind everything," Mom added. "If you explain things by saying they happen because this imp is fighting with that spirit, how are you going to look deeper?"

"So you think that's true?" Annette asked.

"I don't know. It can't be the whole answer—I'm sure of that," her mother replied. "But it may be part."

It seemed neat and clean and logical. Of course, plenty of things that seemed neat and clean and logical were also wrong. "I'll be studying all this stuff when I get to college, won't I?" Annette said.

"You'd better believe it," Mom said. Dad nodded.

So did Annette. Travel across timelines was the biggest thing that had happened to people since the discovery of the New

World, maybe since the discovery of writing and the wheel. As far as Annette was concerned, anybody who didn't want to get involved with it probably would have thought Columbus would fall off the edge of the world or that wheels ought to be square. If seeing all the different ways things might have turned out didn't interest you, odds were you didn't have a pulse.

And the home timeline needed the alternates, too. They had all the things the home timeline was running out of when Galbraith and Hester discovered crosstime travel. Trade for a little here, trade for a little there—the alternates would never miss it. Sink oil wells in a world where men had never evolved, and you could take whatever you needed.

Not everything was perfect. When was it ever? Some diseases had reached the home timeline. These days, biotech usually blunted them in a hurry. People who didn't work for Crosstime Traffic often complained the company had too much power. Annette thought they would have grumbled the same way about scribes back when writing was new. CT had to be the most closely watched company in the history of the world. The early days had seen a few scandals—again, nothing was perfect. But nobody's found any trouble like that for as long as she'd been alive.

"College," she murmured.

Her father chuckled. "Seems far away, doesn't it, when you're in a world where you get sick because your humors go out of whack, where they've forgotten what the Romans used to know about plumbing, and where they've got markets to sell human beings just like we've got markets to sell beans and watermelons?"

"Markets to sell human beings. Slave markets." Annette's mouth twisted. She'd seen one of those markets, down in Marseille. She understood that people in this alternate needed other people to do their work for them. They didn't have machines, the

way the home timeline did. Even if she understood that, the idea
of slavery gave her the cold horrors. To sell people like beans, to
use them—or use them up—like farm animals . . . The day was
cool, but that wasn't why she shivered.

Mom understood. She reached out and set a hand on Annette's shoulder. "It's a nasty business," she said. "Our hands
are clean of that, anyhow."

"They'd better be!" Annette exclaimed. "We shouldn't just
sit back and watch it, though. We ought to try to stamp it out."

"Where we can, we do," Dad said. "In an alternate like this,
it's not easy. People here don't think slavery's wrong. They
think it's natural. And it helps make the wheels go round.
Sooner or later, the time will come when that's not so. But it
hasn't got here yet."

To Annette, *sooner or later* might as well have been forever.
To anybody in this alternate who was bought and sold like a
bushel of beans, *sooner or later* was much too late. She could understand what Dad was driving at. Even in the home timeline,
people hadn't started questioning slavery till the eighteenth century. Nobody—except maybe the slaves—questioned it here.
Annette's heart said that was wrong, that was wicked, that
needed to be changed yesterday—if not sooner.

It wouldn't happen. She knew that, too. Crosstime Traffic
had way too many other more urgent things to worry about. *Too
bad*, she thought. *Oh, too bad!*

Jacques worked hard on his pike drill. He wished he were a mus-
keteer. But he was big and strong. That helped him most of the
time, but it didn't help make his wish come true. Size and
strength counted for more with a pike than they did with a musket. Jacques didn't suppose he could blame Duke Raoul for

making sure the men best suited to the pike were the ones who used it.

His target was a post driven into the ground. He lunged, withdrew, lunged again. The gleaming iron head of the pike tapped the post at what would have been belly height. He imagined the post was one of King Abdallah's men, a bearded infidel screaming, "*Allahu akbar!*" He'd scream, all right, when the spearhead went home. Jacques stretched forward and lunged again.

"That's very smooth," a dry voice said from behind him.

Jacques whirled. There stood Duke Raoul. He was a little gamecock of a man, short and skinny but tough. He had a long face, a scarred cheek, a pointed chin beard going from seal-brown to gray, and the coldest blue eyes Jacques had ever run into. Those eyes saw everything that went on in Paris, and almost everything that went on in the Kingdom of Versailles. They even saw the pike drill of a no-account young soldier.

"I thank you, your Grace. I thank you kindly," Jacques said.

"If you bend your back leg a little more, you'll be able to extend the lunge," the duke said. "Let me show you." He took the pike from Jacques. He might not have been big, but he was plenty strong—he handled the sixteen-foot shaft like a toothpick.

Raoul went through the same drill as Jacques had. Watching him, Jacques was much less pleased with his own performance. Oh, he wasn't bad. But Duke Raoul was supple as a dancer, quick as a serpent. Jacques wouldn't have wanted to face him across a battle line.

After just enough work to break a sweat, the duke straightened and handed back the pike. "Here—run through it again," he said. "Remember that back leg. It really does make a difference."

"I'll try, sir." Jacques did his best. He still felt clumsy and slow next to Raoul. And he had to think about that back leg now.

Thinking was bad on a battlefield. It cost time. You needed to *do*, on the instant. Speed counted for so much. But he did see he could extend the lunge that way. Reach counted, too.

Duke Raoul was nodding. "Not bad. You were trying to bend that leg. I noticed. Now you've got to keep doing it till it turns into a habit."

"Yes, sir. I was just thinking the same thing. I don't want to have to try to remember it if I'm out there fighting."

"Don't blame you. I wouldn't, either. But keep practicing—it'll stick. 'Patience is rewarded. The fool shows his folly and gives way before the end.' So Henri said, and I'm sure He's right." Duke Raoul paused. Then he changed the subject even faster than he'd shifted the pike: "Tell me—what do you think of the traders from Marseille you were talking with the other day?"

How did Raoul know about Muhammad al-Marsawi and his wife and daughter? Jacques hadn't said anything about them. Had the boatman talked to the duke? Did Raoul have spies in the market square? "What do I think, your Grace?" Jacques echoed. "I wonder if the daughter is pretty." At the least, an answer like that bought him time.

It made Raoul laugh. "That I can't tell you. I don't know anybody who's seen her without her veil. You don't want to mess with things like that. Offend a woman from King Abdallah's country and we're liable to have a war on our hands." A clear warning note rang in his voice.

"Oh, I know, your Grace," Jacques said quickly. He didn't want the duke to think he was stupid enough to do something like that.

"All right. Good." Raoul stroked that neat, pointed beard. With his clever face and cold eyes, it made him look a little like the Devil. Jacques couldn't imagine anyone, not even King Charles, having the nerve to come out and say that to Raoul. After the pause for thought, the nobleman went on, "Did you notice anything . . . odd about those Muslims?"

"Odd?" Jacques scratched his head. "I'm not sure what you mean, sir. They did seem to be clever people—not just Muhammad but his wife and daughter as well."

"Yes, I've heard that from others as well. I've said it myself, in fact—I've met them." Duke Raoul paused again. "How many other women from down south do you know—or know of—who have much of anything to say in public? They're rich, too, these traders, or at least a long way from poor. Did they have any slaves or servants with them?"

"Not that I saw." Jacques did some more scratching, and hoped he wasn't lousy again. "That *is* funny, isn't it?"

"Well, I've never heard of any other Muslims with goods as fine as theirs who didn't," the duke said. "I don't know what it means. I can't swear it means anything. But when you find something that doesn't fit in with the rest of what you've seen over the years, you start wondering why it doesn't."

He'd had many more years than Jacques to form patterns like that in his mind. For the first time, Jacques began to see getting some wrinkles and some gray in your hair might have advantages. Did they make up for bad teeth and sore joints and all the other ills of age? Not as far as he could see, but they might be there even so.

"Another thing," Raoul said. "Did they speak French while you were around?"

Jacques had to think about it. "Yes, they did," he answered after a moment. "I know some Arabic, but not a whole lot."

"Good you know some," Raoul told him. "How did the traders sound to you?"

"I don't know." Now Jacques was lost. "Like people speaking French. How are they supposed to sound?"

"Like this, the way most people from down in the south sound." Duke Raoul talked through his nose, as French-speakers from the south did. He was a good mimic. And he'd noticed what Jacques had missed—those traders didn't talk like that. He went back to his usual way of speaking to say, "If you listen to them, you'd think they came from Paris, wouldn't you?"

"Yes, your Grace, you would," Jacques agreed. "What can that mean?"

"I don't know, any more than you do," the duke said. "But I'd like to find out. How would you like to give me a hand?"

"Me?" Jacques almost dropped the pike. "What do I have to do?"

"Well, they're going back to Marseille soon. They won't travel by themselves, not unless they're idiots—and they aren't. They'll go in a group, with other southbound traders," Raoul said. Jacques nodded. That was how things worked, all right—numbers brought safety. The duke pointed a scarred forefinger at him. "How would you like to be a guard in that company?"

Jacques bowed. "Whatever you want me to do, your Grace, you know I'll do it." You had to talk that way around Duke Raoul. If he thought you didn't want to do something he told you to do, he wouldn't tell you to do anything—and you'd never move up if he ignored you. Jacques wanted to move up, and winning the duke's favor was a good way to do it. Besides, he really did want to do this. Raoul had made him curious. "How can I serve you best?" he asked.

"Keep your eyes and ears open and your mouth shut," Raoul answered bluntly. "Think you can manage that? Some people can't. If you're one of them, say so now. I won't hold it against you—I'll be glad you're honest. You'll get other chances, I promise. But if you go along and you mess things up by blabbing . . . I won't like that a bit."

He had ways, painful ones, of making his dislike felt. Jacques gulped a little, but he managed a nod. "I don't talk out of turn, sir," he said.

"Well, I hadn't heard that you did," the duke said. "If I had, I wouldn't have offered this to you. We'll see what happens, then. Don't make it obvious you're snooping, either. If you do, you won't learn anything worth having. Do you read and write?"

"I read some. I've picked it up on my own, mostly. I might be able to write my name. Past that—" Jacques shrugged. He'd never needed to write before. Now maybe he did. He went on, "I read some French, I should have said. I can't make head nor tail of the funny squiggles the Muslims use."

"All right. Don't let it worry you. If you want to, after you come back I'll have someone teach you more. It comes in handy all kinds of ways."

"Thanks, your Grace. I'd like that." Jacques bowed again. "I'll never make a scholar, but I like to learn things."

"That's a fair start for a spy. Of course, it's also a fair start for a gossipy old granny." Even when Duke Raoul praised you, he liked to jab you with a pin, too. He smiled a crooked smile at Jacques. "And if you do get too snoopy, maybe Muhammad there will think you're trying to see under Khadija's veil, eh? And maybe he'll be right, too." He nudged Jacques with his elbow and strode off whistling a bawdy tune.

Jacques stared after him. Raoul wasn't wrong—he wouldn't mind finding out what Khadija looked like. That wasn't why he stared, though. He understood why the duke knew Muhammad al-Marsawi's name. The merchant was wealthy, and Raoul was interested in him. But that Raoul also had Muhammad's daughter's name on the tip of his tongue . . . She was just a girl. Jacques wouldn't have thought she was important enough to stick in a duke's mind. But Raoul kept track of all kinds of things. That was part—a big part—of what made him what he was.

The pikeman practicing next to Jacques sent him a jealous glance. "His Grace spent a lot of time with you," the man said. He was probably twice Jacques' age. Though short, he was broad-shouldered and strong. He made a good enough soldier, but no one would promote him to sergeant if he lived to be a hundred.

Since Jacques didn't want trouble from him, he tried to shrug it off. "He wanted to know about . . . some things I saw on my way up from Count Guillaume's fortress." Everybody knew he'd been there. He'd almost talked about Muhammad and Khadija. But hadn't Raoul told him to keep his mouth shut? If he didn't, the duke might—likely would—hear about it.

"He spent a lot of time," the older man repeated. "I've fought for him since you were born, and he's never spent that kind of time with me."

"Duke Raoul does as he pleases," Jacques said. The other pikeman couldn't very well argue with that. There were ways to get the duke to notice you. Jacques had found one—he'd done well at what Raoul told him to do, and he'd dealt with people Raoul found interesting. If you made a big enough mistake, that would make the duke notice you, too. Afterwards, you'd wish it hadn't, but it would. Jacques feared the other pikeman would draw the Duke of Paris' eye that way, if he ever did.

Caravan guard! That was something. It beat carrying messages back and forth. And he'd get a chance to see what the Muslims' country was like. People in the Kingdom of Versailles were jealous of their southern neighbors. The Muslims were richer. People said they were smarter. They lived more comfortable lives. Paris tried to be like Marseille. No one had ever heard of Marseille trying to be like Paris.

All at once, Jacques wished he hadn't let Muhammad al-Marsawi and his family know he understood Arabic. Now they would be on their guard around him. If they'd thought he only spoke French, they might not have watched what they said in their own language. But he'd wanted to show off. He'd wanted to impress the merchant—and the merchant's daughter. He hadn't worried about what might come of that.

Duke Raoul would have. Jacques was sure of it. The duke always thought before he did things. He was as clever as any Arab. Jacques wished he could be like that. He'd never be a duke, of course—he didn't have the blood. But he might make a captain, or even a colonel. And if he made colonel, his children, when he had them, could marry into the nobility. Oh, snobs would sniff, but they could do it. And his grandchildren might be nobles themselves. If you were going to rise in the Kingdom of Versailles, that was how you went about it.

Jacques laughed at himself. Here he was, seventeen years old, not even a sergeant, and dreaming of being a captain or a colonel. Dreaming higher than that, in fact—dreaming as high as any man in this kingdom could dream. If Raoul found out he wanted his grandchildren to be nobles, what would the duke do?

That was a scary thought. Or was it? Wouldn't Raoul grin and wink and nudge him and whisper, "Good luck"? Somewhere two or three hundred years ago, hadn't one of Raoul's many-times-great-grandfathers gone and done what Jacques dreamt of now? Sure he had. Noble families, except the king's, hadn't come down from before the days of the Great Black Deaths. They had their start in the newer days, the days of Henri, the days of the Final Testament.

Muslims sneered at Christians for following Henri. They said Muhammad was the last man through whom God spoke.

Jacques made the sign of the wheel over his heart. He didn't care what Muslims thought. He knew what *he* believed.

But he didn't like the idea of Muhammad al-Marsawi laughing at him because of his religion. And he really didn't like the idea of Khadija laughing at him because of it. He didn't know what he could do about that, short of converting.

Christians did, every now and then. The Kingdom of Berry had been all Christian once. Little by little, the people there were giving up their faith. Some wanted to escape the higher taxes Christians had to pay in a Muslim kingdom. Others, though, others decided God was on the Muslims' side. Didn't their wealth and power show that? Lots of people must have thought so, because Berry didn't have many Christians left in it these days.

Things were different here in the Kingdom of Versailles. The only mosques here were for traders up from the south. If you converted to Islam, you couldn't even stay and pay extra taxes. You had to leave the kingdom. Except for the clothes on your back, you couldn't take your property with you, either.

In spite of that, people did convert and go into exile. Not a flood of them, but a slow, steady trickle. Some thought they had a better chance of getting rich down in the Muslim lands. Others, again, really believed in what they were doing. They had to, or they wouldn't have put themselves to so much trouble.

Jacques didn't like the idea that his kingdom and the other Christian kingdoms to the north and east were the Muslims' poor, backward cousins. *One of these days, we'll know as much as they do,* he thought. *One of these days, we'll be as rich as they are. And then . . . And then they'd better look out, because we'll have a lot of paying back to do.*

He lunged with the pike one more time. It was perfect. Duke Raoul would have been proud of him.

"Are we ready?" Dad asked for what had to be the twentieth time.

Mom finally lost patience with him. "I don't know about you," she said, a certain edge in her voice, "but *I* am."

The sarcasm didn't faze him. When he was in one of these moods, nothing fazed him. He just turned to Annette and said, "And you, Khadija? Are you ready?"

"Yes, my father," she answered. Her mother snapped back at Dad. Annette mostly didn't. Life was too short. She let him work the jumpiness out of his system.

"Are you sure?" he persisted. "You have everything you will need to take back to Marseille?"

"Yes, my father," Annette said again. Now, whether she wanted it to or not, a certain edge found its way into *her* voice. The room they were staying in, like any room in any inn in this alternate, held no more furniture than it had to. It had beds, stools, a chest that now stood open. Nobody could have much doubt about whether her stuff was packed. Dad . . . got the fidgets.

"God be praised!" he said now. He let it go at that, a sign that this case wouldn't be so bad as some of the ones Annette had seen him have.

"Let's go," Mom said. "I want to head back to the south as soon as we can. This caravan has taken too long coming together."

"It's here now," Dad said. "*If* we have everything out of the room, let's load the mules and get on our horses and be on our way."

Annette was ready to go. Back to Marseille, back to the home timeline, back to the United States . . . Fieldwork was an adventure, but going off to college would be an adventure, too. And the dorms, unlike this inn, would have showers and computers and fasartas, and wouldn't have bugs. There was something to be said for adventures that didn't smell bad.

The innkeeper met his departing guests in the stables. He wasn't fat and jolly, the way innkeepers were supposed to be. He was scrawny and looked like a man who worried all the time. He had a pinched mouth and deep lines between his eyes. He also had horrible bad breath. In the home timeline, a dentist would have fixed his troubles long ago. Here, all you could do with a rotting tooth was pull it. They had no anesthetics but wine and opium. You went to the dentist as a last resort.

He bowed and made the sign of the wheel. "May the roads be fair for you. May God watch over you. May your travels bring you back to my inn once more," he said in pretty good Arabic. Annette was sure he meant the last part. Her father had paid him well.

"It will be as God wills," Dad said, which sounded impressive and meant exactly nothing. Then he asked a question that did mean something: "Have you heard any news of how the roads are?" He didn't mean whether they were muddy or dry. That would change with the weather. He meant whether bandits had been raiding lately.

"What news I have is good," the innkeeper said. "King Abdallah is supposed to have smashed Tariq's band of thieves. If that is true, they will not trouble you on your way home."

"May it be so!" Dad sounded as if he meant it, and he did mean it. The Kleins were at risk till they got back to Marseille. Dad had the disguised pistol. He also had a radio that looked like a set of worry beads. If they got in trouble, they could let the Crosstime Traffic people in Marseille know what had happened. But help couldn't reach them faster than the speed of a galloping horse, and that might not be fast enough.

After exchanging one more set of bows with the innkeeper, Dad led the horses and mules through the winding streets of Paris to the riverside market square where the caravan was assembling. Shopkeepers popped out of their stores to try to sell him medicines or brass candlesticks or carved wooden figurines or bullet molds or whatever else they had for their stock in trade. He waved them all away. "Next time, my friends, next time," he said in French, again and again. That was as polite a way as Annette could imagine to tell them to get lost.

Merchants and pack animals swarmed in the market square. The chaos and the noise and the smell were very bad. People shouted and swore in half a dozen languages. Muslims in flowing robes made broad, sweeping gestures. Traders from the Kingdom of Versailles got excited over trifles, much as Frenchmen might have done in the home timeline. Men from the Germanies wore tight breeches and brimless round caps. They stood with their arms folded across their chests and waited for things to get moving. A couple of Englishmen wore breeches like the Germans but had on flat, broad-brimmed hats that looked like leather pancakes.

Listening to them, Annette could follow their brand of English about half the time. Chaucer had lived in this alternate, too, and had written, though the plague killed him here before he started *The Canterbury Tales*. The merchants' English was a lot like his—German with a French overlay. It didn't have most of the layers of vocabulary that had come afterwards in the home timeline. In this alternate, England had never been a great power. The British Isles were a backwater in Europe, which was a backwater in the world. Scotland was still independent here. Ireland held half a dozen little kingdoms that fought among themselves all the time.

"What dost tha mean, tha great gowk?" one of the Englishmen shouted at another. Annette wondered what a gowk was. Nothing good, plainly. Maybe she would have done better with this dialect if she'd grown up in Yorkshire or somewhere like that.

The merchants chatted about what they'd bought and what they'd sold and the prices they'd got. They argued about who would go where in the southbound caravan. Nothing got settled in a hurry. A lot of them took squabbling over such things as a game. Haggling over prices was a game here, too. You had to play along, or the locals would think you were peculiar. It wasted a lot of time, but then, so did sitting in front of a TV screen. People who didn't find one way or another to waste time probably weren't human.

While the traders talked and bickered, the men who would guard them on the way south stood around and waited. Some of the guards would be mounted when the caravan finally got moving. They had big, clumsy matchlock pistols in holsters on their belts, and spares tucked into their boot tops. Dad's was made to look like theirs. Unlike his, the locals' were single-shot muzzle-loaders. Reloading a pistol like that on horseback was as near impossible as made no difference. That was why they all carried more than one.

Musketeers had matchlocks, too, but longer ones that would fire farther. They would march on foot. They wore iron back-and-breasts—most of them had light linen surcoats on over them—and high-crested helmets. Feathers or plumes of horsehair topped some of the helms. They marked sergeants and officers.

Pikemen wore similar armor. They and the musketeers looked a lot like Spanish conquistadors from the home timeline. No conquistadors in this alternate—the plague had left Spain almost empty. The pikemen were careful to keep their long spears upright. They could have snarled traffic even worse than it was already if they'd let the pikes drop to the horizontal.

Pikemen, musketeers, and cavalrymen all wore swords along with their main weapons. If a spearshaft broke, if they couldn't reload a matchlock fast enough, they could still defend themselves. Even in the home timeline, officers sometimes wore ceremonial swords to this day. These, though, weren't ceremonial blades. Their leather-wrapped hilts were plain and businesslike, and bore dark sweat stains that said they'd seen use.

One of the pikemen looked familiar to Annette. She needed a moment to figure out why, because he hadn't worn a helmet the last time she saw him. She nudged her mother. "Look," she said. "That's the fellow we were talking with here the other day."

Her mother looked that way. "Why, so it is," she said. "We'll have to watch what we say when he's around. His Arabic isn't bad." Her gaze sharpened. "I wonder if that's why he's along. It seems like something Duke Raoul would do."

"Spy on Muslim merchants, you mean?" Annette asked.

"Maybe," Mom said. "Maybe just spy on *us.* We come from a lot farther away than Marseille, after all. Even though we try our best to fit in, even though we speak the languages perfectly, we're strangers here. Maybe it shows enough to make the locals wonder. I hope not, but maybe."

The pikeman—Jacques, his name was—noticed Annette and her mother looking in his direction. He nodded back at them. His smile, Annette suspected, was aimed at her in particular. She pretended not to notice it. The trip south could get complicated all kinds of ways.

Three

As long as nothing went wrong, guarding a caravan was easy duty. Jacques laughed at himself. As long as nothing went wrong, any duty was easy. But he'd had to hurry down to Count Guillaume's fortress, worrying every step of the way. If you were alone, you always had to worry.

Well, he was anything but alone here. A small town might have gone on parade—and on slow parade at that. Animals ambled along. People either walked or rode beside the beasts of burden. Everybody gabbed with everybody else. Nobody seemed to care when the caravan got to Marseille. The merchants had nobody to haggle with but one another. They might as well have been on holiday.

As for Jacques' fellow guards . . . Most of them were older men, in their twenties or thirties or even forties. To him, men in their forties were almost as old as the Cathedral of Notre-Dame. That was a good age for a ruler, for someone like Duke Raoul. For a man out in the field? He had his doubts.

He needed a while to realize the older men had their doubts about him, too. They called youngsters tadpoles, and seemed to think he couldn't do anything his mother hadn't taught him. That made him furious. He needed a while to realize they thought his fury was funny. He stopped giving them the satisfaction of steaming where they could see it. They treated him better after that—he'd shown he could figure something out, anyhow.

When he left Paris, he thought he would spend most of his time spying on Muhammad al-Marsawi and his wife—and his daughter. Things didn't work like that. The caravanmaster rotated his guards three or four times a day, so nobody kept the same station too long.

Jacques didn't need long to see that that was fair. A few hours as a rear guard, eating everybody else's dust, drove home the lesson. But it meant he couldn't even get close to Muhammad and his family most of the time. At first he thought Duke Raoul would be angry at him for falling down on the job. He was hustling up to the front of the caravan so everyone else could breathe *his* dust for a while when he saw he was being silly. Raoul knew how caravans worked. He knew better than Jacques did, and that was for sure. So he couldn't have expected Jacques to spend every waking moment around Muhammad al-Marsawi . . . and Khadija. Marseille was a long way from Paris. *I have time*, he thought.

He breathed a great big sigh of relief. He didn't have to keep twisting his head to see where the Muslim trader was and what he was up to. A lot of Henri's preaching was about the patient man and what he could do. Jacques had listened to endless sermons from those verses in the Final Testament, but they hadn't made much sense to him. Now, all at once, they did.

He got his first chance to talk with Muhammad when the caravan encamped the second night out from Paris. The caravanmaster had stopped in a meadow that gave the animals good grazing and the people enough room to pitch their tents. Swallows swooped overhead, hawking bugs out of the sky. A white wagtail—actually, the bird was mostly gray and black, though it had a white face—hopped in the grass. Chaffinches called from the bushes around the meadow.

"I hope you are well," Jacques said to the merchant, and then, "Do you need help with your tent?"

"I am well, thank you. May God grant that you be the same. As for this tent"—Muhammad al-Marsawi paused to drive a peg into the ground with a rock—"again, I thank you for the offer, but it is not being too troublesome right this minute."

"Good. I am glad to hear it." Jacques watched the trader drive in another peg. He suddenly understood why this man puzzled Duke Raoul. Everyone else he knew, Christian or Muslim, would have said something like, *I'm not having any trouble with the tent*. Jacques had no trouble understanding what Muhammad al-Marsawi meant. The trader's phrase, which gave the tent a life of its own, was more vivid than the usual way of putting things. But it wasn't anything most people would have said. How had he come to put things like that?

"Have you heard any word of bandits on the road?" the merchant asked.

Anyone traveling in a caravan might ask a question like that. Anyone might sound anxious when he asked it, too. Muhammad al-Marsawi certainly did. The trader had a pistol stuffed into his belt. Jacques thought he was as likely to shoot himself in the foot with it as he was to bring down a raider.

Hiding his scorn, Jacques answered, "As far as I know, the road is clear. Of course, I do not know everything there is to know."

"I hope you know the truth," Muhammad said. "Yes, I hope that very much. God grant it be so."

"Yes, God grant it." Jacques sketched the wheel over his heart. The trader looked away when he did it. Muslims accepted Jesus as a prophet, even if they didn't believe He was the Son of God. But they thought Satan, not God, spoke through Henri. Their Muhammad had said he was the last prophet. To them, anyone who came after him had to be a fraud. To Jacques, that only proved how ignorant they were.

Muhammad al-Marsawi coughed. "My family and I were surprised to see you here after we talked a few days ago."

Jacques' cheeks heated. What could that mean but, *Why are you spying on us?* The merchant might be strange, but he was smart. Well, that wasn't anything Jacques didn't already know. He said, "Duke Raoul chose me for this duty. How could I say no to my liege lord?" The last two words had to come out in French. Arabic didn't have quite the same notion—you could say *master* in Arabic, but not *liege lord*. Any superior could be a master, but a liege lord had obligations to his men in return for the duty they owed him.

"Well, anyone owes his master obedience." The trader didn't bother with the difference between the one and the other. He spoke French as well as he did Arabic, but that didn't mean he understood there was a difference. He went on, "And what do you think of this duty he gave you?"

"I like it," Jacques replied. "I get to go places I have never gone, and I get to meet people I have not met before." He bowed to Muhammad al-Marsawi. "And I get to know better people I have already met."

The trader's eyes twinkled. "Ah, but is it me you want to know better, me with my beard and with my hair going gray, or is it Khadija?"

Another blush set Jacques' face afire. "I do not wish to be a trouble," he said.

"Have I said you are?" the merchant asked. "But I am not a blind man, either."

Most Muslims, from what Jacques had seen and heard, would have been furious if a Christian looked at their daughter. Muhammad al-Marsawi didn't sound furious. He sounded . . .

amused? That relieved Jacques and puzzled him at the same time. He was glad the merchant didn't want to pull out that pistol and aim it at him. But why didn't Muhammad act like most other men from his kingdom?

What would Duke Raoul have to say when he heard this? Probably that it was one more piece that didn't fit in the puzzle. Why was Muhammad al-Marsawi so different? Jacques almost asked. That would have given him away, but the trader might have answered just because he was so different.

Was Khadija different, too? If she was, did that mean she wouldn't mind if Jacques got to know her better? He could hardly wait to find out.

Annette didn't like riding sidesaddle. To her, if you rode sidesaddle you were a fall waiting to happen. But women in this alternate didn't ride astride, so she was stuck. If she didn't care to ride sidesaddle, she could walk. She did a good deal of that, too—not so much as her father, but a good deal even so.

She let out a silent sigh of relief when the caravan left the Kingdom of Versailles and passed into the Kingdom of Berry. She felt safer among Muslims here than she did among this alternate's strange Christians. Western Europe here had been through a lot. It was at last starting to emerge from the new dark age the Great Black Deaths had clamped down on it. In another couple of hundred years, it might be a very lively, very exciting place, the way it had been in the home timeline between 1600 and 1700. For now, this alternate's Western Europe was still a borrower, not a creator.

At the border, the customs inspectors went easy on the Muslims and searched the Christians' goods with great care. It had been the other way around when Annette and her family entered the Kingdom of Versailles this past spring. The inspectors took away a fine bell a trader from the Germanies wanted to bring into their kingdom. He squawked in bad French and worse Arabic, but they wouldn't listen to him.

"He should have known better," Annette's father said as the caravan got moving again. "That can only be a church bell, and churches aren't allowed to have bells in Muslim kingdoms. The Muslims are willing to let them exist—as long as they pay their taxes—but they can't advertise, you might say."

"What do you want to bet the Muslims find something to do with the bell themselves?" Mom said.

"Oh, sure they will." Dad nodded. "Either that or they'll sell it back across the border and make a nice profit on it. But the Germanies are a long way away. Nobody there can go to war with the Kingdom of Berry over how it treats their traders."

The merchant kept spluttering and fuming and complaining till the caravanmaster got tired of listening to him. "Quit grumbling," he told the German. "You got caught with a church bell, so you're stuck. Thank Jesus and Henri that they didn't confiscate the rest of your goods. Then you'd have something to howl about."

"You do not help me!" the trader said.

"I'm sorry." The caravanmaster sounded anything but. "I know a lost cause when I see one." He wheeled his horse and rode away from the German. The man started to ride after him. A couple of guards stepped up and persuaded him that wouldn't be a good idea.

One of the guards was Jacques. After he helped get the merchant from the Germanies calmed down, he looked over in Annette's direction. As soon as he did, she looked away. She knew he was interested in her. This was one of the times when a veil came in handy. Wearing one meant he couldn't see her expression.

He wasn't bad-looking. He seemed nice enough. She might have liked him . . . if he bathed, if he were deloused, if he were dewormed. She might have liked him . . . if he didn't despise people who weren't of his religion, if his head weren't packed full of superstitions. She might have liked him . . . if he weren't from this alternate.

People from Crosstime Traffic were warned not to get too close to the locals when they left the home timeline. People being people, they broke the rules every now and then. When they did, things almost always turned out bad. The rules were there as much to protect people from the alternates as they were to make sure nobody gave away the Crosstime Traffic secret.

On an alternate like this, giving away the secret was only a small worry. The idea of traveling between alternate worlds was beyond most people's mental horizons here. Even if it hadn't been, the locals couldn't do anything about it. The closest thing they had to a computer here was the abacus. People who knew how could do arithmetic amazingly fast with those beads on wires. Even so . . .

Keeping the secret mattered a lot more on alternates with breakpoints closer to the present. A lot of them had had an industrial revolution and a scientific revolution, too. Some of them had technology nearly as good as the home timeline's. A few had technology better than the home timeline's, at least in things that didn't have anything to do with crossing from one alternate to another. Annette's world had learned a lot from them. And if they ever got the idea for crosstime travel, they could run with it.

The guard with Jacques said something. They both laughed. They were probably talking about what a fool the German trader was. Human nature didn't change much from one alternate to another. The other guard slapped Jacques on the back. This time, Jacques said something, and he got a laugh. Annette didn't think the trader would be happy if he could hear them. With the small crisis solved, they separated.

Jacques came over toward Annette and her family. She might have known he would—he did whenever he got the chance. He didn't talk directly to her. That would have been rude, even offensive. But he kept an eye on her while he talked to her father. He was interested, all right. She knew the signs. They weren't much different here from what they would have been in the home timeline.

"God grant that you and yours are well," Jacques said to Dad in his accented Arabic. He'd had to learn it the hard way—no implant for him. You could hear the French underneath.

"God grant you the same," Annette's father said. "I am glad the commotion is over and done with."

"So am I," Jacques replied. "You would not be foolish enough to bring something into the Kingdom of Versailles that is not allowed there."

"Well, I hope not," Dad said. "Life is simpler when you do not go out of your way to make a nuisance of yourself. Not everyone can see that, though."

"Very true," Jacques said gravely. Did he see that he was making a nuisance of himself by coming around and chatting with the Kleins when they didn't want his company? If he did, would he have kept doing it?

Annette waited for her father to show it to him if he didn't see it. But Dad just went on talking about the weather and the road and the likely price of olive oil next year. He passed on some gossip he'd picked up in the caravan, and he listened while Jacques passed on some of his own. Back in the home timeline, Dad wasn't so patient. When he came to this alternate, he gave people the benefit of the doubt. Biting their heads off when they acted like fools would have got him talked about, and he didn't want to draw notice to himself that way.

Instead, he drew notice to himself another way. People from Marseille all the way up to Paris thought Dad was one of the nicest fellows they'd ever met. *Even if he is a Muslim*, Christians would always add when they talked about him. They might apologize for liking him, but like him they did.

It might have been better if no one remembered him, or if people remembered him as an ordinary person. But how could you tell your own father to be less nice? You couldn't—or Annette couldn't, anyhow. And so innkeepers and people he bargained with smiled when they thought about him.

Jacques said, "It must be hard, bringing your wife and your daughter with you on such a long journey."

In the home timeline, Paris and Marseilles were a couple of hours apart by bullet train, less than that by airplane. Here Jacques was right—a long journey separated them. With a smile and a shrug, Dad said, "Well, being separated from them seems a bigger hardship, and so they travel with me."

"Don't you worry about bandits and robbers?" Jacques asked, adding, "I would, if I were traveling with women."

In the home timeline, that would have been a sexist thing to say. In this alternate, as in others that hadn't known an industrial revolution, it was just common sense. On the average, women were smaller than men, and not so strong. And they had babies, which was a dangerous business without modern medicine. In the home timeline, women had a longer life expectancy than men. That wasn't true here, or in other low-tech alternates. Childbirth was the main reason it wasn't true. Some women died of it. Some who didn't were weakened so they died of other things instead.

And no one here had any contraceptives that worked. Once women became sexually active, they *would* get pregnant.

"May God keep bandits and robbers—far away from me," Dad said. Jacques laughed. And Dad was joking, but at the same time he wasn't. Things *could* go wrong on the road, and he knew it. He went on, "It would take a bold band of robbers to attack a caravan this size."

"And one with such brave guards," Mom put in.

Jacques smiled. He had a nice smile. His teeth were straight, and he still had all of them—but then, Annette didn't think he was even her age. His beard was still mostly fuzz. "Maybe the lady your wife gives me too much credit," he said to Dad.

"Maybe she does—but she'd better not," Dad answered.

That made Jacques smile. He bowed to Annette's father. He was careful to keep his long pike upright while he did it. Then he pointed to the pistol on Dad's belt. "If—God prevent it—some cowardly wretches attack us, surely your own great courage and ferocity will make them flee like the jackals and wolves they are." Arabic was a wonderful language for flowery compliments, and for insults that would have sounded over the top in English.

Dad smiled back. Annette thought the curve of his lips looked a little strained, and hoped Jacques wouldn't notice. That pistol seemed ordinary, but it wasn't, not by the standards of this alternate. It was nice to have, but it was for emergencies only. Dad said, "Any caravan that has to depend on me to save it is in more trouble than it knows what to do with."

"And here until now I thought you were a hero, a man without flaws," Jacques said. "Now I see you have one after all—you are too modest." In English, he would have been laying it on with a trowel. In Arabic, the teasing came out just right.

"I am a modest man—a man with plenty to be modest about," Annette's father replied. Annette had heard him use that line before. It really belonged to a twentieth-century British politician. Nobody in this alternate had ever heard it before. It passed for Dad's own wit. If you were going to steal, you should steal from the best.

Jacques shook his head. "Oh, no, sir. Oh, no. You are a man of accomplishments." He shifted from Arabic to French. "I know that many of your countrymen have learned my language. Many of them speak it well—if you are patient and work hard in spite of troubles, you will have your reward in the end." That was straight from Henri's New Revelation. Still in French, Jacques went on, "But never until now have I met a Muslim man who spoke my language *perfectly*, as if he were a Parisian himself. And your lady wife and your daughter are just as fluent. Maybe it is a miracle from God." He made the wheel sign Christians here used instead of crossing themselves.

Annette didn't think he really believed it was a miracle. No—he'd found a polite way to ask, *How do you do that?* The answer was simple . . . if you had the home timeline's technology. Implants made learning a language easy. The information went right to the speech center in your brain, so you used your new tongue as smoothly as if you'd been born speaking it.

Here, the Kleins spoke this alternate's French a little *too* well. Whoever had prepared the language module must have done it from a native speaker. She should have done it from someone whose native language was the local Arabic but who also spoke good French. Then Jacques wouldn't have had any reason to wonder about it.

He waited to see what Dad would say. Dad, for once, didn't seem to know what to say. If he claimed French-speaking relatives, Jacques would check on that. Well, Jacques probably couldn't, but people he knew would be able to. Pretty plainly, he hadn't asked the question at random.

"We learned the way you would think—from slaves in Marseille," Annette said—in Arabic. However much she despised slavery, it came in handy here. She added, "And we have always been good with languages. All of us have."

If snoopy Jacques wanted to check on that—well, good luck. By his grin, he knew he couldn't. He spoke to Dad, not directly to her: "If your charming daughter says it, my master, why then it must be so."

Mom started to laugh. After a moment, so did Dad. Annette and Jacques joined in a heartbeat later. He was looking at her. She wished he could see her. He'd got her good, and he had to know it, and she wanted him to know she knew, too. He'd sounded as if he meant every word of what he said, which only made him more sarcastic than he would have been if he sounded sarcastic.

Annette pointed at him. "You are a demon," she said, as she might have said, *You're a devil* to a friend at high school.

At her high school, though, nobody took demons and devils seriously. They were things you joked around with, things you watched in bad movies, things you killed in computer games, and things that tried to kill you there. They couldn't kill you for real, and you knew it.

It wasn't like that here. To the people in this alternate, demons and devils were as real as cheese and olive oil. When you didn't really know what caused diseases, when you looked to religion to answer your questions about the world because you had nowhere else to look, of course demons and devils seemed real. Annette should have remembered that, but she hadn't. She'd liked Jacques, and so she'd treated him like someone from the home timeline.

And that was a mistake. Only a handful of words, but they horrified him. He made the sign of the wheel again. "By God, by Jesus, by Henri, I am no such evil thing," he said, speaking straight to her for the first time. "I am only a mortal, praying for heaven and afraid of hell and the things that dwell in hell."

"I'm sorry," she said, but he wasn't listening to her. He gave Dad a coldly formal bow, spun on his heel, and stalked away. He was graceful as a cat—a cat whose fur she'd rubbed the wrong way.

"Oh, dear," Mom said.

"He made a joke, and so I made a joke," Annette said helplessly.

"Except that kind of thing isn't a joke here," Dad said. "They broke Henri on the wheel because they thought he was a demon—and no doubt he was." He spoke the last few words louder than the rest, in case anybody else was listening. As someone playing the role of a Muslim in this world, he couldn't have a good word to say about Henri.

"Maybe it's for the best," Annette's mother said. "Jacques was asking a lot of *pointed* questions, wasn't he? He'll think twice before he does that again."

Dad laughed. "He'll think twice before he gets anywhere near us. Either that or he'll want to exorcise us with a bucket of holy water apiece, the way that French priest did with the salamander."

"Salamander?" Annette said, and then, "Oh." He didn't mean a little four-legged creature that lived in damp places and ate bugs. He meant a fire elemental. But that still left her confused. "What French priest?"

"Why, the one in *The Devil's Dictionary*," her father replied, as if she should have known without asking. "A very fitting book for the circumstances, don't you think?" And so it was, but Dad always thought *The Devil's Dictionary* was a fitting book. In it, Ambrose Bierce didn't have a good word to say about anybody or anything, and all his prods and pokes and gibes had style. Dad grinned wickedly. "Can you imagine what would happen if I translated it into the French they use here?"

"*I* can," Annette's mother said before she could answer. "They wouldn't understand half of it, and they'd want to burn you at the stake for the other half."

That sounded about right to Annette. Dad mimed being wounded. As far as Annette was concerned, he was the biggest ham left unsliced. He knew it, too, and took advantage of it. It probably made him a better merchant than he would have been otherwise. And people in this alternate were less restrained than they were in the home timeline. They had no TV, no movies, no radio, no recorded music, no computer games. If they wanted fun, they had to make their own. Overacting when they haggled was part of it.

Another caravan came up the road from the south. It was even bigger than the one coming down from Paris. The two edged past each other. Traders made a few hasty deals as they did. Caravan-masters screamed at both groups to keep moving. The dust they churned up was amazing. Annette's veil kept some of it out of her mouth and nose, but not enough. The guards from each caravan eyed those from the other as if they were about to fight. Nothing came of that, but it worried Annette just the same.

She walked and rode, rode and walked. Peasants in the fields stared at the caravan. A lot of them wouldn't have traveled more than a day's walk from where they were born in their whole lives. Little by little, the weather grew warmer and drier. Marseille had a Mediterranean climate, like that of Los Angeles or Melbourne or Cape Town. The rugged North Atlantic ruled the weather in Paris.

A hoopoe flew by, a bird that looked as if it had no business existing. It was salmon pink, had a feathery crest on its head, and made the strange noises that gave it its name. Birds of all sorts were more common here than they were in the home timeline. Over on the other side of the Atlantic that this world's sailors were only now beginning to cross, passenger pigeons still flew by the billion.

Annette understood why birds and other wildlife were more common here—people were less common. They didn't have the tools to kill on a large scale, either. They didn't have many tools at all, in fact. Those peasants plowed behind oxen. They used hoes and spades and a few other hand tools. In good years, they raised enough to feed themselves and the towns. People went hungry in bad years.

Seeing the towns made her want to cry. Paris was a real city—a raw, smelly city, a twisted ghost of the Paris in the home timeline, but a real city even so. Marseille, too. But even Lyon was just a little country town here. It huddled inside walls that followed the lines of the ones the Romans had built. People said wolves had howled outside those walls not long before the caravan got there.

"Is there any alternate that has enough technology to let people be comfortable but hasn't messed up the environment getting it?" she asked her father in the hostel in Lyon.

He thought for a minute, then shook his head. "Not that I've ever heard. If you've got technology, what do you use it for? To change the environment. That's what technology *does*. You do what seems best for yourself right then. You chop the head off the big bad wolf that ate your granny. You bake four-and-twenty blackbirds in a pie. And you worry about what happens later, later—if you worry at all."

In this alternate, wolves still ate grannies. They hadn't got anybody when they prowled close to Lyon, but they could have. Blackbirds in Europe were different from the ones back in America. They were thrushes, and acted and sounded a lot like American robins. Europe had birds called robins, too, but they weren't closely related to the American kind. It all got confusing. People who studied birds used scientific names to clear up confusion like that. Annette wasn't a scientist, and got confused.

She did know people here baked blackbirds in pies, even if they didn't make rhymes about it.

When she thought about blackbird pie, she missed Burger King and Tuesday's Tapas and Panda Express even more than she had before. "I can't *wait* to get home!" she exclaimed.

"Won't be long now," Dad said.

The farther south Jacques got, the richer the countryside seemed to him. Traveling in the Muslim kingdoms rubbed his nose in how backward his own was. Everybody here seemed well fed. People ate wheat bread all the time. They didn't bother with barley or rye, let alone oats. When they grew oats, they fed them to their horses. Well, so did people in the Kingdom of Versailles. But Jacques had eaten plenty of oat porridge himself. He even liked oats—as long as he was with other people who ate them, too. Down here, it would have taken a torturer to get him to admit he'd ever touched them.

And the farther south he went, the more he found himself speaking Arabic. A lot of the peasants were still Christians. They paid taxes to their overlords so they could keep their religion. And most of them spoke French. But Jacques couldn't always follow them when they did, and they couldn't always understand him, either. Their dialect was so nasal and singsong, it might as well have been another language.

They had no trouble with his Arabic. Theirs sounded pretty much the same. When he mentioned that to Muhammad al-Marsawi, the merchant said, "Arabic has dialects, too. When I talk with a man from Egypt, or from Baghdad, we have to go slowly and figure out what we mean. Sometimes we even have to write things down. The written language is the same everywhere—well, almost—but people from different places pronounce the letters differently."

"But Egypt and Baghdad—they're far, far away. They're over the sea. They're at the edge of the world." To Jacques, those all meant about the same thing. "No wonder people talk funny in places like that. We haven't come anywhere near that far, though, and already these people talk French like . . . like . . . I don't know what."

"It is different from what you hear in Paris," Muhammad agreed.

"It sure is." Jacques took off his helmet, scratched his head, and put the helm on again. "Why don't you speak French the way they do down here? Really, this time."

"Oh, I can talk like this," the Muslim trader said through his nose. That was what Jacques thought he said, anyhow. The Devil might have invented this dialect to torment him. When Muhammad al-Marsawi spoke again, it was in the French of Paris: "But if I did talk like that, people up there couldn't follow me. And so I talk the northern way when I'm with folk from the north."

"Right." Thwarted again, Jacques wondered if there was anything Muhammad couldn't do. "Why don't you know all the other Arabic dialects, too?"

"I don't hear them so often or need them so much," the trader answered as easily. Jacques couldn't trip him up no matter how he tried. He wondered what kind of luck Duke Raoul would have had. Raoul was about the cleverest man he knew. But he'd started to think Muhammad al-Marsawi was just as clever. The Muslim was slick as boiled asparagus.

Jacques glanced over to the shrouded shape of Khadija. He was happier thinking about her than about her father. She gave signs of being clever, too, but—when she wasn't talking about demons—she didn't intimidate him the way Muhammad al-Marsawi did. For one thing, she was female. For another, he thought she was around his own age—though how could you be sure from a pair of eyes? And, for a third, he thought she liked him.

Oh, he didn't think she liked him like *that*. She'd given no sign of it if she did. But she talked at him as they traveled south. She couldn't very well talk *with* him, not when he answered through her father. Still, she did talk. And he thought he heard a smile in her voice every now and then. He even thought he saw a smile in her eyes once or twice. People always talked about how expressive eyes were. And eyes told a lot—when you saw them with the rest of somebody's face. By themselves, they were a lot harder to judge.

"Good day," she called to him in French two mornings after they left Lyon. "I hope you are well. I hope you slept well."

"Please thank your daughter and tell her I am very well, and that I rested well," Jacques said to Muhammad al-Marsawi. He also used French. Speaking his own language felt good. "Tell her also that I hope the same is true for her."

The trader bowed. "By some miracle, I think she will hear you even if I do not speak. Perhaps an angel will whisper your words into her ear. What do you think, eh?"

He was grinning. He might have been inviting Jacques to share the joke. The only trouble was, Jacques wasn't sure there was any joke to share. It sounded more like blasphemy to him. Of course Khadija could hear Jacques even if her father didn't pass his words on to her. Jacques had just done his best to be polite instead of talking straight to her. He hadn't imagined anybody, Muslim or Christian, joking about angels. God's messengers were serious business—just like demons.

"My father . . ." Khadija said in Arabic. Her voice held no

smile now. Instead of being a daughter, she might have been a mother scolding a naughty little boy.

"Yes, I know. I went too far," Muhammad al-Marsawi answered, as if he deserved that scolding. He looked back to Jacques. "Never mind me, my young friend. There are times when my tongue runs away like an unbroken horse, and I do not even have the fun of getting drunk first. Life is full of sorrows." His face turned sad, comically sad. He made fun of himself as easily as he made fun of angels.

But this, at least, was a familiar kind of foolery. Jacques had heard other Muslims act sad that they couldn't drink wine or beer or spirits. He'd also seen some who went ahead and drank whether they were supposed to or not. To them, that was a sin, but all men were sinners, weren't they? Muslim or Christian, that didn't matter. Nobody acted the way he—or even she—should all the time.

"Easy to make peace with me," Jacques said. He lifted his pike a few inches, aiming the point toward the heavens. "Have you made your peace with God?"

"I hope I have," the trader answered. "But that's my worry, don't you think?"

The question made Jacques scratch his head. He scratched his head a lot around Muhammad al-Marsawi and his family. They seemed to look at the world through a different window, and they saw different things. And then they went and talked about them! Wasn't salvation everybody's business? Jacques had never known anybody, Christian or Muslim, who didn't think so. Society on both sides of the border was set up with that in mind. If Jacques understood Muhammad al-Marsawi—and he thought he did—the merchant said what other people thought didn't matter.

Jacques didn't ask him about that. One of these days, Muhammad and his family would come back to Paris. Duke Raoul could worry about it then. It was too much for a messenger and caravan guard to get to the bottom of.

And Jacques had other things to worry about. The road from Lyon went south and a little east. The country rose. There were fewer farms and more forests. Some places, trees and brush hadn't been cleared back far enough from the road. Some places, they'd hardly been cleared back at all. He muttered to himself. All the guards were muttering and fuming. If this wasn't ambush country, he'd never seen any that was.

He breathed a sigh of relief when they made it to Grenoble, in the valley of the Isère. But a look south from the town told him the worst part of the journey still lay ahead. Real mountains still stood between the caravan and Marseille, mountains with forests of oak and ash and elm and hickory on their lower slopes and darker, gloomier pine woods farther up their sides. They might have been daring honest men to come through them.

A long, slogging day and a half out of Grenoble . . .

Four

Annette thought the countryside south of Grenoble some of the most beautiful she'd ever seen. The woods, the blue, blue sky, the crisp air, the little streams leaping down over rocks and making miniature waterfalls—it all reminded her of walking through a national park back in the home timeline. But this was no park. It was just part of the countryside.

Choughs were raucous overhead. They looked like skinny crows, except they had red legs and feet. Some had red beaks, too. Others had yellow. Dad said they were two different kinds of bird. Annette didn't worry about that one way or the other. She was happy enough admiring them. They swooped and tumbled in the air like Olympic gymnasts. Unlike gymnasts, they didn't have to worry about falling.

Having branches in new leaf overhead was nice. Annette enjoyed the shade. When she got to Marseille, her hands would be suntanned. So would a rectangle that included the bottom of her forehead, the skin around her eyes, the top of her nose, and the top of her cheeks. The rest of her? Fishbelly white. When you saw people with really strange patterns of tan and pale skin in the home timeline, you could bet they'd been out working in the alternates.

Mom was as bad off as Annette was. Dad wasn't, not quite— at least his whole face saw the sun. At the moment, he looked worried. "This is the worst part," he said for the third or fourth time that morning. "If we can get through this stretch, it's all downhill from here." He meant that literally as well as figuratively.

Something changed, up in the air. Annette looked up, trying to see what it was. She didn't see anything for a moment. Then she realized that was the problem. The choughs were gone. The caravan hadn't bothered them. What would have?

Up ahead, the road turned a corner. She couldn't see what lay around the corner because of the trees. She didn't think much of it when her part of the caravan stopped. That happened every now and then. You didn't need a freeway to make a traffic jam. Horses and mules and people and a narrow road would do the job just fine. If another good-sized party was trying to come up this dirt track while her caravan was going down it . . .

The caravanmaster's horn blew urgently from the head of the column. Guards pounded up toward the van. Annette couldn't see how the pikemen kept from fouling one another with their long-shafted weapons, but they did.

"I don't like the look of that," Mom said.

"Neither do I." Dad pulled the pistol from his belt. He was one of the most peaceable men in the world, but even peaceable men had trouble staying that way if the people around them wouldn't.

The volley of musket fire came from the woods on both sides of the road. The roar was like the end of the world. Wounded men screamed. So did wounded horses. Their cries of pain were terrible. Women on the rack might have shrieked like that. Dad cried out and stared at his hand. He was only slightly wounded—but the precious pistol went flying. In the movies, cops shot pistols out of bad guys' hands all the time. In real life, that was wildly unlikely. But unlikely didn't mean impossible. Whoever fired at him doubtless hadn't tried to knock away the handgun. He'd done it, though, try or not.

Another volley boomed. Thick smoke showed where the musketeers hid behind trees and rocks. It smelled like a Fourth of July fireworks display in a park. Warm summer nights and fireflies didn't belong in this chaos, but Annette couldn't help thinking of them. The smell of gunpowder smoke summoned them to her mind.

"Get the gun!" Dad said urgently. He was opening and closing his right hand, trying to make it work again, while blood dripped from the webbing between his thumb and forefinger.

Annette took two steps toward the pistol. Then a spooked horse bowled her over. She squawked and fell. The horse didn't trample her. That was good luck, the way Dad's losing the handgun was bad luck. The beast's hooves thumped down all around her. It could as easily have kicked her in the head.

As soon as the horse thudded away, Annette's mother pulled her to her feet. "Are you all right?" Mom asked in a strange, shaky voice.

"Get the pistol!" Dad said again, and then, "Where the devil did it go?" The horse that had knocked Annette down wasn't the only one going crazy. One of the animals must have kicked it away—in the chaos, who could say where?

And Annette and her mother got no time to search for it. Men were running out of the woods. Some wore robes, others tunics and breeches. Some had swords, some had spears, some had pistols. A few wore helmets. None seemed to have any other armor. They were all screeching like banshees.

"Run!" Dad shouted. "I'll hold them off!"

But there was nowhere to run to, nowhere to hide. The brigands were coming from both sides. One of them grabbed Annette. She flipped him over her shoulder and slammed him to the ground. She'd taken years of judo classes. She'd never imagined they would come in handy against a ruffian who might not have had a bath in his whole life. But they did. Nobody in this world fought like that. The bandit landed on his head and lay still afterwards. Annette hoped she hadn't killed him, but she didn't hope very hard.

She sent another man flying a moment later. Then somebody clouted her just above the ear with a spearshaft. All the judo classes in the world couldn't help her with that. The world flared red for a moment, then went black. She crumpled, and never knew when she hit the ground.

The caravanmaster's horn call meant trouble up ahead. Clutching his pike, Jacques trotted forward to see what had gone wrong. Up till now, nothing had. Older men who'd made a lot of these journeys were talking about how smooth this one was. Talking too soon was never a good idea.

If a robber band wanted to strike the caravan, this was a good place to do it. The forest came down close to the road on either side. They weren't close to any towns. All the same, Jacques had trouble believing anyone would try to bother this particular caravan. Its guards and merchants could put up a good fight.

Then he saw the roadblock ahead. The tree trunks and boulders made sure nobody was going forward. From behind the roadblock, a man shouted in Arabic: "Surrender, you dogs! You cannot hope to get away!"

"If you want us, you'll have to take us!" the caravanmaster yelled back. He was up on horseback. His sword leaped free of the scabbard. The blade flashed in the sun. He shouted again, this time in French: "God and Jesus and sweet Henri with us!"

A dozen men popped up behind the barricade. They rested their muskets on the timber and stone to steady their aim. The boom of the volley stunned Jacques' ears.

Something slammed Jacques in the chest. He groaned and staggered. Breathing hurt, but not the way it would have if he'd got a bullet in the lungs. He tore open his surcoat and looked down at himself. His back-and-breast was lead-splashed and dented, but it had held the bullet out.

Not everyone was so lucky. Men went down, some dead, others wounded. The caravanmaster's horse fell, too. The master had kicked free of the stirrups, though, and was on his feet, still waving that sword. "Come on, men!" he cried. "We can beat these swine!" If the robbers spoke French, that would make them angry. You couldn't call a Muslim anything worse than a pig.

Those musketeers ducked away from the barricade to reload. Another dozen or so took their place. They poured another volley into the guards at the head of the column. More brigands were shooting from the woods to either side. Jacques ground his teeth. Whoever'd planned this attack knew just what he was doing.

"Forward!" the caravanmaster shouted, aiming his sword at the roadblock. "They can't have any more men with guns back there now!" He trotted toward the jumble of stones and felled trees. Cheering, the guards still on their feet followed.

But he was wrong. A man aimed a cavalry pistol at him and shot him in the chest. The caravanmaster was unarmored. He hadn't thought he would need to be a general, too. He groaned. He gurgled. He dropped his sword. He staggered and fell.

The charge he would have led came to a ragged halt. More musketeers popped up behind the barricade and gave the guards another volley. This one was more ragged than the two that had gone before. Jacques knew what that meant. The bandits who'd fired the first volley had reloaded, and the faster men hadn't waited for the slower ones to finish.

A bullet cracked past his ear. That was the noise bullets made when they came too close. Jacques laughed, not that it was funny. How could you come any closer than getting hit square in the chest? But his face wasn't armored. His arms and legs weren't, either.

Another bullet flew by. An instant later, it struck home with a soft, wet, slapping sound. A horse screamed. Jacques thought it was a horse, anyway. With sounds of pain, you couldn't always tell.

"What do we do?" somebody cried, panic in his voice. "Jesus and Henri, what *can* we do? Do they aim to murder us all?"

If they did, they were like no bandits Jacques had ever heard of. Part of the profit in robbing a caravan came from selling its goods. The rest came from selling people into slavery—or, if they were rich enough, from holding them for ransom. Jacques wasn't rich. Fear made his limbs feel light. He didn't want to fall into slavery. But he didn't want to die here, either.

Screams and shouts and curses rose from farther back along the length of the caravan. He knew what that meant. The bandits were seizing traders, who couldn't fight back so well. They had the guards right where they wanted them.

He started running back. He couldn't help anybody where he was, not even himself. Farther back, he might be able to do Khadija and her family some good. As he ran, he realized he should have thought of Muhammad al-Marsawi and *his* family. Well, too bad. He'd thought the way he'd thought, and he'd meant it, too.

He got shot a few heartbeats later.

One moment, he was running as fast as he could. The next, he lay in the dirt by the side of the road, howling like a wolf. Blood turned the calf of his left trouser leg red. He pulled up the trouser leg to look at the wound. It could have been worse. A bullet had torn a chunk of meat out of that big muscle. But it hadn't hit a bone, and he dared hope it hadn't torn the tendon. If the wound didn't fester, he might not even limp in a few weeks.

But that would be in a few weeks. Now . . .

He took his knife from his belt and cut a strip of cloth from the trouser leg to bandage the wound and slow the bleeding. He'd just finished, biting his lip against the pain, when a man with a sword ran up to him. "Yield or die!" the bandit shouted, first in Arabic, then in French.

Jacques let the knife fall in the dirt. "I yield," he said in Arabic. Even if he killed this robber, he couldn't hope to get away.

"Ah, you speak a real language. That means you will sell for more." The bandit sounded happy. Jacques had used Arabic for just that reason. If he was going to be a slave, he wanted to be a valuable one. He'd get treated better. The man who stood over him asked, "Can you walk?"

"I don't think so," Jacques answered. "Not far, anyway."

"All right." The bandit shouted for a friend. The friend came up leading a horse. Earlier that morning, one of the merchants in the caravan had been riding it. Now it was just loot. Jacques realized he was just loot, too. The only reason the robbers kept him alive was to make money selling him. He was glad they had any reason at all.

He couldn't mount by himself, not with the wounded leg. The brigands helped him up onto the horse's back. They tied his feet together under the animal and tied his hands to the reins. By then, the fighting was almost over. A last few bangs, a last few screams, and it ended. The merchants and the guards were either dead or captured. All their trade goods were spoil for the bandits.

Unwounded men who'd surrendered were put to work clearing the roadblock. Jacques got to watch that. He was no good as a laborer, not right now. One of his captors gave him water to drink. He would rather have had wine, but took what he could get. Up there on horseback, he looked around for Khadija and her father and mother. He didn't see any of them. He hoped she was all right—and her parents, too.

When Annette Klein woke up, she wished she hadn't. In those first horrible seconds, in fact, she wasn't sure she had. She was convinced she'd died and gone to hell. For one thing, her head still felt as if it wanted to fall off. Most of her wished it would. She'd seen plenty of movies and TV shows where the hero got knocked cold and was running and jumping and fighting again five minutes later. Real life didn't work like that. She felt as if her brain had just banged off the inside of her skull—and it had.

For another, her eyes didn't want to focus. And even when they did, she didn't want to believe they had. The ground seemed much too close, and everything else was upside down.

She tried to raise a hand to her aching head, and found she couldn't. What with everything else that had gone wrong, she wondered for a panicky instant if she was paralyzed. Then she realized she couldn't move her hands because they were tied to her feet. After she got clouted, somebody'd slung her over a horse's back and tied her up so she couldn't fall off—or get away.

The world made more sense. That didn't make her feel any better, though. The pounding pain in her head and the unnatural way the ground going by looked combined to make her seasick or horsesick or whatever the right word was. She threw up all over the dirt below.

Somebody in robes came up to her. She could see only the

bottom half of him, and that was as upside down as anything else. "So—you are awake, are you?" he said in Arabic.

Annette spat a couple of times before answering, trying to get the vile taste out of her mouth. She didn't have much luck. "I—think so," she said.

He laughed. It was the laugh of someone who'd seen plenty of people in the same boat as she was. It was, in other words, the laugh of a man who took slaves. Ice and fire ran through her. She hated him and feared him at the same time. Whatever else he was, though, he wasn't a man who was more cruel to his livestock than he had to be. "Would you like some water?" he asked. "Can you sit right side up on a horse?"

"Water? Oh, please!" Annette said. The other took more thought, and thought wasn't easy. "I'll try to sit up. It has to be better than this." Maybe she could escape when they untied her. It worked in the movies.

By the time they got through dealing with her, she decided she would never take another movie seriously as long as she lived. She was still too sick and woozy to run, let alone to fight anybody. But even if she hadn't been, the man who let her down from the horse called a couple of friends over. One of them had a pistol. The other one had a musket. Those weapons weren't accurate out to any distance. But the bandits couldn't very well miss if she was only a meter or two away.

They didn't come any closer than that, either. "You're the one who sent Ibrahim flying, aren't you?" the fellow with the pistol said.

Her memory of the fight was fuzzy, but she nodded. A moment later, she wished she hadn't—pain stabbed through her battered head. She was lucky she didn't have a fractured skull— or, for all she knew, maybe she did.

"In the name of God, the compassionate, the merciful, could you teach others that trick?" the bandit asked eagerly. "We're all still laughing at Ibrahim because of the way he came down, thump!"

"Maybe," Annette said vaguely. She had to try three times before she could climb up into the saddle. She sat there swaying, doing her best not to see double. She pointed a shaky finger at the pistoleer. "And how dare you call God 'the compassionate, the merciful' when you speak of fighting tricks?"

All the bandits thought that was the funniest thing they'd ever heard. "Hear how she talks—like a *qadi al-Islam*," the pistoleer said.

"She was an honest judge, Daud, for you did wrong," replied the man with the musket.

The brigand who'd let Annette down from the horse now tied her feet under it. He straightened up, another length of rope in his hand. "She is a warrior maid and a scholar, both at once," she said. "Truly she will bring a great price."

"*Inshallah*," the other two murmured—*if God wills it.*

"Here," the first man said to Annette. "Give me your hands, and I will tie them to the reins. We don't want you getting away—oh, no, indeed."

Numbly, she did. He knew what he was doing with ropes. He tied her tight enough to keep her from getting loose, but not tight enough to cut off her circulation. This all seemed more like a bad dream than reality—except for her headache, which was much *too* real. *But I'm supposed to start at Ohio State soon!* She wanted to shout it. She wanted to scream it. But she knew too well it wouldn't do her the least bit of good.

She looked around. If she moved her head very slowly, she could do that without hurting herself too badly. "Where are my mother and father?" she asked. It wasn't quite like screaming, *Mommy!*—although she felt like doing that, too.

The bandits put their heads together. After half a minute or so, the one with the pistol said, "Our friends who are going on to Marseille must have taken them."

"We're . . . not going on to Marseille?" Annette asked. Another hope crashed and burned. Dad might have been able to use his radio—if a robber hadn't stolen it. Even if a robber did, she and her family might have been recognized there. Crosstime Traffic people could have bought them or stolen them away. That might still happen with her mother and father. Annette gulped. "Where—are we going?"

"Madrid," the pistoleer answered. "A really great city with a really great market. Madrid!"

Now Jacques knew what Khadija looked like. The slavers had stripped the veils off all the Muslim women they'd captured. Their modesty wasn't worth protecting any more—a slave *had* no modesty, except what the master granted. And buyers would want to see what they were getting before they parted with their dinars.

Some of the Muslim women took it very badly. By the way they fussed and carried on, the bandits might have stripped them naked. And so the bandits might have, if they'd wanted to—who could have stopped them? Those women tried to cover their faces with their hands and turned their heads away whenever they saw a man looking at them. When men looked at them from two directions at once, they didn't know what to do. It might have been funny if it weren't so sad.

Khadija wasn't like that. She rode along like a captive

princess—her attitude told the world that, whatever had happened to her, it wasn't her fault. She had a big, nasty bruise on one side of her face. A slaver must have had to hit her hard to make her give up. Somehow, that didn't surprise Jacques.

But for the bruise, she was very pretty—not beautiful, but very pretty. He'd already known she had large brown eyes. Her nose was strongly arched, but not too big. She had the finest, whitest, straightest teeth of anyone he'd ever seen. His own teeth were good. Even his wisdom teeth were coming in without giving him torments, the way so many people's did. But her teeth were better. He had to admit it. A good thing the bandit hadn't broken them when he hit her. Of course, he might have been careful about that, because broken teeth would make her worth less. The bruise would go away. Broken teeth were there for good.

The brigands didn't mind if friends among their captives rode with other friends. Jacques was shy at first about moving up next to Khadija, but he soon did. She was the only person in this luckless crew he cared anything about. His fellow guards—older men—were gloomy and sour, and they had reason to be. They had to know they'd likely go to the mines or to galley slavery or something like that—a short life, and not a merry one.

All Khadija said when they first got close enough to talk was, "So they caught you, too."

"I'm afraid so," Jacques said. "How are you?"

"My head hurts," she answered matter-of-factly.

"I believe it," he said. "The whole left side's all over purple."

"Is it?" Her mouth twisted. "Well, I'm lucky not to have a mirror, then. What happened to you?"

He knew what she was asking. *Did you just give up?* She would have scorned him if he'd quit without putting up a fight. But he hadn't, and he had the wound to prove it, even if it was on the side away from her. "I got shot in the leg," he said, not without pride.

"Oh!" Khadija's mouth got bigger still. "How is it?"

"It hurts." He was as matter-of-fact as she had been. "But it's not too bad. No broken bone, and I'm not hamstrung. As long as the wound doesn't go bad, I'll be all right in a while." Telling that to himself—telling that to the world—made him feel a little less as if a wildcat were gnawing on the leg. A little.

"I hope so." She sounded as if she meant it. "They're taking us to *Madrid*. Isn't that dreadful?"

Jacques only shrugged. "Madrid? Marseille? Naples? What difference does it make to a slave?"

"It makes a difference to me," Khadija said. "My family and friends are in Marseille. If I went on the block there, they'd buy me and set me free. My father and mother are on the way there now, with the rest of the slavers." Up till then, she'd been strong as an iron bar. But at last her face crumpled. "And I'm all alone here, and I don't know what to do."

He couldn't even reach out and pat her hand, not when he was tied to his horse's reins. In French, he said, "You're not alone here unless you want to be." He wasn't sure he could get the exact meaning across in Arabic, and he didn't want her to misunderstand him here.

She didn't say anything for most of a minute, and her face didn't show anything, either. He remembered she was a master merchant's daughter. She would have more ways than a veil to hide her thoughts. When at last she smiled, the sun might have come out, even though it was already shining. "That is very kind," she answered, also in French. "Truly we are partners in misfortune." She added, "That is the kind of fortune that never misses."

In spite of everything, Jacques laughed. "Well said! You have a way with words."

"You give me too much credit," Khadija said. "It is a saying from—a book of proverbs, I guess you might call it."

"It doesn't sound like any proverb I ever heard," Jacques said. "What is the name of this fabulous book?"

To his surprise, Khadija blushed. "It's called *The Devil's Wordbook*," she answered. With his hands tied, Jacques couldn't make the sign of the wheel, but he started the gesture anyway. She saw him do it. "There—I knew that would happen," she said. "It's not a bad book, just a . . . sharp-tongued one. It's been one of my father's favorites for a long, long time, and he taught me to like it, too."

"*The Devil's Wordbook*." Jacques tasted the name. It sounded unsavory. It sounded downright unholy. But Muhammad al-Marsawi had struck him as not only a clever man but a good one. And Khadija was the closest thing to a friend he had in the world right now. He didn't want to think ill of her. "Tell me another proverb from this wordbook, then," he said, a challenge in his voice.

She frowned, then nodded. "All right. It calls a beggar someone who has relied on the assistance of his friends."

Jacques needed a couple of heartbeats for that to sink in. When it did, he winced. "Whoever wrote that book dipped his pen in bile, didn't he?"

"Oh, yes," Khadija answered.

"Give me another one," Jacques said. Anything that helped pass the time was good.

Khadija frowned again. Then she gave him one that struck close to home—probably too close to home—for both of them: "It says an auctioneer is a man who proclaims with a hammer that he has picked a pocket with his tongue."

Paris had plenty of pickpockets, so Jacques got that one right away. He winced again, more painfully this time. He and Khadija would both go under the hammer before long, and some auctioneer would feed his children because of them. He said, "Tell me another one."

"Do you know what an interregnum is?" Khadija said the word in both Arabic and French. Jacques hadn't known the Arabic term. The French . . .

"When a kingdom has trouble with the succession, it's the time between kings."

"That's right." He won a smile from Khadija, which felt even better than praise from Duke Raoul. She went on, "Well, *The Devil's Wordbook* calls an interregnum the period during which a monarchical country is governed by a warm spot on the cushion of a throne."

Tied up or not, on his way to be sold as a slave or not, Jacques laughed out loud. For three or four heartbeats, he forgot all about his troubles. He wondered if anyone had ever given him a more precious gift. "They ought to hear that in Ireland and the Germanies," he said. Those lands had lots of rulers and lots of strife, so they also had lots of interregnums.

"Maybe they should." But Khadija's smile faded like sunshine after the clouds rolled in. She tried to lift a hand to her head. Her bonds wouldn't let her, any more than Jacques' let him shape the sign of the wheel. "I'm sorry," she muttered. "Sometimes it feels like they're mining for lead between my ears, and they've just sharpened their picks."

"That can happen when you get hit," Jacques said sympathetically. Sometimes people got better in a few days or a few weeks. But he knew men who still got headaches and had trouble thinking clearly years after they were hurt. He didn't say anything like that to Khadija. It would have lowered her spirits. And lowering hers would have lowered his.

———

What was southern France in the home timeline held four Muslim kingdoms—actually, one was a principality and one was an emirate—in this alternate. Annette got to see them all, in what seemed a slow-motion journey. One field of wheat looked like another. So did one vegetable garden or meadow or vineyard or olive grove.

Cows and horses and sheep and goats and (on Christian farms) pigs were their familiar selves. They weren't so highly bred as they were in the home timeline. Many more of them looked sickly than they would have in her France. Anthrax wasn't a terrorist weapon here. It was an ordinary disease, a livestock-killer that sometimes killed farmers and herdsmen, too.

Little by little, her headaches eased. They came less often, and didn't—quite—make her wish someone would cut off her head. One of the slavers made her a sort of tea from willow leaves. It tasted nastier than anything she'd ever drunk. To her surprise, though, it did take the edge off the headaches. Then she remembered that willow leaves had salicylic acid in them, and salicylic acid was most of the way toward being aspirin. Some folk remedies really worked.

She kept wishing Crosstime Traffic people would swoop down out of the sky in a helicopter and rescue her. There were only two things wrong with that. This alternate had no helicopters. And nobody in Marseille knew where she was. Crosstime Traffic hadn't been here very long, and was still setting down, setting up, and exploring. And southern France might not look big on a map, but it sure did when you rode across it on horseback.

She thought she would have gone straight round the bend if not for Jacques. To her, being captured and sold was something out of a nightmare or a bad movie. To him, it was just something that happened. It wasn't good, but it was part of the world he was used to. He would have had trouble believing how most people in

Columbus took fender-benders for granted. Nobody liked them, but an awful lot of people ended up in one every once in a while. Annette would have traded this for a fender-bender a week the rest of her life. She didn't get choices like that, worse luck.

She didn't need long to figure out that Jacques wouldn't have been so friendly, or would have been friendly in a different way, if she were a boy and not a girl. He didn't make a pest of himself, which was something.

Even without that one, she had plenty of other things to worry about. She'd thought she might escape and try to get back to Marseille alone, or maybe with Jacques. But she never got the chance. Her captors were professionals at what they did. Nobody in the USA had ever had a job like this. There'd been slave trackers, slave hunters, before the Civil War, but slave catchers, people who caught free men and women to turn them into slaves? No, not inside the United States. And the slavers made sure they always posted guards. They made sure their prisoners' bonds were secure at night. Nobody got loose. Nobody got away.

After Jacques' leg healed enough for him to limp around, he had the same idea. But his luck was no better than Annette's. "I had a little knife stashed in my boot," he said mournfully. "They found it when they searched me."

"Too bad." Annette meant it. She'd had a little knife strapped to her leg. She didn't have it any more. She didn't remember getting searched, which was probably a mercy. They must have done it while she was still out cold.

The Pyrenees rose in the southwest. Farmers raised some herb in their gardens. Its smell on the breeze was familiar, but Annette couldn't place it. When she asked Jacques, he said, "That's fennel, isn't it?"

"Fennel! Of course it is!" Annette said. Now she knew what the odor reminded her of—the Italian sausage on a pizza.

Jacques was giving her a curious look, and she knew why, too. She should have been more familiar with a southern spice than he was. To cover herself, she said, "That knock in the noggin scattered more of my brains than I'd thought. I'm lucky to remember my own name, let alone fennel."

It worked. "Oh, yes," Jacques said seriously. "That can happen."

She wondered why keeping her secret mattered now. What difference would telling him the truth make? Odds were he wouldn't believe it. And even if he did, what could he do about it?

In the end, training told. She kept quiet. Jacques might get away or buy his freedom after she told him. Even if he didn't, he might tell his master or his fellow slaves. Word might spread. And whatever word did spread would be garbled. She was as sure of that as she was of her own name. Surer—since the concussion, she sometimes really did have to fight to hold on to who she was. But talk here about Crosstime Traffic would be talk about witches and wizards, or at best talk about alchemists. The company didn't need that kind of talk, and this alternate didn't need it, either. It could send people here looking in too many wrong directions, just when they were finally starting to come out from under the shadow of the Great Black Deaths.

Crossing the mountains meant crossing a border, as it did in the home timeline. On the other side, the people who didn't speak Arabic spoke Catalan, the same as they did back home. It wasn't quite the same Catalan, any more than the French and the Arabic were the same. Annette could pick out a word here and there, but that was about all. She hadn't learned it through her implant or studied it on her own. She did a little better with signs, but there weren't many signs to see. Gutenberg had never been born in this alternate. No one had invented printing here.

They kept on to the south and west. They crossed the Ebro at

Zaragoza. By then, lisping Castilian Spanish had replaced Catalan. Annette had an even harder time with that, especially when
she heard it. The country was broad and high and rolling, hot and
dry, with herds of sheep and also camels—on its way to being a
desert if not quite there. The camels didn't seem out of place, even
if Spain in the home timeline had none. She wanted to say something to Jacques about the camel being the sheep of the desert.
But the pun worked only in English, not in French or Arabic.

Maybe that was just as well. She wondered if such a bad pun
meant her wits were coming back or if she had more brain damage than she thought.

Madrid in the home timeline was an enormous city, not much
smaller than Paris. In this alternate, Madrid was bigger and more
important than Paris. That didn't make it an enormous city, but
did make it a fair-sized one. At a guess, Annette thought it held
somewhere between a quarter-million and half a million people.
In an alternate without good roads, that was about as big as a city
could get.

Suburbs straggled out beyond the big, thick walls that de-
fended the city's heart. Houses showed the street nothing but
walls and doors and narrow, shuttered windows. They centered
on their courtyards, where only family and friends would come.
The richer homes had whitewashed walls and red tile roofs. They
looked a little like houses in California in the home timeline.
Those houses were often called California Spanish. The weather
was similar, so the colonists coming up from Mexico had brought
with them what worked in their Spain.

Poorer homes weren't whitewashed. Their walls were of
plain mud brick, their roofs often thatched. And hovels could be
made of anything at all, which meant mostly wood and rubble.
People here didn't have sheet iron and plastic.

Madrid was richer than Paris as well as being bigger. Even the suburbs outside the wall had cobblestoned streets. That made the way less dusty than it had been. Less dusty, yes—less smelly, no. Madrid had no sewers. People threw slops and garbage into the street from rich homes and poor alike. Flies buzzed. Dogs and pigs rooted through the rubbish. So did skinny children, looking for things they could use that their richer neighbors didn't want.

Annette had seen that in Paris, too. It made her sad and angry at the same time. People shouldn't have to live as scavengers off other people. But in so many alternates—and, even now, some places in the home timeline—they did.

Jacques took the scrounging children for granted. From things he'd said, he hadn't been that poor when he was a little boy, but he knew plenty of people who had. Wrinkling his nose, he said, "You forget how much a city stinks till you've been away from one for a while."

"They shouldn't smell this bad," she said. "People ought to be cleaner. They shouldn't throw trash and slops every which way."

"What are you going to do with that stuff, then? You can't just leave it in your house." Jacques sounded like someone who'd just heard something silly being reasonable. By this alternate's standards, he was.

They passed over a drawbridge and through a gate and into the walled part of Madrid. Two low, broad buildings stood side by side next to a market square. Annette and the female captives were herded into one, Jacques and the men into the other. Annette needed only a moment to realize what the buildings were—slave barracks. And that market was bound to be a slave market. Some time before very long, they were going to sell her there like a bit of mutton. And she couldn't do a thing about it.

Five

As far as Jacques was concerned, the slave barracks were just . . . barracks. They were more crowded than the ones in Paris or in Count Guillaume's fort. The beds weren't as good—thin pallets of musty straw wrapped in scratchy fabric. The food wasn't as good, either, and they didn't get as much of it. But he *could* sleep on his pallet, and they didn't starve him. He had nothing to do but wait. A lot of soldiering was like that, too.

He did have interesting people to wait with. Some of the men in the barracks were black as ebony, almost as black as coal. When he first saw them, he thought they were captive demons. When they found out, they thought he was an idiot. They spoke better Arabic than he did, though with an odd accent.

"We were taken in war," one of them said. "It must have been God's will, though what we did to make Him angry at us, I cannot say." He spread his hands, palms up. Those palms were pale. So were the soles of his feet. That fascinated Jacques. The black man—his name was Musa ibn Ibrahim—went on, "And what of you, stranger? Till we came here, all the men we ever saw had brown eyes and black hair, whether their skin was light or dark."

Jacques' hair was an ordinary brown, his eyes gray. He said, "Some in my kingdom have hair darker than mine, some lighter. Some have yellow hair."

"Yes, I have seen this," Musa agreed. "It is peculiar."

"Not as peculiar as a black hide," Jacques said. But Musa only thought that was funny. Everyone in his kingdom was black, and so to him people were supposed to be that way. Jacques went on, "Some people—a few—in my kingdom have hair the color of polished copper."

"This I have not seen." Musa ibn Ibrahim raised an eyebrow. It was hard to make out against his dark skin. "I think you are telling stories to see what I will believe."

"By God and Jesus and Henri, I am not," Jacques said indignantly. "Ask any of the men from the north who are here. They will tell you the same."

Musa sighed. "Who knows what a Christian oath is worth? Muhammad was the seal of prophets, so Satan must have sent this Henri."

Muslims always said that. Jacques' fists bunched. He didn't feel like hearing it now. "You take it back!" he said. He was bigger than the black man, but Musa was older and no doubt more experienced. Musa also looked ready to fight, but he didn't throw the first punch.

"Hold up, both of you," an older man said. "They whip you if you brawl. They don't want you damaging the merchandise."

"I am not merchandise," Musa ibn Ibrahim said with dignity. "I am a man."

"Well, so am I," Jacques said, "and I'm a man you insulted."

"I did not insult you. I insulted your foolish religion," Musa said.

"Same thing!" Jacques said. "Shall I tell you what Christians think of Muhammad?"

"Who cares about such ignorant opinions?" Musa said, but Jacques saw him get angry. To Jacques' surprise, Musa saw himself getting angry, too. He started to laugh. "We are in a mirror, you and I. But which of us is holding it and which the reflection?"

Jacques knew what he thought. He needed a little while to realize the black man would think the opposite. He said, "If there were any Jews here, they would tell us we're both wrong."

"Ah, do you have Jews in your country?" Musa ibn Ibrahim asked. "I know there are some in the Maghrib, the land between my kingdom and Spain, and they say some of these Spaniards are Jews, too. In my land, though, we have none."

"You're lucky. We have a few," Jacques said. "We'd have more, too, if we didn't give them a hard time."

Musa looked at him. "We feel that way about Christians."

The Kingdom of Versailles felt that way about Muslims, too. But it couldn't treat them as badly as it treated Jews. The rich, powerful Muslim lands to the south would have gone to war to protect the Muslims in the kingdom if it did more than make them pay a special tax. Jacques didn't want to admit his land was too weak to do everything it wanted to. He changed the subject instead, asking, "What kind of dangerous animals do you have?"

"You mean, besides Christians?" Musa said slyly. Jacques spluttered. The black man laughed. He'd wanted to hit a nerve, and he had. He went on, "Well, the beast a warrior measures himself against is the lion."

"Lions? You really have lions?" Jacques said. Musa gave back a sober nod. The idea of lions impressed Jacques almost as much as the other man's color. "Have you hunted them?"

"I have killed three," Musa ibn Ibrahim declared with somber pride. *Believe me or not—I don't care. I know what I have done*, his manner seemed to say. Because of that manner, Jacques did believe him. Musa asked, "And what beasts have you? Not lions, by the way you speak of them. You are lucky if you do not."

"We have wolves and bears," Jacques said.

They were just names to the other captive. Jacques had to

explain what they were. At first, Musa wasn't much impressed. "Wild dogs? We have wild dogs, too. I did not think to name them."

"*Big* wild dogs," Jacques said. "They can weigh almost as much as a man. And they hunt in packs. A lion could kill one wolf, I suppose. But I don't think a lion could beat a pack of wolves."

"Lions hunt in prides, too," Musa said, which Jacques hadn't known. "What of these other beasts, these beers?"

"Bears," Jacques said, laughing. "A beer is something else." As well as he could, he told Musa about bears. He wondered how much sense his words made to the black man. Then he wondered how well he understood Musa. Which of them was the looker, which the image he looked at? Or were they just two mirrors, looking back at each other?

Annette found herself bored in the slave barracks. She'd expected a lot of things, but not that. She asked permission to write a letter to her kin in Marseille, asking for ransom. The men who'd caught her refused. "It would take too long," one of them said. "We need the money now, as soon as the next auction comes. And we would have to pay to send the letter all that way, and find someone who was going there to carry it."

They plainly meant it. They'd stopped worrying about her judo tricks, too—they didn't seem to have time to worry about them. In the home timeline, she could have telephoned or e-mailed or faxed or, when speed wasn't too important, put a stamp on an envelope and thrown it in a mailbox. Mail here was catch-as-catch-can. If you wanted to send a letter, you found someone who was going your way and paid him to take it. The person who got it would usually pay him a little something, too.

The other women in the barracks thought she was odd for

knowing how to read and write. If any of them could, they didn't want to admit it. To amuse themselves, they spun wool into thread, rolled dice for pebbles they dug out of the rammed-earth floor, and chattered. The chatter didn't amount to much—mostly how they'd got caught and how many men would be sorry they weren't coming home. The Muslims among them also complained about how naked they felt without their veils.

To keep from seeming like a white crow, Annette complained about that, too, even if she didn't mean it. But she said, "Even if we don't have men to take care of us, we've got to do the best we can for ourselves. After all, we're people, too."

A couple of the others nodded. More looked at her as if she'd lost her mind. "What can we do?" one of them said. "They're going to sell us, and then we'll be stuck with whoever buys us."

"Even so," Annette said stubbornly. "We can make things better, or we can make them worse. Look at Sheherezade and the stories she told to Harun al-Rashid. She was just a harem girl, but she ended up a queen." The *Arabian Nights* were popular in this alternate, too. Not all the stories were the same as the ones in the home timeline, but lots of different versions circulated there, too.

"Yes, but Sheherezade was beautiful," said the other woman, who unfortunately wasn't.

"So what?" Annette said. That made all the other women exclaim. To them, if you weren't beautiful, you weren't anything. "So what?" Annette repeated. "Harun al-Rashid had lots of beautiful girls in his harem. He was the caliph. He could have as many beautiful girls as he wanted. If Sheherezade had been beautiful and stupid, he would have called her once and never bothered to do it again. She didn't get where she was because she was beautiful. She got there because she was smart. And if you're smart, you can get somewhere, too."

In the home timeline, that would have been water to a fish.

Here, Annette might have been preaching revolution. Some of the women saw what she was driving at. One of them said, "If you're really smart, you won't let your master know just how smart you are."

That might have held some truth in the home timeline, too. Bits and pieces of sexism lingered there even at the end of the twenty-first century. They sometimes popped up in surprising places, too. Things were better than they had been a hundred years before, though, and much better than they had been two hundred years earlier. Here, what the woman said was plain old good advice.

"If you want to show off how clever you are, you'll end up in trouble," another woman predicted.

"If you need to show off, you aren't as clever as you think you are," Annette said. "I didn't mean that. But if you act helpless and foolish all the time, what will happen to you?"

"You'll catch a man, and he'll take care of you." The other woman looked down her nose at Annette. "Well, *you* probably won't. Your tongue is too sharp."

"I'd rather have a sharp tongue than an empty head," Annette said. The other woman squealed. For a second, Annette thought she'd end up in a fight, which she hadn't done since she was in the fourth grade. She remembered using that judo throw against one of the slavers—it was about the last thing she *did* remember for a while. The other woman would fly through the air with the greatest of ease, too, if she came after her.

But she didn't. She just said, "You'll find out," and went back to her spinning.

Most of the time, the comeback would only have annoyed Annette. The way things were, it held too much truth for comfort. One way or another, she *would* find out, and sooner, not later. Before long, there would be another auction, and someone would buy her. Then she would see firsthand what slavery was like. If she ever escaped, that might come in handy as research. If she didn't . . .

Or maybe no one would buy her, and she'd have to come back to the barracks. Would that be better or worse? She had a hard time deciding. At least she wouldn't turn into property. But she would have to face the humiliating notion that nobody wanted her, even as a slave.

A slave. Back when she was training, they'd warned her, *Anything that can happen to anyone else in that alternate can happen to you.* Oh, she was immunized against diseases the locals could catch. Drinking the water probably wouldn't give her the galloping trots. She had had insect repellent to keep away bedbugs and lice. Now she didn't, and she itched. But the idea that they could sell her in the market square like a kilo of corned beef seemed ridiculous.

In the home timeline, it would have been. They took slavery for granted here. The only time the locals saw anything wrong with it was when they were being sold instead of doing the buying. To Annette, that was the wrong attitude. The thing was wrong all the time. Why couldn't they see it?

The home timeline had slaves, too. But its slaves had plugs or batteries. In this alternate, as in so many others, they didn't have machines to do things for them. They had to use people instead. And they did, and they didn't lose a minute's sleep over how unfair and evil it was.

It still didn't feel real to Annette, right up until the morning they took her out to the market square.

Every so often, Jacques had had daydreams about buying a slave. Owning one would make life easier for him. It would also be a sign that he'd arrived, that he'd become somebody. He knew lots of people who had dreams like that. In fact, he hardly knew anybody who didn't.

But who had daydreams about getting sold into slavery?

They tied Jacques' hands together behind him. They tied his left leg to Musa ibn Ibrahim's left leg. They tied another man's left leg to Jacques'. When they had all the men who were going up for sale in a line, they marched them all out into the market square. It was a slow, awkward march. They had to get used to staying in step with one another. Nobody fell down, which would have made things even worse. Jacques stumbled once. Catching himself without flailing his arms wasn't easy, but he managed.

Another line of luckless people was coming out of the women's barracks. Was Khadija there? Jacques smiled when he spotted her. A familiar face was nice. A familiar pretty face was nicer.

Guards with matchlock muskets stood not far from the auctioneer's platform. Slow, small trails of smoke rose from the men's lengths of match. The matchlocks were ready to shoot. If anybody tried to get away—if anybody could try to get away—he (or she) would be sorry.

Jacques looked out at the crowd in front of the platform. Some of the people out there would be customers. Others would just be out for a morning's entertainment. They would look over the men, ogle the women, and listen to the bidders going against one another. Then they would head off to their eateries and coffeehouses and gossip about what they'd seen and heard.

The auctioneer stepped up onto the platform. He was a small, dapper man with spotless white robes and a neatly trimmed black beard with a few streaks of gray. Bowing to the crowd, he said, "Welcome, my masters, welcome, three times welcome." His voice was bigger and deeper than Jacques would have expected from a man his size. It easily filled the square. Bowing again, the auctioneer went on, "In the name of God, the compassionate, the merciful, we have several fine lots of slaves to present to you this day."

In the name of God, the compassionate, the merciful. Where was the compassion here? Where was the mercy? Did the auctioneer even notice they were missing from what he did? Jacques didn't think so. Would he notice if he went up on the block himself instead of selling others? Jacques nodded to himself. Yes, very likely he would.

Up went the first man out of the barracks. He was middle-aged and scrawny. "He will work hard for you," the auctioneer said, trying to make him sound as attractive as possible. "See how honest he looks?"

Musa ibn Ibrahim laughed softly. "As if any slave is likely to be honest! Or is it different in your country, man who knows not lions?"

"Not a bit," Jacques whispered back. Musa laughed again. Jacques didn't intend to be any more honest than he could help once he got sold. He owed himself more than he owed any master, especially one he hadn't chosen for himself.

A few bids came in for the scrawny man. In spite of everything the auctioneer could do, he went for thirty dinars—less than half a pound of silver. That wasn't much of a price, and the auctioneer didn't look thrilled to get his silver. For that matter, the fellow who bought the scrawny man didn't look thrilled to have him.

Up came another man. He looked as ordinary as the one who'd gone before him, but he said he was a skilled mason. A big man out in the crowd asked him a couple of questions. He answered without any trouble. "See how clever he is!" the auctioneer cried. "He will do well for you!" The second man did better for the auctioneer, bringing in almost twice what the scrawny fellow had sold for. The big man who'd questioned him sent a flunky up with the money.

The big man bought several other slaves, including a couple of Musa's countrymen. He and an older fellow bid against each other time after time. More often than not, the big man outspent his rival. The older man looked less and less happy each time it happened. At last, he burst out, "A plague take you, Marwan! Have you all the silver in the world to call your own?"

The big man bowed. "Not all of it, sir, but enough for my needs, for which I thank God. What man could ask for more?"

"That is well said," declared the auctioneer, who didn't care where money came from as long as it came.

"Ten years ago, who in Madrid had heard of Marwan al-Baghdadi?" the older man said, playing to the crowd. "Who? Anyone? And now he dares to bid against me—*me*, Hassan ibn Hussein! Has my family not led here for generations? Where is the justice?"

"I have silver. I earned it honestly. I am free to spend it as I see fit," Marwan replied. "That's justice, as I see it." He had backers in the crowd, too, and they nodded and clapped their hands.

Hassan ibn Hussein frowned. "Silver goes only so far, sir. There is also blood."

Jacques would have agreed with that, but Marwan didn't. "Blood says your great-great-great-great-grandfather made your family's silver," he answered, politely but firmly. "It says nothing about what kind of man you are yourself. But silver you've earned on your own—well, that may say *you* have done well in the world."

His followers clapped again. They weren't rich enough to buy slaves, but they probably dreamt of the days when they would be. Hassan ibn Hussein muttered under his breath. He didn't say anything more, not out loud. But when the next man came up on the block, he bid the fellow's price up and up, even though the new slave didn't look very strong and didn't seem very smart.

His last bid raised the price to more than three times what the man looked to be worth. He glared over at Marwan al-Baghdadi, waiting for him to bump things up still further. By the way Hassan's eyes gleamed, he thought they'd both put their prestige on the line over the slave. Maybe he thought so, but Marwan didn't. With a smile and a bow, he said, "He's all yours, my friend."

Hassan ibn Hussein gaped. He looked like a fish just pulled from the water. Marwan had left him as high and dry as if he *were* a fish just pulled from the water. Now he had to lay out all that silver on a slave who wasn't worth it. That left him less money to buy slaves he really wanted at prices he could really afford to pay.

"That is an angry man," Musa ibn Ibrahim whispered to Jacques. "I hope he doesn't buy me. He would make me pay for his own folly."

Looking at the fearsome scowl on Hassan's face, Jacques nodded. "He tried to make this Marwan into a fool, but Marwan turned the tables on him."

A helper undid the rope that bound Musa's leg to Jacques. The black man got up on the platform. "See what a fine figure of a man we have here!" the auctioneer exclaimed. He asked Musa, "How were you taken?"

"In war. I was unlucky. It was the will of God," Musa answered.

"Do you see? He speaks Arabic well, and he is a pious man," the auctioneer called to the crowd. "He will work hard for you!"

Marwan al-Baghdadi bid on Musa. So did a couple of other

men. Hassan ibn Hussein kept out of the auction. Marwan won it, and probably paid a little less than Musa might have brought.

That helper undid the rope between Jacques and the man behind him. He gave Jacques a little push, muttering, "Go on." Jacques went. He took his place where the others for sale had stood before him.

"See how white and fair he is!" the auctioneer said. "A Frank from the North!" Muslims called all Christians Franks, after the vanished Kingdom of France. The auctioneer eyed him. "Do you speak Arabic, fellow? Do you understand it?"

"No, I'm sorry, your Excellency, but I don't understand even a word of Arabic," Jacques answered—in Arabic.

The auctioneer threw back his head and laughed. "Clever as well as fair!" he said, and looked back to the crowd. "How much for this big, strong, smart slave? He will be a foreman in a few years, if God is kind."

Hassan ibn Hussein opened the bidding. Another man raised it a couple of dinars. Then Marwan al-Baghdadi spoke up. Jacques hoped Marwan would buy him, as much because the man was a great traveler as for any other reason. He'd come here to Madrid all the way from far-off, fabled Baghdad.

Hassan and Marwan and two other men bid Jacques' price up and up. When it got over a pound of silver, the other men dropped out, first one, then the other. At not quite a pound and a half of silver, Hassan sent Marwan a look that should have killed him. Marwan smiled back, which only made Hassan angrier. Angry or not, he threw both hands in the air instead of raising his bid again.

"Going once! Going twice! Sold!" the auctioneer chanted, and pointed toward Marwan al-Baghdadi. "Sold to this fine gentleman here!" He shoved Jacques, not too hard. "Go to your new master. Serve him well." Jacques got down off the platform. One of Marwan's men took charge of him. The fellow tied his left leg back to that of Musa, the last slave Marwan had bought.

"There," the man said, straightening up. "You're not going anywhere."

"No, I suppose not." Jacques hoped that sounded like a nice, meek answer. No, he wasn't going anywhere—not unless he saw a chance.

Annette had expected it to be ladies first, but it wasn't. They sold the men before they got around to the women. She had to stand out in the sun for two or three hours before things started happening with her. It wasn't torture or anything. The day was warm, but it wasn't hot. A man with a clay jar of water and a dipper went up and down the line. The waiting women could have a drink whenever they wanted to. The water in that jar was surprisingly cool. Had the jar been metal, the water would have been warmer. Sure enough, evaporation caused cooling, just the way they said it did in physics.

She watched Jacques get sold. He got down off the platform and went over to his new owner. Like the others who got sold, he didn't seem especially upset. This was part of life here—not a part anybody liked, but a part everybody knew how to handle. Annette didn't—couldn't—understand it. Why weren't they all screaming their heads off? This was *wrong*. And so it was, to her. But not to them.

Then the women started going up on the block. The auctioneer made his dumb jokes. He asked them questions about what they'd been before they got caught. If their answers showed they had two brain cells to rub together, he praised them to the skies.

He wanted them to go for high prices, because that meant his commission went up.

Every so often, mostly with women who said they'd had children, he would look at their teeth. Whenever he did, Annette would grind hers. He really might have been selling horses up there, not human beings at all.

Except he was. And her own turn came closer every time someone else stepped down from the platform. And then she was stepping up onto it. "Here is a fine girl, good for all sorts of things!" the auctioneer said, and then, "Tell them your name, sweetheart."

"I am not your sweetheart, God be praised," Annette said coldly, which only made him chuckle. She went on, "I am Khadija, daughter of the merchant Muhammad al-Marsawi. If you send to Marseille, my father will pay far more than I cost to ransom me."

"There you go!" The auctioneer beamed at her. He beamed out at the crowd. "Hear that, my friends? Do you hear that? Spend a little money now, make more money later. How can you go wrong?" He looked back at Annette. "So you're a merchant's daughter, are you? What can you do?"

"I read and write Arabic and French," she said, adding, "I speak French, too," in that language. Returning to Arabic, she went on, "And I can cipher. I could keep your books better than whatever cheating fool you use now."

The auctioneer blinked. Annette wondered if she'd laid it on too thick. Women here weren't usually able to do things like that. If they could, they weren't supposed to brag about it. "Hear what a clever maid this is!" the auctioneer cried after that little startled pause. "You can put her to the test, if you like. And if she fails, by God, you can beat her as she deserves!"

Out in the crowd, men were nodding. If a donkey balked, they would beat it to make it go. And if a slave failed, they would beat him—or her, too. Why not? A slave was just as much their property as a donkey was.

"What am I bid, then?" the auctioneer called. "If she is as good as she says she is—and I believe her—you will get your money's worth from her even if you never see a copper of this ransom."

It boiled down to Hassan ibn Hussein against Marwan al-Baghdadi. She thought the older man wanted her for the ransom, the younger one for what she could do. She hoped Hassan would win—that gave her a better chance of getting free. But Marwan seemed to have more silver than he knew what to do with. Every time Hassan bid, Marwan raised the price. Finally, a horrible look on his face, Hassan turned away. "Going once!" the auctioneer called. "Going twice! . . . Sold!"

Numbly, Annette got down off the platform. Sold. She'd been sold.

Jacques was glad Marwan had also bought Khadija. At least there would be someone else he knew in the household. He had no idea how often he would have the chance to see her, but you could often work those things out. A lot of the time, it just depended on getting in good with a steward or a butler or maybe a head cook. He would have to look around and see which way the wind blew.

After the auction was over, Marwan paraded his new slaves through the streets of Madrid. Here as in the Kingdom of Versailles, you showed off if you were a rich man. Showing off was a big part of being rich. And the story of how he'd outbid Hassan ibn Hussein time after time would race through the city faster than wind-whipped fire. His prestige would rise. Hassan's would fall.

Marwan himself swaggered along at the head of the procession. He was having fun, laughing and joking with passersby and throwing coins to beggars and cripples and children.

"He acts like a prince, or a man who wants to be a prince," Musa ibn Ibrahim whispered.

"He does, doesn't he?" Jacques said. "I wonder what the men who *are* princes in this city will say to that."

"My very thought," Musa agreed. "I wonder what they will say after Hassan ibn Hussein whispers in their ears. And he will whisper in them, unless he shouts in them instead."

"Nothing we can do about that," Jacques said, and Musa nodded. What could a slave do about anything? Not much. Back in Paris, Jacques could have whispered into Duke Raoul's ear. The duke might not have paid any attention to him—but then again, he might have. Here, the only people Jacques knew were Musa and Khadija, and they were both slaves, too.

"Almost there," one of Marwan al-Baghdadi's men called.

From up on a roof or behind a shuttered window, someone said, "More slaves for the demons to eat up!"

"I don't like the sound of that," Jacques said. "I hope he's just a friend of Hassan ibn Hussein's."

"I fear no demons," Musa said stoutly. "As long as I worship God, how can demons harm me?" But in spite of his bold words, the black man nervously looked this way and that. Jacques wondered what he thought demons looked like. Jacques had thought they looked like him.

Marwan's man laughed. "Pay no heed to what foolish folk say. Sometimes we take slaves out to my master's country estates while it is still dark, so they can start work as soon as the sun comes up. The ignorant and lazy do not see them go, and so they think something bad has happened to them. In the name of God, it is a lie."

That sounded fair enough. All the same, Jacques would have scratched his head if his hands weren't tied behind his back. What the hidden man had said was so strange, he didn't know what to make of it. If someone had warned him that he'd be beaten or that he wouldn't get enough to eat, those threats would have made sense. But talk about demons? He supposed Madrid had its share of crazy people, like any other place.

Marwan al-Baghdadi's house was larger than most of the others on its block. Its outer wall was freshly whitewashed. The tiles on the roof were new and bright red—sun and rain hadn't faded them yet. All those things were signs of wealth, but didn't prove it. Coming back to the house with a new troop of slaves—that proved it.

Once the last slave went inside, Marwan's men closed the door and barred it. They undid the ropes that tied one slave's leg to another's, and also the bonds on their hands. Jacques chafed at his wrists where the rope had rubbed them raw. He looked around the courtyard in which the slaves stood. It held a fountain, a garden of flowers and herbs, and an old-looking statue of a lion.

"If you work well for me, I will treat you well," Marwan said. "You will have plenty to eat. You will have plenty to do, too, but not too much. If I work you to death, I lose the money I paid for you. But if you try to run away, you will be very, very sorry. I promise you that. You have no idea how sorry you will be. And you will not escape. I promise you that, too."

As usual, he sounded like a man who knew what he was talking about. Jacques didn't intend to try to disappear right away. He wanted to wait till he had a better notion of the lie of the land

and what things were like here. If he saw a chance then . . . That would be a different story.

The stew Marwan's cooks served was full of mutton and barley and onions. You could have seconds if you wanted. Jacques did. His new owner seemed to be telling the truth about the food, anyway. And the beds in the men's hall were real cots with wood frames and mattresses on leather lashings, not just pallets on the floor. He hadn't slept so soft since he left Paris. It wasn't what he wanted, but it could have been worse.

It could have been worse. Everyone around Annette said so. She supposed the locals knew what they were talking about. Marwan al-Baghdadi did seem to give his slaves enough to eat. He worked them only till they got very tired, not till they fell over dead. No law told him he had to be so generous. No custom did, either. Everybody seemed to know stories about masters who made him look like a saint by comparison. But if he was such a saint, why did he own slaves?

Like the others, Annette had to get up at sunrise. After breakfast, she went to Marwan's kitchens. They were always full of women, and the women always had plenty to do. In low-tech kitchens, there always seemed to be more work than people to do it.

Something as simple as the heat under a pot wasn't simple. You couldn't just turn a valve or a switch to control it. You had to keep a real live fire going, feeding it sticks every so often so it didn't get too big or too small. If it did, whatever was in the pot either burned or didn't cook at all. And you got in trouble.

Annette had had practice back in Marseille. She needed all of that not to give herself away a dozen times a day. She didn't lose her breakfast when she had to gut freshly beheaded ducks or chickens or pigeons. She just thanked heaven she didn't have to use the hatchet herself.

Washing dishes was as bad as getting food ready for cooking. There was no hot water. There was no dishwashing soap—even people-washing soap was an expensive luxury. Plates and cups mostly weren't glazed. Things stuck to them and soaked into them. There were no scouring pads, either. There was sand and there was elbow grease and there was time, lots and lots of time.

People talked. People sang. People scrubbed in rhythm. People chopped vegetables in rhythm. Every so often, people wandered out into the courtyard for a break. If you didn't do it too often or stay out there too long, nobody yelled at you. Annette was cautious. She didn't want to get in trouble. Some of the other women stayed out more. They did get yelled at. Nobody pulled out a cat-o'-nine-tails and whipped them, though.

Every so often, Annette and Jacques took a break at the same time. Then, not quite by accident, it was more than every so often. Some of the older women in the kitchens smiled behind their hands. But Annette wasn't the only one with a friend. Nobody made any big fuss about it.

Jacques said, "It could be worse," too. He was pleased with the way he'd helped repair a wagon.

"You should be working for yourself," Annette said.

He shrugged. "I suppose so. I hope I will again one of these days. But for now . . ." He shrugged again. Slavery was part of his world. He didn't like it at all, but it didn't sicken his spirit the way it did Annette's.

"We have to get away," she said. She wouldn't have said that to anyone else. Trusting anyone from an alternate didn't come easy for somebody from the home timeline. But you couldn't stay all alone, either. The poet who said nobody was an island knew what he was talking about.

Jacques looked around to make sure nobody could overhear. "Wait till they relax about us," he said in a low voice. "Wait till they think we're all right. Then . . ." Annette nodded.

But they left sooner than that, though not in the way they'd intended. A woman shook Annette awake in the middle of the night, saying, "Come with me. We are going to take you to another of the master's properties."

She yawned and got out of bed. Several more slaves were already up. The woman woke a couple of others. Then she led them all out of the female slaves' barracks. Annette thought they would go out on the road, but they didn't. Instead, the woman who'd wakened them led them to a doorway that looked like all the rest. When she opened it, it showed nothing but a stairway leading down.

One of the slaves laughed nervously. "Does this take us to the underworld?" she asked.

"No, no, no. Don't be foolish." The leader sounded as businesslike as if she came from the home timeline. "Just go down. Others will be waiting for you."

Down they went, farther than Annette had expected. The chamber at the bottom of the stairway was bigger than she'd thought it would be. Torches on the walls cast a dim, yellow, flickering light. As the woman had said, other slaves—men— already stood there. After a moment, Annette spotted Jacques. He saw her, too, and waved.

"Stay back near the edges of the chamber, everyone." Marwan al-Baghdadi's big voice raised echoes from the ceiling. "Do not go out near the center. It is not safe. By God, no harm will come to you as long as you do what I tell you to do."

Annette yawned again. What *was* he talking about? You'd almost think . . .

One instant, the middle of the underground chamber was

empty. Then, silently and without any fuss, a huge, shiny metal box appeared out of nowhere. Slaves screamed and shrank back against the walls. Annette screamed with them. Her amazement was mixed with delight, not fear. That was—could only be—a Crosstime Traffic transposition chamber.

Six

Jacques blinked several times. The great metal box stayed there, right before his eyes. He wasn't drunk. These Muslims didn't even give their slaves beer or wine. All he'd had with supper was a tart, orange juice from some kind of fruit that didn't grow in the Kingdom of Versailles.

A door in the box slid open. Bright light spilled out, light far brighter than that from the torches. It might almost have been daytime inside the box. Jacques sketched the sign of the wheel. Beside him, Musa ibn Ibrahim murmured, "Truly there is no God but God, and Muhammad is the Prophet of God."

"Go inside. Take seats," Marwan al-Baghdadi called. "I say again, no harm will come to you. This is a . . . traveling chamber. It is like a ship or a wagon. There are seats inside. You will be comfortable as you go."

It wasn't like any ship or wagon Jacques had ever seen. He wasn't the only slave who hung back instead of going forward. But then, to his surprise, Khadija went in as calmly as if she were swinging up onto a horse. If she wasn't afraid, Jacques figured he didn't have to be, either.

As he was a couple of steps behind Khadija, so Musa was one step behind him. "Let no one claim you go where I dare not follow," the black man said. He sounded angry, not at Jacques but at himself.

Seeing that nothing bad happened to the first ones who went into the box, others went after them. Inside the box, a voice spoke in Arabic from out of the air: "Please take your seats. All passengers, please take your seats."

Try as Jacques would, he couldn't see anyone talking. What he could see was Khadija's face, shining as brightly as the lamps inside the box. What about those lamps? He saw no torches or candles—no oil lamps, either, such as they used in these southern parts. He smelled nothing burning, either. The whole top of the box—the ceiling, he supposed you'd have to call it—glowed. It wasn't too bright to look at, but it shed better light than anything he'd ever seen except the sun.

"Please take your seats," that voice from the air repeated. "All passengers, please take your seats."

Khadija sat down right away, still smiling as if she'd just been promised heaven. She knew about boxes like this—knew about them and liked them. That encouraged Jacques to sit down beside her. The chair was comfortable enough, but what was it made of? Something hard and smooth and . . . orange? It wasn't metal or wood or stone or cloth or even bone. What did that leave? Nothing Jacques knew of.

"What is this place?" he whispered to Khadija in French.

"It's a transposition chamber," she answered in the same language. That told him nothing he didn't already know. She went on, "It will rescue us. It will take us back to . . . to where I come from."

"To Marseille?" Jacques said, more confused than ever. "It's only a box in the middle of an underground room."

"No, not to Marseille," Khadija said impatiently. "To . . . Oh, never mind. You'll see when we get out. And it's not just a box. It—"

As if to prove what she said, the door slid shut all by itself.

With all the people inside the box, the air should have got hot and stuffy in nothing flat. It didn't—it stayed fresh and cool. Jacques tried to decide whether that was more marvelous than the lamps or the other way around. He couldn't.

"What are you two talking about?" asked Musa ibn Ibrahim. He had no more reason to understand French than Jacques did to follow whatever language he spoke besides Arabic.

Before Jacques could explain—no, could answer, because he *couldn't* explain—some lights at the front of the box started winking on and off. They reminded him of candle flames seen through stained glass. Some were red, some amber, but most a clear green. "We're going," Khadija said. Now she spoke in Arabic, so Musa could also make sense of her words.

Jacques shook his head. "No, we're not," he said. "We're just standing still." He knew what motion felt like. He felt none of it here. The box might have been nailed to the floor of the underground room. Musa ibn Ibrahim nodded agreement with him.

But Khadija said, "Remember how the transposition chamber came out of nowhere at Marwan al-Baghdadi's? Well, when it stops it'll come out of nowhere someplace else."

She sounded very sure. Musa leaned forward so he could look at her past Jacques. "How do you know these things?" he asked in a low voice.

She bit her lip. "Never mind. It doesn't matter right now, anyway. But I'm right. You'll see."

Musa eyed Jacques. "What do you think?" the black man asked.

"I think she has to know more about this—chamber?—than I do, because I don't know anything," Jacques replied. "As for the rest . . . I don't know. Let's see what happens when that door opens again. One way or another, we'll find out then."

Musa ibn Muhammad pursed his lips. He looked up at the

ceiling—the ceiling that glowed. Maybe the impossible but un-
deniable glow helped him make up his mind. He nodded. "This
is good sense, Jacques of the north. When the door opens
again—however it opens—we shall see what we shall see."

"How long will it take?" Jacques asked Khadija. If anybody
knew, she did.

"It will seem like about half an hour," she said, an odd answer. Then she added something even odder: "It really won't
take any time at all."

It seemed like more than half an hour to Jacques. By the way
Khadija frowned and fidgeted, it seemed like more than half an
hour to her, too. He wondered if something was wrong. He could
only wonder—it wasn't as if he could do anything about it. Then a
green light on the front panel turned red. A heartbeat later, the
door slid open. "All passengers out," said the voice without a
source. "All passengers please leave the chamber at once. All
passengers out. All passengers please leave . . ."

Jacques and Khadija and Musa and the others filed out.
What else could they do? They found themselves in an underground room. But it wasn't the room where they'd got into the
chamber. It was bigger and better lit. When Jacques looked up,
he saw glowing tubes that shed the same kind of bright light as
the transposition chamber's ceiling. Khadija was nodding to herself and smiling. She'd seen tubes like those before, even if
Jacques and Musa hadn't.

"Over this way! Up these stairs!" a man shouted in Arabic.
He wore a tunic and trousers of mottled green and brown. He had
stout leather boots on his feet, and wore a helmet with a cloth
cover of the same mottled fabric as the rest of his clothes. He
carried what was obviously a weapon. It looked something like a
matchlock musket, but was much shorter and more compact.
And it had a knife sticking out below the muzzle, so it could dou-

ble as a short thrusting spear. *What a clever idea!* Jacques thought, wondering why no one in the Kingdom of Versailles had ever thought of it.

"Be careful," Khadija whispered to him. "It can shoot many bullets quickly, without reloading between shots." Her smile had gone out. Whatever she'd expected, this wasn't it.

"Up the stairs! Get moving!" yelled the man with the gun-and-knife combination. Unlike the strange voice in the chamber, he didn't repeat himself exactly.

Up they went. These stairs were iron, and clanged under Jacques' boots. They must have cost a fortune. More men with weapons waited as people came up from below. "Male slaves to the left!" one of them shouted. "Female slaves to the right! Get moving, if you know what's good for you!"

"No," Khadija whispered. "No, no, no, no!" But the men with the weapons didn't look as if they would take no for an answer. Jacques and Musa went to the left. Still with that look of astonished disbelief on her face, Khadija went to the right.

Annette had thought she was living a nightmare ever since she got captured and separated from her parents. Now she discovered what nightmare really was. That had been a Crosstime Traffic transposition chamber. She'd thought it would take her back to the home timeline. She hadn't known why it was taking so many people from that alternate with her, but she hadn't worried about it. Why worry when she was on her way home?

But she wasn't. This seemed more like hell than home—industrialized hell. The rest of the slaves, the ones who really had come from the alternate of the Great Black Deaths, didn't realize what was wrong. How could they? The only timeline they'd ever imagined was their own.

Wherever this was, it was in a different alternate. The house and grounds above the underground room where the transposition chamber came and went were bigger than the ones in the other Madrid. The house and the other buildings had solar panels on their roofs, too. Those would generate at least some of the electricity this place used. And if the locals were low-tech, they'd have no idea what the panels were for.

Even before Annette got to the barracks, she decided the locals *were* low-tech. For one thing, she couldn't see any sky-glow from street lamps over the outer wall. For another, the stench of sewage and garbage filled the air. Again, the other slaves took no special notice. They'd lived with that smell all their lives. They took it for granted.

They did exclaim when they found fluorescent tubes lighting the barracks. "Our new master must be a strong wizard!" one of them said. She sounded more proud than otherwise, as if being owned by such a man gave her extra status. For all Annette knew, it did.

She made herself exclaim, too. If she took those glowing tubes too much for granted, the others might wonder why. If they wondered why, Marwan al-Baghdadi—or whatever his real name was—might start wondering, too. Or maybe he didn't even come to this new alternate. Maybe he was just a hired man like the goons with the guns. But having the boss here wonder about her would also be very bad news.

Slaves! One of Crosstime Traffic's strongest rules was the one against buying or selling other people. Annette wouldn't have thought the rule even needed to be there. It had been almost 250 years since the United States fought a civil war over slavery.

But . . . That was a CT transposition chamber. She'd been in enough of them to recognize another one. It didn't come from some other alternate that also knew how to travel between time-lines. That had always been Crosstime Traffic's worst nightmare. This trouble, though, this trouble was homegrown. To Annette, that made it worse, not better.

She lay down on a bed just like the one she'd had in that other Madrid. The rest of the newly arrived slave women soon went to sleep. They didn't fully understand what had happened to them. Annette did, and her whirling thoughts kept her tossing and turning. People inside Crosstime Traffic were dealing with—dealing *in*—slaves. They'd got their hands on their own private transposition chamber. If that didn't mean there was corruption in *very* high places, Annette would have been amazed.

Why would they want slaves? She worried at that as if it were gristle stuck between her teeth. Whatever they dug up or grew here, Crosstime Traffic could surely get it somewhere else. And besides, how many people connected to Crosstime Traffic needed money? Most of them made more benjamins than they knew what to do with.

She yawned. However upset she was, she was tired, too. What else besides money would make people want to own other people? For a while, she couldn't think of anything. She yawned again. She was going to fall asleep in spite of herself.

She'd almost drifted off when she suddenly sat bolt upright instead. Maybe just the thrill of doing something this *wrong* would be enough. In the home timeline, people didn't wear furs. Up till this moment, Annette had never asked herself why they didn't. That she hadn't asked said a lot about how strong the taboo was. She'd always just taken it for granted.

Every once in a while, though, you would hear stories on the news . . . Reporters would talk in hushed voices about how so-and-so—sometimes somebody famous, sometimes someone no-body'd ever heard of—had been caught with a fur jacket or a mink stole in the closet. You could only wear something like that where no one (except maybe someone as twisted as you were) saw you do it. The only reason you *would* do it was because everybody else thought it was sick. You got some sort of perverted pleasure from going against the way everyone else felt.

Well, if wearing furs was a perverted kick, wasn't buying and selling and owning people an even bigger one? It sure looked that way to Annette. The idea made more sense than anything else she'd come up with, that was for sure.

Finding something that made sense, even if it was something horrible, helped her relax. She lay down again and began drifting off.

She began, yes. But then she jerked and twisted, there on that slave's bed. Sleep wouldn't come after all. Maybe part of the thrill of slavery was buying and selling and owning people. But wasn't the rest of it doing anything you wanted to them while you had them? Anything at all? Why not? They were just property, weren't they?

Annette lay awake the rest of the night.

When Jacques woke the morning after the strange ride in the transposition chamber, he found that not all the slaves in the barracks were men who'd come with him. He also found he couldn't speak with the strangers. They didn't use Arabic or French. They didn't use Spanish, either—he knew what that sounded like, even if he couldn't speak it. Some of them had a language that reminded him a little of Arabic, though he couldn't follow it. Others made noises that hardly sounded like speech at all to him. Their tongue was full of sneezes and hisses and coughing sounds, and he couldn't tell where one word stopped and the next began.

"I think it is the Tower of Babel," Musa ibn Ibrahim said gravely. "God has confused our speech."

The only answer Jacques could find was, "Why would God want to do that to the likes of us?"

"God is God," Musa said. "He may do as He pleases. We have not the right to question Him."

How could you argue with that? Jacques couldn't, and he knew it. But he did say, "God didn't put us in that—that chamber, Khadija called it. People did. And the people who did know more about it than we do."

"Then we will learn—when God wills that we learn," Musa replied. Jacques gave up.

A man stood in the doorway. He shouted a couple of incomprehensible words. Then he said, "*Iftar!*" That was *Breakfast!* in Arabic. Jacques guessed he'd said the same thing in the other two languages. Next time the man said those words, Jacques told himself, he would remember what they were. He wasn't sure he could pronounce one of them, but he'd try.

He didn't know where to get breakfast here. The slaves who spoke the strange languages did. He followed them. So did Musa and the other slaves who'd come here in the chamber. A bored-looking cook ladled porridge into bowls. Those bowls, and the spoons that went into them, were of some hard white stuff Jacques hadn't seen before. It reminded him of the orange stuff that went into the seats in the transposition chamber. Maybe Khadija had a name for it. Even if she did, though, would it mean any more than *transposition chamber* did?

To his relief, the benches and tables where the slaves ate were of ordinary wood. He got a splinter in his hand when he sat down. As he dug it out with a fingernail, it made him feel at home.

This place didn't try to keep its slaves hungry. The bowls were big, and the cook had filled them full. The porridge even had bits of meat in it. Jacques spooned it up. Things could have been worse—and how many times had he had that thought?

"What is this flesh?" Musa ibn Ibrahim asked after eating for a little while. "It does not taste like anything I have had before."

"Ham, I think," Jacques answered with his mouth full. And then, a heartbeat slower than he should have, he said, "Oh."

Grimly, Musa shoved the bowl away from himself. "You are a Christian," he said. "This food is not forbidden for you." By the way he said it, he meant, *You don't know any better.* Iron in his voice, he went on, "You will know, though, the swine is an unclean beast for Muslims." He called out, "Muslims! My brethren! My sisters! The food has forbidden flesh in it!"

Some of them cursed. Some of them prayed. Some of the women screamed. They all stopped eating breakfast. Some of the other slaves, the one who'd been here before, looked at them as if they were crazy. Others moved away from them on the benches. Jacques knew what that meant. They thought trouble was coming, and they didn't want to get stuck in the middle of it.

Jacques went on eating. He felt guilty about it—Musa and the other Muslims were going hungry—but nothing was wrong with the food for him. Even Musa had said so. He was hungry now, and he thought the porridge tasted fine.

In tramped three guards with those muskets with the blades attached. "What's going on here?" one of them yelled in Arabic.

Musa stood up and bowed to him. "You will excuse me, please, sir, but this porridge has pork in it. It is *haram*—forbidden." He spoke respectfully. He knew he was a slave here. He knew how slaves were supposed to act. But he also knew he had a problem, one the guards and their superiors needed to hear about.

The guard who'd spoken before glared at him. "You can eat,

or you can starve. Those are your choices. But you're going to have to work any which way."

Musa bowed again. "Thank you, sir. In that case, I will starve. When I am dead, God will welcome me into Paradise. I hope you have a care for your own soul." He sat down.

"You're a troublemaker! You'll be sorry. It's not like you can hide around here," the guard warned. He was bound to be right about that. Only three or four black men had traveled in the chamber. Still glaring, the guard spoke to all the Muslims: "You'd better watch yourselves. We don't have time for your foolishness. You'll all be sorry if you aren't careful."

"I hope you won't get into too much trouble on account of that," Jacques whispered to Musa as the guards stomped out.

"Let them do as they please," the older man said with a shrug. "God may have made me a slave. All right—His will be done in that as in all things. But God would not make me break His commandments. That has to be Satan."

"I suppose so." Jacques wondered what he would do if these people tried to make him break a rule set down by Jesus or Henri. Would he have the courage to stay stubborn? He hoped so, and knew he wasn't sure.

People inside the dining hall were still muttering back and forth when the guards returned. One of them pointed his musket at Musa. "Come with us," he snapped.

"I obey." Musa got to his feet. "What will you do with me?"

"You say you won't eat pork, eh?" The guard had a nasty grin on his face.

"That is right," Musa ibn Ibrahim said with great dignity.

"Well, we'll see." The guard's smile got nastier still. Jacques hadn't thought it could. "We're going to stick you in a cell. You can have all the water you want. But if you want food, you'll eat pork or nothing—and if you do starve, too bad for you." He gestured with the musket's muzzle. "Come on. Get moving."

"I come." Musa murmured something else, so softly that Jacques thought he was the only one to hear it: "Truly there is no God but God. Truly Muhammad is the Prophet of God." The black man took a couple of ordinary steps toward the guard. Then he lowered his head and rushed him.

It wasn't the worst bet in the world—or it wouldn't have been against a matchlock musket. The guard would have time for one startled shot. If he missed, Musa would be on him. If Musa could wrestle away the musket, he had at least a chance of smashing down the other two guards. Maybe the other Muslims would join him. Maybe this would turn into a full-scale uprising.

Khadija had said the guards' weapons could fire more than one bullet without reloading. Musa ibn Ibrahim might not have heard it. If he had, he might not have believed it or understood what it meant.

When the guard pulled the trigger, his musket made a sound like a giant ripping a sheet of canvas. Jacques had no idea how many bullets hit Musa ibn Ibrahim. They were enough to come close to cutting the black man in half. For a moment, there was a horrid pink mist as the bullets tore his insides out. Some of them went through him and hit other people. They screamed. He didn't. He fell and scrabbled at the floor with his hands for a little while. Then he died.

The iron smell of blood and the stink of his bowels filled the air. Smoke didn't. Jacques needed a moment to notice that. He didn't smell gunpowder, either. What sent the bullets flying, then?

Whatever it was, it was plenty to do the job and then some.

"Anybody else?" the guard asked. Except for the shrieks of the wounded, no one said a thing. The guard gestured with his musket again. "Anyone who's hurt, go on out. You'll be treated.

If you can't walk, somebody near will help you." He spoke in the other two languages that seemed to be used here, probably saying the same thing. Close to half a dozen people had been shot. Out they went—except for a woman who'd taken a bullet between the eyes.

After more shouted orders, two men dragged her out by the heels. Her blood made a long trail across the floor. When the men came back, the guards made them drag Musa's body out, too. Flies had already started landing in the gore pooled under him. Jacques usually thought Muslims were bound for hell. He hoped God would make an exception for the black man.

He looked down at his bowl of porridge. He was glad he'd eaten most of it, because he sure didn't want any more.

Was Khadija all right? He hadn't seen her limp away, but he knew that impossible burst of gunfire might have unnerved him. No, there she was. Her face was pale and drawn—no surprise, for most of the people in the dining hall were pale and drawn. Jacques probably was himself. Khadija nodded to him when their eyes met, but then quickly looked away.

At first, that offended Jacques. Then he realized she might be smarter than he was. They'd got into the transposition chamber together—and together with Musa ibn Ibrahim. She might not want to remind their new master that they were friends, and also that they'd known a slave who'd tried to rebel. Jacques had never been a slave before, but he could see that staying as close to invisible as you could was likely to be a good idea.

He could see that—once he'd thought about it for a while. Khadija must have seen it in the wink of an eye. Forget that *maybe*. She *was* smarter than he was.

One of the guards came back in. As usual, he gave his orders in three languages. Jacques could follow the Arabic: "Men are on the roadbuilding detail today. Women will work in the garden plot—except those on duty inside the manor. You know who you are. Any questions?"

Nobody said a word. If he'd told them to jump off the wall around the manor, most of them would have done it without a peep. Whatever happened when they hit the ground had to be better than facing one of those terrible muskets.

Roadbuilding. Jacques muttered to himself. That didn't sound easy, and it didn't sound like much fun. But he was young and strong and—except for the leg that pained him now and again—healthy. He could do the work. It wasn't as if the guard had said he was going to the mines. That was a mankilling job, one where you might as well rise up because you had nothing left to lose and nothing left to live for.

Out into the courtyard he went. He and the rest of the newly arrived slaves stuck together. They couldn't even talk with the ones who'd been there longer. They weren't friends, but they all spoke Arabic. That made them companions.

Another guard, a big, beefy fellow, took charge of them. "You will come with me," he barked. "You will do what I tell you. You have work you need to do, and you will do it. Do you understand me?"

"Yes, sir," Jacques and a few other slaves said.

"*Do you understand me?*" the guard roared.

"Yes, sir!" This time, everybody spoke up.

"That's more like it." The guard nodded. Jacques felt oddly reassured. The man didn't sound like a cruel master. He sounded like a sergeant drilling raw recruits. If he spoke French, Duke Raoul would have hired him in a heartbeat.

Under his lead, the road gang marched out of the manor. As soon as Jacques saw what lay outside, he knew Khadija told the truth. The chamber had taken the slaves somewhere new. He'd already partly realized things were different here. He hadn't heard city noises, and he hadn't smelled city smells. But seeing bare countryside, as if noisy, smelly, brawling Madrid had never existed, jolted him to the core.

As the guard inside the manor had said, there were vegetable plots. There were fields of growing grain. And there were what would be olive groves when the saplings got bigger. Beyond them, the near-desert of central Spain stretched out as far as the eye could see.

"Where did the city go?" one of the Muslim women asked as she weeded in the garden.

"They must be mighty wizards, to make it disappear!" another one exclaimed.

Annette said things like that, too. She didn't want the people who ran this place to think she took travel between alternates for granted. That would have been dangerous. Right now, she couldn't imagine anything that would have been more dangerous. If they decided she knew about travel between alternates . . .

They'll kill me, she thought as she grubbed a weed out from between a couple of tomato plants. The people who were doing this were committing so many crimes, one more murder might not even make it into the balance sheet. The one thing they could not have was anyone in the home timeline finding out what they'd done.

Slavery. Moving low-tech locals from one alternate to another. Using high technology against low-tech locals. Importing life-forms to alternates where they didn't belong—highly bred tomatoes were as much out of place here as assault rifles. At least two murders that Annette had seen, plus who could say how many more? Who could say what other acts of cruelty went on here, either?

Where did the slaves who didn't speak Arabic come from? Were they from this alternate? Or had the slavers brought them in from somewhere else? Did this alternate have any people at all, or was it one of those where human beings had never evolved? Those were all important questions, and she had answers to exactly none of them.

Even starting to find out wouldn't be easy. Annette had never tried to learn a foreign language on her own, without the help of her implant. People did it. Even in the home timeline, people in countries that weren't so rich had to do things the hard way. If you learned words, you could figure out grammar a bit at a time . . . couldn't you? She had to hope so.

One of the rifle-toting guards in camouflage clothing tramped past her. She worked faster while she thought he was looking at her, then slowed down again. How many slaves in how many alternates had done something like that over how many thousand years? She watched the man out of the corner of her eye. Did he carry that rifle to protect himself from the slaves and from wild beasts, or did he worry about wild men, too?

The woman weeding in the next row said something in the language that sounded a little like Arabic but wasn't. She looked over at Annette and smiled. She was somewhere close to forty, her skin tanned and leathery. Her teeth were crooked, a couple of them broken. She spoke again, then cocked her head to one side, waiting.

"I'm sorry, but I don't understand you," Annette replied in Arabic.

More gutturals came from the other woman. She was probably saying she couldn't understand Annette, either. She jabbed a thumb at her own chest and said, "Emishtar."

Was that the older woman's name? Annette didn't see what else it could be. Pointing to the other woman, she said, "Em-

ishtar." The woman smiled and nodded. She pointed to Annette
and made a questioning noise. "Khadija," Annette told her. She
had to be Khadija—that was the name under which she'd come
here. Changing it would make people wonder, which was the last
thing she could afford.

"Khadija," Emishtar said. She rattled off something that
made no sense to Annette. It didn't sound like a question. Maybe
it was a prayer.

They taught each other names for parts of the body and tools
and the sun up in the sky. Some of the words Emishtar used did
sound something like the Arabic ones Annette had picked up
through her implant. Annette wondered how long she would be
able to remember them. She had to try. The other woman didn't
seem to have any trouble remembering her words. That made
Annette more determined not to let somebody from a low-tech alternate get ahead of her.

Sun was *shams* in Arabic. It was *shamash* in Emishtar's language. That was pretty plainly a Semitic tongue, too—related to
modern Arabic and Hebrew in the home timeline, and to ancient
Aramaic and Assyrian and Babylonian. But Annette was almost
sure it wasn't any Arabic dialect.

"*La ilaha illa'llah—Muhammadun rasulu'llah*," she said.
There is no God but God, and Muhammad is the Prophet of God.
Emishtar just looked at her and shook her head. The older
woman didn't know anything about Islam. She would have recognized the *shahada*, the profession of faith, if she did. In all the
alternates Annette knew of where Arabic was used in Spain,
Muslim conquerors had brought it here. That pretty much nailed
it down. Whatever language Emishtar used, it wasn't one of the
many varieties of Arabic.

But what *was* it? For a while, Annette couldn't think of any
other Semitic tongues that had been spoken in Spain. Then she

remembered the Punic Wars, where Carthage had fought Rome. Carthage—in modern Tunisia, in North Africa—had been a Phoenician city, and the Phoenicians spoke a Semitic language. Carthage had planted colonies of its own in Spain.

"Carthage?" Annette asked, making sure no guard could hear her do it. She pointed east and a little south. "Carthage?"

Emishtar just looked at her and shrugged. She didn't get it. *Carthage*, of course, was the English version of the Latin version of the real name of the place. It wasn't close enough to the original to make sense to Emishtar—if Annette had guessed right in the first place about how this alternate got started.

She laughed at herself. It was either that or pound her head into the dirt. How much she didn't know! She didn't know the right name for Carthage, the one that would have made sense to a real Carthaginian. And she didn't know whether Emishtar came from this alternate. Maybe she'd got here in a transposition chamber, too. If she had, all of Annette's guesses about this place were worthless.

How many alternates did these slavers visit? How long had this been going on? Annette had no way to be sure, except by noting that the manor seemed new. The roadbuilding Jacques and the other men were doing also argued this place hadn't been here very long. If it had, the road would already have been in place, wouldn't it? Annette thought so, but she couldn't prove a thing.

If word of this ever reached the home timeline . . . Somewhere under downtown Madrid was a subbasement with an outlaw transposition chamber. What would people do? Say they were coming into town on business or on vacation? Travel to this alternate or the one with the Great Black Deaths or some other unknown one and play at being masters for a while, then go back to the home timeline with a suntan and with memories they didn't dare share? Again, that was how it looked. Again, Annette knew she couldn't prove it.

She couldn't prove it as long as she was here. Even if she could prove it while she was here, it wouldn't do her any good. But if she could get back . . . If she could ride that transposition chamber back to the home timeline . . .

Most chambers had a human operator in them to take over if anything went wrong with the computers. The slavers hadn't bothered here. Annette could see why not, too. An operator would be one more person, maybe one person too many, who knew the secret. And the computer hardly ever went wrong. Even when it did, the operator couldn't do much about it most of the time. But transposition chambers did have manual controls.

Annette laughed at herself again. It was either that or break down and cry, which she didn't want to do. Suppose everything went just right. Suppose she could hop into the transposition chamber and pilot it back to the home timeline. Then what? Then somebody in that Madrid would knock her over the head, and she would have wasted a thrilling escape.

It wouldn't have worked out like that in a video game. There would have been some puzzle to solve. You might have to look real hard for it, but it would be there. You could win the game.

Here . . . She laughed one more time—those tears she didn't want to shed were much too close. The only way she saw now to win the game and get out of that subbasement in home-timeline Madrid was to look like a master on the way back from her time as lord of all she surveyed. Only one thing was wrong with that.

She couldn't do it.

All she had in this alternate were the clothes on her back. They wouldn't convince anybody she was anything but a slave. She hadn't seen any women from the home timeline here. Even if she did, how likely were any of them to be eighteen years old?

Young people weren't likely to do anything like this to begin with. The passion to lord it over other people, to set yourself up as a little tin god, got worse with age.

"You!" a—middle-aged—guard yelled at her in Arabic. "Work harder!"

As long as he was watching her, she did. Then she slacked off again. She'd already learned one lesson of slavery—never do more than you had to.

Seven

When these people built a road, they didn't fool around. Jacques found that out in a hurry. A track already led east. The road went in the same general direction, but ignored the track. The track meandered and took the easiest way across the hot, dry country-side. The road went straight as a string. In fact, strings stretched from posts driven into the ground marked out the way it would go on.

It was about twenty feet wide, and built on a foundation four or five feet deep. Digging out that much dirt was hard work. The slaves traded off with pick and with shovel and with a wicker basket with which to dump out the spoil. They argued about which job was hardest, using both signs and words. Everybody claimed whatever he was doing at that moment was the hardest thing in the world.

Jacques learned Arabic curses he hadn't known before. He learned some curses in the other two languages, too. He didn't always know what they meant, but liked the way they rolled off his tongue.

The one good thing he could say was that the guards gave the slaves plenty to drink. Without that, men would have died like flies, and they wouldn't have got much roadbuilding done. Some of the swarthier men and the few blacks left after Musa ibn Ibrahim got killed worked stripped to the waist. Jacques couldn't do it. This hot southern sun burned him wherever it touched his skin. He kept his shirt on. He sometimes thought the breeze blowing through the sweat-soaked linen helped cool him. Other times . . .

"I feel like a sausage in an oven," he said, grunting as he lifted a basket of earth and rocks and dumped it to one side of the trench.

"You're still wearing your casing," a slave named Muhammad said with a grin. Four or five of the slaves who'd come over to this place—wherever it was—had that name. This one was short and lean and tough and a brown that staying out in the sun only made browner. He had no trouble shedding his shirt.

Behind the gang that dug down to the foundation came another that filled in the trench to make the roadbed. They threw in dirt mixed with sand, then gravel, then bigger pebbles. Once they'd built the roadbed up close to ground level, they tamped everything down so it was good and firm. Then they set flat, close-fitting paving stones on top of the foundation. Another gang somewhere was probably cutting those stones. Curbstones defined the edge of the road.

There were highways like this in the Kingdom of Versailles. People said they went back to the days of the Romans. Jacques didn't know a lot about the Romans. They'd been strong before Henri's time, before the Great Black Deaths. And they'd crucified Jesus, Henri's older brother. Once you know that much, what else did you need to know?

Because the road was so much work, it didn't move forward very fast. That didn't seem to worry the guards, as long as the road gang worked hard. They kept an eye on the slaves and talked among themselves. Sometimes they used Arabic, sometimes one of the two tongues the slaves who didn't speak Arabic spoke, and sometimes another language Jacques didn't understand. The sounds of that one reminded him a little of the ones in the speech of traders from England.

One day a couple of weeks after Jacques got to the manor, a guard pointed down the track. It ran straight east here—the fancy road was eating it a foot at a time.

A horsemen rode up the track toward the roadbuilding crew. As he drew near, Jacques saw he was waving something in his right hand. It was an olive branch—no mistaking the small, gray-green leaves. A sign of peace? The rider wore a baggy tunic, something that looked like a divided skirt, and rawhide boots. He had on a floppy hat that shielded his face from the sun. Jacques wished he had one like it. The man's face was strong and square, with a big, straight nose, a thick black beard, and bushy eyebrows that grew together in the middle.

The stranger reined in about fifty yards from Jacques and the closest guards. He yelled something in the sneezing, hissing language some of the slaves used. One of the guards shouted back in the same tongue. When he did, the one-eyebrowed man on horseback looked as if he'd got a big mouthful of vinegar. He called out again. The guard answered, and gestured with his musket. *Come ahead*—Jacques could figure that out without understanding a word.

Still with that sour expression on his face, the horseman rode forward. His mount's hooves thumped in the dirt, then clattered on the paving stones of the finished section of road. A guard near Jacques talked into something small that he held in the palm of his hand. Jacques thought he heard the—the thing answer back. That was impossible, though. *Or maybe not*, he thought, remembering the voice that had spoken out of the air in the transposition chamber. Who could say for sure what these—wizards?—were able to do?

Khadija might know, Jacques thought. He hadn't had much

chance to talk with her since they got here. Both of them were too busy. He promised himself he would ask when he did get the chance.

As the stranger rode on, the guards started to laugh. "What's so funny, sir?" Jacques asked the closest one. If you stayed polite to them, they would sometimes answer.

This one did. Still smiling, he said, "The flea-bitten fool is angry because we speak his language as well as he does."

Jacques scratched his head. His hair was filthy and matted with sweat. "I don't understand, sir," he said.

"His people say foreigners can't learn their language," the guard told him. "They say demons tried to learn their language and couldn't do it. But we can." He laughed some more.

And what does that make you? Jacques wondered. He didn't ask. He didn't think the guard would tell him. He wasn't sure he wanted to know, either.

Annette was weeding when she heard a sound that reminded her heartbreakingly of home: a telephone rang. A guard took it out of his pocket, listened, and said, "Yeah?" He listened some more, then said, "Okay," and put the phone away again.

Emishtar was weeding next to her. They'd got into the habit of doing that, so they could teach each other bits of their languages. The guards didn't seem to mind. Emishtar made strange gestures in the direction of the guard who'd used the telephone. To her, it had to be some sort of magical gadget. Maybe she was trying to make sure the magic didn't come down on her.

The guard pointed down the road. Annette looked that way, too, when she was sure nobody was looking at her. A stranger! The first man she'd seen who didn't belong to the manor. He looked . . . like a man. The olive branch seemed to serve as a flag of truce. His horse trappings and his clothes all seemed made by hand. He probably wasn't riding for fun, then, the way he would have in the home timeline. He was riding because this was the best way he knew to go from one place to another. Annette nodded to herself. She'd known this couldn't be a high-tech alternate.

Another guard stepped out into the roadway as the horseman neared. He held up his hand, palm out. The rider reined in. The guard spoke to him. The language sounded like the one some of the slaves used, not Emishtar's tongue but the other one. The horseman answered in what seemed like the same language. After some back-and-forth, the guard waved him on toward the manor.

Once the horseman rode off, the fellow who'd spoken to him came over to the guard near Annette. They were both grinning. Annette wouldn't have wanted those nasty grins aimed at her.

"Lord Wog's not so high and mighty any more?" one of them said.

"Nope," the other answered. "We taught the savages that all kinds of horrible things happen to 'em if they mess with us. They're like any other dogs. Kick 'em a few times and they'll roll over and show you their bellies." He laughed. So did his pal.

Annette kept her head down. She didn't want them to see the look on her face. *Savages* was bad enough. But *wog!* And *dogs!* In the home timeline, calling people names like that was almost as sick as wearing furs. Crosstime Traffic training went on and on till everyone's eyes glazed over about how the people in the alternates *were* people just like anybody else. They might believe some things that weren't so, but that was because they didn't know better, not because they were stupid. Annette could have repeated those lessons in her sleep. She'd believed them, too. She'd thought everybody believed them.

Shows what I know, went through her head.

She'd had some notion of what the masters here got from keeping slaves. It sickened her, but she thought she understood how it worked. What the guards got out of being here—besides piles of benjamins—hadn't been so obvious. She wouldn't have trusted money alone to make people keep their mouths shut. And it didn't look as if the slavers did, either.

If you thought you were better than someone else because you came from here and he came from there, or because your skin was this color and hers was that one, you couldn't show it in the home timeline. If you did, nobody would want anything to do with you. You had to keep those feelings to yourself, to hide them. If you came to a place where you could let them out instead . . .

Wouldn't that be fun? It sure would, if you were the right kind of wrong person.

What had the guards done to the locals? Taken slaves from among them, plainly. What else? *Do I really want to know?* Annette wondered. Her stomach twisted. The locals would have swords and bows and arrows. The guards had assault rifles and body armor and night-vision goggles and all the other tools of twenty-first-century war. They'd won. They probably thought they were heroes because they'd won, too.

Or maybe this was like a duck-hunting trip for them, not even war at all. A lot of people in the home timeline looked down their noses at hunting, but some still enjoyed it. If Annette had her opinion, she knew it was only an opinion. On other things, where just about everyone around her thought the way she did, she sometimes confused her opinions with laws of nature.

People in other alternates were apt to do the same thing. The difference—to her mind, anyway—was that they were likely to be wrong. She couldn't imagine sensible people approving of slavery, for instance, or of male chauvinism, or of furs.

"What are you doing sitting there like a mushroom?" a guard shouted at her in harsh, guttural Arabic. "You didn't come out here to get a suntan, sweetheart. You came out here to work. You'd better remember it, too, or you'll be sorry."

Annette started weeding like a machine. The guard scowled. He didn't have a whip, like an overseer in the South before the Civil War. But he did have a billy club on his belt to go with his automatic rifle. Guards didn't hit slaves here very often. That didn't mean they wouldn't if you gave them an excuse, though, or sometimes just if they felt like it.

"He bad man," Emishtar whispered in bad Arabic.

"He very bad man," Annette agreed in the older woman's language. They'd taught each other *man* and *bad* by pointing at the guards. Annette wished she could ask Emishtar about the man who'd just ridden into the manor, but she didn't have the words. Trying to remember the ones she'd learned without an implant wasn't easy, and she knew she was pronouncing them wrong.

An accent. I've got an accent. She'd never had to worry about that before. The implant let her speak perfectly when she used it. Emishtar had an accent when she used Arabic. That made Annette feel a bit better.

A small bit better. Feeling good about something else while you were a slave was like feeling good about something else while you had two broken legs. You could do it, but not for long and not very well. After a while, you got over a broken leg. How did you get over being a slave if you couldn't escape and there was nobody in this whole alternate to ransom you?

Yes, how did you? Did you? Could you?

When Jacques came in from a day of work on the road, he began to understand how a pack horse felt. The guards insisted on get-

ting so much work out of him. If he could do that much work
without trouble, all right. If he couldn't . . . They insisted on getting that much work out of him anyway, and out of the other
slaves. "You've got to do it!" the guards yelled. "You'll be sorry if
you don't!"

And if men didn't, if men couldn't, the guards made them
sorry. They did excuse people who were really sick. But if you
goofed off, they made you regret it. Those sticks they carried
could raise welts almost like a whip. They didn't always bother
with them, though. Sometimes they would use a boot or a musket
butt to get their point across.

Once, brutality led to tragedy in short order. A guard clouted
one of the men who'd come here in the transposition chamber
with Jacques. The man leaped to his feet and smacked the guard
in the face. Taken by surprise, the guard fell down and dropped
his musket. With a roar of triumph, the slave snatched it up. He
squeezed the trigger.

And nothing happened.

The slave cried out again, this time in despair. The other
guards gave him the ultimate insult—they took the time to laugh
at him before they shot him. The muskets worked fine for them.
They spat bullets like a boy spitting melon seeds to annoy his
sister. The slave fell, with as many holes in him as a colander.
The bullets made horrible wounds, worse than any Jacques had
ever seen. When they tore through a man, they tore his insides
out with them. Jacques wondered why they were so much nastier
than any other musket balls. Maybe they traveled faster. The
gunshots certainly sounded quicker and harsher than any he'd
known before. They went *crack!* instead of *boom!*

After the slave lay dead, his blood soaking into the dirt, the
guards rounded on the rest of the roadbuilding gang. "Anybody
else feel brave?" one of them shouted in Arabic. "Anybody else

feel stupid? You mess with us, only one thing happens—you end up like this." He stirred the body with his boot. Then he shouted some more, in the other languages the slaves here used.

None of the roadbuilders said a word. What could you say? The guards even seemed to have a spell on their muskets, so they could use them and no one else could. How were you supposed to fight men like that? Jacques saw no way, however much he wished he could.

"You and you and you." The guard who'd shouted picked a pikeman and two shovelers near Jacques. "Get off to the side of the road and dig him a grave. You don't need to make it too deep—just enough so the animals won't dig him out."

"May we pray for him?" one of the shovelers asked.

By the look on the guard's face, he wanted to say no. He wanted to, but he didn't. "Yes, go ahead," he said gruffly. "And while you're at it, pray he's got more sense in the next world than he did in this one."

The gravediggers set to work. It was the same work they would have been doing preparing the roadbed. The dead slave would never get out of this bed once they laid him in it, though.

Jacques eyed the guard. The man seemed vicious but not stupid. The slaves needed to see they couldn't hope to get away with rising up. But if he hadn't let them pray over the dead body, that might have given them reason to rise whether they had hope or not. Reluctantly, Jacques decided the men in the mottled tunics and trousers knew what they were doing. *Too bad*, he thought. He would rather have had a bunch of bungling idiots watching him.

Even for three men, digging a grave took a while. When the hole was big enough and deep enough, they dragged the dead man over and slid him down into it. That shoveler murmured prayers in Arabic. All the Muslims paused and lowered their heads in respect. The guards rolled their eyes, but they didn't complain out loud.

Thud-thump! Dirt falling on a body made a dreadfully final sound. The gravediggers filled in the hole, compacting the dirt with their shovels. Then they took some of the stones the crew behind them were using to fill in the roadbed. They tamped those down on top of the grave, too, so wolves or foxes or wolverines would have a harder time digging in. Again, the guards let them do it.

That could have happened to me. A chill ran through Jacques in spite of the heat of the day. If somebody thumped him, he knew he might lose his temper and go after his tormentor. And if he did, he would lie dead moments later. He would go into the ground without even the proper last rites. As far as he knew, he was the only Christian here. If he died without confession, without forgiveness, where else could he go but straight to hell?

But if anybody treated him like a lumpish farm animal, if he snapped and hit back without even thinking . . .

Did all slaves feel this way all the time? Jacques hadn't, not up till now. That other death made him feel the possibility of his own in a way he never had before. He was close to the edge of doing murder, and just as close to being murdered on account of it.

Once the brief funeral was over, the roadbuilding gang went back to work. The guards didn't even have to order the slaves into action. They just fell to, as if they had nothing else to do with their time. Jacques found that he wasn't sorry to be swinging the pick again. The harder he worked, the less he had to think about what had happened there that afternoon.

Along with the rest of the gang, he tramped back to the manor for supper. After he ate, his time was his own. He usually did what the rest of the roadbuilders did: he went straight to sleep. Sometimes, when he had more spirit than usual, he would wash a little before falling into bed. The Muslims washed a little more often than he did. So did the men whose language was all sneezes and snorts. The ones who spoke the language that sounded a little like Arabic washed less often. To him, it didn't make much difference one way or the other.

This evening, though, he walked in the courtyard with Khadija. He was glad she wasn't too tired to come walking with him. In a low voice, he told her what had happened. He spoke French, hoping no one else here understood it.

"That poor fool," she said in the same language when he finished. "Oh, that poor, brave fool."

"The musket wouldn't even shoot for him," Jacques said bitterly. "Are these people evil wizards with spells on their weapons?"

Khadija shook her head. "No, no, no. It's only a trick that poor slave didn't know. I do know about these muskets." How did she know? The same way she knew about transposition chambers? How was that? Jacques didn't even have the chance to ask, for she went on, "They have a little lever on the side that clicks back and forth." She showed him what she meant with a stiff forefinger. "It's called the 'safety.' When it's in one place, the musket can't shoot even if someone pulls the trigger. It can't go off by accident, either. You have to move the safety to the other place before the musket will work. The slave wouldn't have known about that."

"I sure didn't. I never thought of such a thing." Jacques scratched his head. "It's a good idea, though, isn't it? With a gun that spits so many bullets, you don't want it spitting them by mistake."

"That's why they have the safety." Khadija cocked her head

to one side, studying him as daylight leaked out of the sky. "You're clever, to figure that out so fast."

"Am I?" Even to himself, Jacques sounded bleak. "But you already knew it, didn't you? How?"

Khadija stopped. She looked up at him, there in the deepening twilight. To a guard watching from the manor's outer wall, it must have seemed like a tender moment. "I'm not going to tell you that," she replied. "If you think about it, you'll probably come up with the right answer. But don't ask me if you do, because I won't tell you if it is, either."

"Why not?" Jacques didn't feel tender. He was angry. "The way you go on about this and that and the other thing, you might as well be one of these people yourself." His wave took in the whole manor—and the road and the gardens outside, too.

Khadija looked horrified. No, she looked terrified. Or was it both at once? Both at once, Jacques decided. She tried to stare in every direction at once. "I just hope to heaven they didn't hear you, or they didn't understand you if they did."

"How come?" Jacques demanded, but her fright made him lower his voice. "The way you're carrying on, you really *are* one of. . . ." He ran down like a water wheel whose stream dried up. Of itself, his hand shaped the sign of the wheel. "Oh, Jesus and Henri," he whispered. "You are."

She didn't answer. For a heartbeat, that puzzled him. Then he remembered she'd told him she wouldn't. She'd also told him he could figure out what the truth was. Well, he had, all right, and plainly faster than she'd thought he would. Maybe he really was clever. If so, he wished he were stupid. Some things hardly seemed worth finding out.

After a moment, she said, "There's a difference between these people and me. You need to remember that."

Jacques nodded jerkily. "I'll say. They're the masters and

the guards. You're a slave just like me. What bigger difference is there?"

"No, that's not what I meant," Khadija said. "The difference is, these people are outlaws. They're the worst kind of outlaws anybody's seen in a long, long time. If I could get to my . . . my duke, I guess you'd say, he'd land on them with both feet. He would, and he could—if I could let him know about this. By whatever oath you want from me, Jacques, I swear that's true." She took his hands in hers.

It must have looked like another tender moment. Jacques' head whirled, but not the way it should have around a pretty girl. If she could get away, she might be able to rescue all the slaves. That was what it boiled down to. "How do I help?" he asked.

"Well, I don't know yet," she answered. "But if I get the chance, I'll take you with me if I can. All right?"

"If it helps me get away from this place, it's better than all right," Jacques said.

Annette lay on her bed in the women's dormitory. She felt sick to her stomach, and it had nothing to do with the food slaves got here. She'd just broken about half the rules Crosstime Traffic set. And she hadn't just broken the rules. She'd thrown down the pieces and danced on them.

No matter what she'd done, and no matter what she might do, nothing she did could come close to what the slavers were doing. Remembering that helped steady her. Yes, she'd given away most of the Crosstime Traffic secret to somebody from another alternate. Well, so what? Look what these people were doing!

As if to prove as much, one of the house slaves came in and lay down on her bed. She was young and good-looking, and she'd been summoned to the master's residence. That was another thing a slaveowner could do—and a slave couldn't stop him, not unless she wanted something even worse to happen to her. There was one more charge against these people, too.

House slaves didn't have to work as hard as the ones who went out to the gardens. For a little while, Annette had hoped she would get called back to the manor. That was the kind of hope a slave had—not to do what she wanted, but to do something a little less nasty than something else. Now, though, Annette decided she didn't mind going out to the vegetable gardens. She didn't want anybody noticing her the way that pretty house slave had been noticed.

To help keep that from happening, Annette didn't keep herself as clean as she might have. If she had a smudge of dirt on one cheek, if her hair was matted and greasy, if she didn't smell very good, if onions filled her breath, who would pay attention to her like that? She wanted to wash. She wanted hardly anything more. One of the hardest things about going to the alternates was dealing with filth. Here, though, it made for protective coloration. Annette shook her head. No, protective discoloration was more like it.

In a bed not far away, Emishtar was snoring. The other woman had as much to worry about as Annette. In fact, since she was older and from a low-tech alternate, she probably wasn't anywhere near as healthy, so she had more to worry about. But she didn't seem to worry nearly so much. She just went on doing as little as she could get away with. The only thing that did seem to bother her was too much work.

I should be so lucky, Annette thought. In spite of her worries, she found herself yawning. All of them put together couldn't keep her awake till midnight, not with the day she'd put in. She yawned again, and fell asleep.

Somebody banging on a gong woke her much too early the

next morning. That was low-tech, which didn't mean it didn't work. She yawned and rolled out of bed. Every time she did that, she shook her head in disbelief. *This* was her life? All she had to look forward to was another day of pulling weeds under the hot sun? Such as it was, this was it, all right.

And she had to move fast, too, or she wouldn't have time to finish breakfast, or maybe even get any. As she left the women's barracks, her eyes went toward the building she'd come out of when she got to this alternate. Somewhere down in the subbasement, a transposition chamber came and went. If she could get aboard it . . .

She laughed at herself. That would have been funny if it weren't so sad. For one thing, she had no idea *when* the chamber came and went. For another, the way down was always guarded. In the movies, one unarmed person could take on a swarm of guards with assault rifles and win. Annette wished life imitated art. The third-quarter moon rode high in the southern sky. She could wish for that, too, while she was at it.

Men and women were lining up for breakfast. They mingled only at meals and in the little stretch of time after supper and before sleep. Whoever set this place up might have been—had been—evil, but wasn't stupid. Far from it, worse luck. Making attachments hard to form let everything run more smoothly. People in love would take chances for the ones they loved that they wouldn't take in ordinary times.

Jacques came in a few minutes after Annette. He waved to her. She smiled and nodded back. If she got out of here, she would have to try to bring him with her, or to come back if she made it alone. It wasn't just that she'd promised, though she had. But getting down to that subbasement might take more muscle than any one person had.

What would Crosstime Traffic do with her—do to her—if she

brought Jacques back to the home timeline? What would the
company do with—do to—Jacques? Annette shrugged. She'd
worry about that when the time came, if it came. She had plenty
of worse things to worry about now.

One of those worries was, what if getting down to the subbasement took more muscle than any two people had? What was
she supposed to do then? Lead a slave revolt? She quailed at the
thought. She didn't like leading any better than she liked following. She couldn't even talk to most of the slaves. And if they did
rise, the guards would massacre them—and would laugh while
they were doing it, too. She was as sure of that as she was of her
own name.

Details, details. She mocked herself. It might have been
funny if it weren't so sad.

She took a bowl. She took a spoon. A cook—another slave—
dipped a ladle in a big pot of porridge and filled her bowl. She
got plenty. The one cruelty they seemed to skip here was starving
the slaves. It wasn't exciting—barley and peas and beans stewed
forever, with chopped sausage and onions thrown in for flavor.
But it wasn't terrible. Some of the slaves said they were eating
better than they ever had in their lives.

Emishtar sat down beside her. "Good morning," Annette said
in the language that sounded a little like Arabic but wasn't.

"Good morning," the older woman answered in Arabic.

"You good?" Annette asked.

Emishtar nodded. "I good. Thank you. *You* good?"

"I good, too. Thank you."

On they went, each using the other's language as best she
could. As long as they stuck to clichés and stock phrases, they
did all right. When they tried to go beyond those, they had more
trouble. Every day, though, each of them learned a few more
words. Almost every day, one of them figured out something new

about the grammar in the other's language. They had a long way to go, but they were gaining.

Emishtar glanced over toward Jacques. "Nice young man," she remarked, her voice very, very casual.

"Is she?" Annette tried to be casual, too. Making a mistake like that didn't help. Emishtar laughed her head off. Annette tried again: "Is *he?*"

"I think so," the older woman said. "I think you think so, too."

Annette's ears heated. "And so?" she said. That made a handy, all-purpose question.

Emishtar grinned at her. "And so nothing. Nice young man, is all." It wasn't all. It wasn't even close to all, not by that grin. She enjoyed teasing Annette. She wasn't mean about it—she did it the way a friend would.

If I'm stuck here for good . . . Annette didn't want to think like that, not when she knew the transposition chamber came and went down there in the subbasement. But the slavers were careful. They had to be. If they slipped up, they knew what kind of trouble they'd land in.

In the movies and on TV, bad guys did dumb things and got caught because of it. Annette supposed that was true a lot of the time in real life, too. But the only mistake these people had made that she could see was buying her for a slave—and they didn't know she was from the home timeline.

"Come on! Time to work!" a guard shouted. Annette understood the words in Arabic, and she understood them in Emishtar's language, too. Was that progress, or was it a sign she'd already been here too long?

Men on horseback trotted up the road from the manor toward Jacques and the rest of the roadbuilding gang. Jacques would have ridden by the side of the road, not on the paving stones—horses liked soft ground underfoot better than hard rock. Maybe the guards on the horses didn't know that. They didn't seem like especially good riders. But they had those quick-shooting muskets slung over their shoulders. They weren't going out there to mix it up. They were going out to shoot whatever got in their way. How good a horseman did you need to be to do that?

The guards keeping an eye on the roadbuilders waved to the riders as they went past. Some of the horsemen waved back. They called out in the language that sounded like the one Englishmen used. That would have done Jacques more good if he'd spoken any English.

Off the riders went, down the track in the direction from which that horseman had come before. On the track, the horses kicked up a cloud of dust. People who were paying attention would have time to disappear before the riders got dangerously close. If a dozen men with muskets like that had been after Jacques, he would have done his best to disappear.

He shoveled some dirt into a basket, then turned to one of the slaves swinging a pick. "If you had to, how would you fight these people?" he asked in quiet Arabic.

"How?" The Muslim paused to wipe sweat off his forehead with his arm. "Carefully, by God—that's how." He also spoke in a low voice.

Jacques laughed, but it was one of those painfully true jokes. "What could you do against them? Hope to catch one alone and stab him in the back?"

"Probably your best chance," the other man agreed. "Odds are bad, though. I wouldn't want to try it at all, not unless I had to. I'd have about as much chance as a farm dog going up against an armored man."

One of the remaining guards strode toward them. "Enough chatter," he said. "Pay attention to what you're supposed to be doing."

With a sigh—a soft, quiet sigh—Jacques shoveled more dirt into the basket. That other slave swung his pick. The guard turned around and walked away. *I might jump him from behind*, Jacques thought. *I know about the safety, thanks to Khadija.*

If he could get a guard's musket and shoot all the other guards right here before they realized he understood how to use the weapon . . . Well, then what? The sound of gunfire would bring more guards. They would open up while he was still explaining to the other men who would snatch up muskets what a safety was and how to move it so their new firearms would shoot. And he could only talk to men who spoke Arabic.

He was ready—he was eager—to take chances to be free. But he saw the difference between taking chances and committing suicide. Trying to jump a guard and steal his musket seemed suicidal. *Too bad*, Jacques thought. *Too bad, too bad.*

What would happen if he just tried to run away? Again, he didn't need to be a monk or a scholar to figure that out. They would go after him, and they would probably catch him. When they did, they would make him very unhappy. He didn't know how, but he was sure they would. Anybody whose slave tried to run away would punish him once they got him back. These people seemed likely to be very, very good at punishment.

He glanced over at another guard. Even if he could grab a musket, even if he could arm his fellow slaves, even if he could get rid of all the guards and capture the manor and kill the master, he'd still be stuck here. He couldn't go back to the Madrid from which he'd been yanked, much less to the Kingdom of Versailles.

But there was a link between this place and Madrid. The

transposition chamber. He had no idea how to make it work. He didn't, no. *Khadija does. She belongs to these people, but she's not bad like most of them.*

He wondered how he was so sure. He knew her better than he knew the ones who'd enslaved him. *And she's too pretty to be bad.* He did laugh at himself this time, and loaded another shovelful of dirt into the basket.

Eight

Day followed day. Annette quickly lost track of which day of the week it was. That didn't seem to matter. About all she had to measure time were the ripening of the vegetables and the slow swing of the sun to the south. The weather got cooler—cooler, yes, but not really cold.

Emishtar greeted the sun with a prayer every morning. At first, it was just noise to Annette. A few words at a time, a few phrases at a time, she learned to understand the whole thing. It was rather pretty. It was also another sign of how much time she'd spent here. *Too much, too much*, she thought.

More slaves, men and women, came up from the subbasement one night. They were blonds and redheads, with fair, freckled skins and eyes of blue or green or gray. When summer's full heat came back, they would roast. None of the slaves spoke a language they understood, while theirs made no sense to anyone else. The guards could shout at them and make sense, but the guards had implants, so they were able to learn languages in a hurry.

What alternate were the newcomers from? One where Crosstime Traffic did business? Or one like this, where the slavers had it all to themselves? Annette couldn't tell on her own, and had no way to ask.

With the newcomers getting the hardest jobs, some of the

women who'd been tending vegetables became house slaves. When Annette stayed put in the garden plot, Emishtar said, "They should have brought you in. You are too smart for this." Her Arabic was getting pretty good, too.

"I do not mind," Annette said.

Emishtar laughed. "I know why you do not mind, too. That is one of the things that can happen to a slave woman."

"I do not want it to happen to me." Annette was proud of herself. She just said it. She didn't scream it.

"It can happen to you if you stay out here, too," the older woman said.

"Don't remind me," Annette answered in Arabic—she didn't know how to put that into Emishtar's language.

Emishtar either understood it or figured out what it had to mean. She laughed again. "I do not think you have to worry so much, though, not for a while," she said.

"No? Why not?" Annette asked.

"The master and the guards will try the new ones. They *are* new. And they look strange. That will make them seem . . . interesting."

Annette thought Emishtar was half right. Blondes and redheads might seem unusual to the older woman, but they wouldn't to somebody from the home timeline. Still, the rest of what the older woman said was true. The blondes and redheads were the new fish, so they probably would seem extra interesting for a while. Who'd said variety was the life of spice? Annette didn't think it was Ambrose Bierce, even if it sounded cynical enough to come from him.

While they were in the garden plots, the guards spent most of their time yelling at the new slave women. The language they used was oddly musical. It reminded Annette a little of an Irish brogue. On a visit to the west of Ireland a couple of years before, she and her folks had stopped at a pub for lunch. She'd needed a while to realize most of the Irishmen and -women eating and drinking there were speaking Erse, not English. The sounds of the older tongue had flavored the way they spoke hers.

So maybe these are Celts, too, she thought. Their looks argued for it. But that didn't say anything about which alternate they'd been stolen from.

They exclaimed at the hoes and trowels and three-tined cultivators they were supposed to use. To Annette, the tools were the most ordinary things in the world. They looked like Home Depot or Wal-Mart specials. They likely were—Annette's skirt had a label that said *Wal-Mart—made in Bangladesh* on it. Why get anything fancy and expensive for slaves? But they seemed something special to the fair-skinned women.

Watching them, Emishtar smiled, showing off her crooked front teeth. "When I first come here, I thinks tools very good, too," she said.

"They're all right." Annette didn't want to get excited about them.

"Gooder than all right." Emishtar's grammar slipped—so did Annette's a lot of the time—but she made herself understood. She went on, "All tools this kind, all tools that kind, all same. All *just* the same. All good, smooth handles. Not too heavy. Not too—" She paused and raised an eyebrow, looking for help.

"Light?" Annette said. She picked up a pebble and easily tossed it up and down. "Light."

"Light. Yes. Thank you. Is the word." Emishtar nodded. "Not too heavy. Not too light. All good to use."

To her, as to the—Celtic?—women, tools were made one at a time, by hand. No wonder they got excited when they saw several that were just alike. *I should have figured that out sooner*, Annette thought, feeling dumb. She might take mass production for granted, but people from a low-tech alternate wouldn't. To them, it was as strange and marvelous as a transposition chamber, maybe more so.

Once she'd read a story—she didn't know if it was true—set in the days when high technology hadn't yet spread all over the home timeline. An African from a tiny village in the middle of nowhere had to come into the big city for some reason or other. He saw an airplane flying overhead, but it didn't mean much to him. Maybe he thought it was magic, or maybe he didn't realize people rode inside it. Then he saw a two-horse team pulling a carriage. He laughed and snapped his fingers and exclaimed, "Why didn't I think of that?"

The horse and carriage lay within the range of what he could understand, even if he hadn't thought of the arrangement till he saw it. The airplane was as far over his head in terms of ideas as it was high up in the sky. In the same way, the Celts—and Emishtar—could admire the gardening tools. They could see what those were for and how well they were made. The transposition chamber was beyond them. Even the safety on an assault rifle had been beyond that luckless slave in Jacques' gang.

"Come on, get to work!" a guard shouted to her in Arabic. "You think you can stand around lollygagging all day long? Things don't work that way around here. You better believe they don't!"

"I am so sorry. Please forgive me," Annette said. She got down on her hands and knees and started weeding. The guard went off to yell at somebody else. Annette hated acting like— well, like a slave. But sometimes the guards didn't just yell. Sometimes they smacked somebody with a billy club or a rifle butt or gave somebody a kick in the backside or in the ribs. Annette thought that enjoying hitting people who couldn't hit back was part of what went into being a guard.

After this one got out of earshot, Emishtar whispered, "I so

sorry, too. I so sorry guard not dead. I so sorry guard not on fire.
I so sorry guard not in pile of manure. I so sorry guard not sick,
horrible sick. I so sorry—"

She went on for quite a while. She might not have known
much Arabic. Everything she did know that was bad, she aimed at
the guards. Long before she ran down, Annette was giggling helplessly. A guard sent her a suspicious look, but she was working as
well as giggling. The guard didn't do anything but look.

Emishtar said some things in her own language, too. Annette
didn't understand all of that. What she could follow was along
the same lines as the Arabic, but even juicier. She tried to remember some of the best parts.

And Emishtar also showed her something else. The older
woman had to do the work, just as Annette did. Even so, her
spirit stayed free. Some of the slave women—and some of the
slave men—seemed hardly more than beasts of burden to Annette. They'd accepted their fate. They were resigned to it. Emishtar reminded her it didn't have to be that way.

And there were times when she needed reminding, too.
Sometimes the home timeline felt a million miles away. Sometimes the transposition chamber in the subbasement also felt a
million miles away. It might come and go, but how could a slave
get down to it? Try as she would, Annette couldn't figure out a
way to sneak past the guards or overpower them. And if she
couldn't, she'd stay a slave forever.

Here came the guards who'd ridden out like knights. Jacques
counted them. They hadn't lost a man. *What a shame*, he
thought. One of them had a bandaged forearm. He seemed more
angry at himself than badly hurt. By the way his friends teased
him, they thought the wound was pretty funny.

For a moment, Jacques wondered why. War was a serious business, and the people on the other side were trying to hurt you just as hard as you were trying to hurt them. His leg still twinged every now and then to remind him the raiders who'd overrun his caravan had put a bullet through it.

But that had been an even fight. Men on both sides used the same kinds of weapons. It didn't look as if the people around here had any firearms at all, let alone quick-shooting muskets like the ones the guards carried. Going up against them wouldn't be war, not in the true sense of the word. It wouldn't even be like hunting wolves, where your quarry was ferocious and had sharp teeth. It would be a lot more like hunting rabbits.

Or, since you were hunting *people*, wouldn't it be a lot like murder?

The guards didn't seem to think so. They were laughing and joking and telling stories. Jacques couldn't follow what they were saying, but he didn't need to know what the words meant. Their smiles and their gestures said they'd had a terrific time doing whatever they'd done out there.

One of them wore a strange necklace. That surprised Jacques—the guards didn't usually go in for display the way soldiers from the Kingdom of Versailles and its Muslim neighbors did. Then the man came close enough to let Jacques see what he'd strung on that cord.

It was a necklace of human ears.

A few bloodthirsty men in Jacques' kingdom kept souvenirs of their kills like that. Most, though, thought it was bragging. Jacques looked at it that way, too. And he wondered why anybody would want to brag about killing enemies who could hardly fight back. It didn't seem sporting.

The guards keeping an eye on the roadbuilding gang called to the ones who'd gone . . . hunting. The horsemen in mottled clothes shouted back. Again, Jacques didn't need to know their language to have a notion of the kind of things they were saying. When a man threw back his head and thumped his chest as he spoke, he wasn't likely to be doing anything but boasting.

One of the guards with the roadbuilders called, "We just taught the chicken thieves and cattle rustlers a lesson. See if they come bothering us any more."

Jacques didn't know they'd come around before. He shrugged. Whatever the locals had done, what the guards did to them was like killing a mouse by dropping a building on its head.

That guard went on talking in the language that sounded a little like Arabic, and then in the one that was full of hisses and sneezes. Jacques kept an eye on the slaves who spoke that tongue. He thought they were from right around here. They didn't look very happy. A couple of them muttered back and forth. But what could they do besides mutter? Not much, not that he could see.

Then the guard spoke to the new men, the fair-haired men, who'd come up from the subbasement a few days earlier. Their speech reminded Jacques of the language men from Brittany used. He knew a few words of that tongue. The Duke of Brittany was a vassal—of sorts—to the King of Versailles. Some of the duke's men hardly spoke any French at all. If you didn't talk to them in Breton, you didn't talk to them.

"Hello," Jacques said to a redheaded man with a droopy mustache. "Understand me?"

He got back a wide-eyed stare. The other man's eyes were almost as green as leaves. "Understand," he said—or Jacques thought he did, anyway. It wasn't the same language as Breton, just one close to it, the way Catalan was close to French. When the redhead went on in a hurry, Jacques couldn't follow him at all.

"No understand," he said, and threw his hands in the air. He knew only a few words of Breton. It wasn't like Arabic, which he actually spoke, even if he didn't speak it well. "Go slow," he added.

Maybe the redhead didn't understand that, because he babbled on, fast as a galloping horse. Jacques put his two index fingers together, then very slowly moved them apart. Maybe sign language would work.

And maybe nothing would. A guard yelled in the redhead's language—*he* had no trouble using it. Jacques wondered how the guards all spoke so many languages so well. Maybe Khadija knew. She knew all kinds of curious things. But Jacques didn't get a chance to wonder much about that. As soon as the guard got done yelling at the redhead, he switched to Arabic and yelled at Jacques: "Go on, you lazy good-for-nothing, dig! You didn't come out here so you could gab!" He set a hand on the club he wore on his belt to show what would happen if Jacques didn't dig.

Jacques dug. Most of the time, the guards didn't threaten more than once. After that, they really walloped you. If you were dumb enough not to work while they were keeping an eye on you, you almost deserved to get clobbered. And if you were dumb enough to work hard when the guards *weren't* watching, you almost deserved . . . what?

To be a slave, that's what, Jacques decided.

After a bit, the man in the mottled clothes decided to bother somebody else. Jacques hadn't expected anything else. As soon as the fellow's eyes weren't on him any more, he slacked off. He had the chance to look this way and that and see what was going on around him. The first thing he saw was that the redhead with the droopy mustache was watching him.

Plainly, the new slave didn't speak Arabic. Jacques tried him with French. So far, the only person here with whom he could speak his own language was Khadija—one more reason for

him to think she was special. The redheaded man shook his head
and spread his hands and shrugged. French didn't work.

It would have to be Breton, then, or Jacques' tiny bits and
pieces of it. He pointed towards a guard and said the nastiest thing
he knew how to say. Would that make any sense to the redhead?

The man's eyes widened again. He snorted. He almost giggled. He turned very red—his skin was so fair, it made the flush
easy to see. He pointed toward the guard and said something
else. Jacques wasn't sure exactly what it meant. He thought it
had to do with horses—parts of horses, anyway. He knew which
part of a horse he thought the guard was. He grinned at the redhead and nodded.

"Dumnorix." The man with the mustache pointed at himself.

Jacques gave his own name. He pointed at the redhead and
tried to pronounce *Dumnorix*. The other man corrected him.
When Dumnorix tried to say *Jacques*, he had trouble with the
first sound. Jacques repeated it. On Dumnorix's second try, he
got it right—or close enough, anyhow.

That still didn't give them much to talk about. They could
swear at the guards, but they'd been doing that before they found
they had any words in common. Now Jacques could follow some
of Dumnorix's bad language. And if Jacques cursed in Breton
instead of French or Arabic, Dumnorix could understand some
of that.

Can I tell him about the safety on the guards' muskets?
Jacques wondered. That was something Dumnorix needed to
know. If he wanted to make trouble, and if he wanted to do it
without getting killed right away, he had to know it.

But when Jacques tried to explain, he ran into a stone wall.
The man with the red mustache figured out he was talking about
muskets. Jacques' sign language and his handful of words were
plenty for that. To Dumnorix, though, the weapons weren't tools

like picks and shovels. If Jacques understood him rightly, he thought they were magical.

Try as Jacques would, he couldn't convince Dumnorix that magic had nothing to do with it. Dumnorix saw a thing that went *bang!* over here and killed somebody over there. He didn't see how the one was connected to the other.

How did gunpowder work? Jacques couldn't explain that, though there were men back in the Kingdom of Versailles who could have. Jacques just knew that it worked. That wasn't enough for Dumnorix.

Sometimes Jacques wanted to knock sense into the older man's foolish head. And then he wondered how Khadija felt when she was trying to explain things like the transposition chamber to him. Would it ever be anything but magic, as far as he was concerned? You got in it, it didn't seem to move, but you were somewhere else when you got out again. If that wasn't magic, what was it?

It wasn't magic to Khadija, because she knew that it worked, maybe even how it worked. Jacques stopped being quite so annoyed with Dumnorix. Weren't the two of them in the same boat?

Emishtar turned out to be right about the newly arrived women. The master forgot about the slaves who'd been there for a while. He started summoning the blondes and redheads who had come out of the subbasement. Some of them just went. Some raised a fuss. They ended up going anyway. They came back in tears.

"Is part of being slave," Emishtar said in her halting Arabic.

"It shouldn't be." Annette was furious. She'd read about things like this, but she'd never dreamt she would see them. She'd especially never dreamt they would happen because of people from the home timeline. "Women shouldn't have to put up with things like this."

Emishtar's laugh sounded old as time. "Go ahead. Make men listen to you." She laughed again.

In the home timeline, there were laws against things like this. Not only that, strong customs backed up the laws there. Annette would have said everybody followed those customs. And she would have been wrong, wrong, wrong. The proof of that was right here. Some people—not many, but enough—behaved the way they should as long as anybody was watching. As soon as the eyes went away . . .

As soon as the eyes went away, they turned into slave drivers. Literally.

What did they say, back in the home timeline, to explain why they were away so much? Were they supposed to be on vacation? On business trips? Working in some foreign country. If you googled them thoroughly, would a pattern show up? Of course it would. It would have to. Keeping a secret these days was next to impossible once somebody decided to look for it.

The only way to keep a secret was not to let anybody know you had one in the first place. Then no one would start searching to see what it was.

Too late, Annette thought. *Much too late. Somebody from the home timeline who isn't in on it knows.* All Annette had to do was get back and start sending e-mail and calling people on the phone.

Now she laughed, almost as bitterly as Emishtar had. Yeah, that was all. Easy. Ha!

Her friend eyed her. "What is joke?" Emishtar asked. If you had a joke, you told it. You didn't just sit on it. There were no written rules here, but that seemed to be one of the strongest unwritten rules. Things that were funny were too precious to be hoarded.

"It's on me," Annette said. "If I could get away, if I could get back to where I come from, I have friends I could tell what's happened, friends who would rescue me." She spoke in short phrases to give Emishtar a better chance to understand.

And the older woman did—or at least she understood the words. "But what is the joke?" she asked again, using her own language instead of Arabic.

"If I could go back where I come from, I wouldn't need rescuing!" Annette exclaimed. "I would be free." She laughed again.

This time, so did Emishtar. "Oh, yes. That is funny. That *would* be funny, only. . . ." She pantomimed laughing and crying at the same time. She was a natural mimic and actress. Annette wondered if they had theaters in whatever alternate she came from. If they did, she wondered whether women could perform in them. Or were they like the ones in ancient Greece and Shakespeare's London, where men and boys played all the parts?

She did the best she could to ask in Emishtar's language. When she ran out of words, she used Arabic. They had to go back and forth several times before Emishtar caught on. "Ah!" she said. "Yes, we have. We do. But we do only with men. In your country, with women, too?"

"Yes," Annette said. "We call them *actresses*." She used the Arabic word. "The men who do it are *actors*."

Emishtar taught her the word for *actor* in that other Semitic language. It sounded nothing like the one in Arabic. The two tongues had plainly got them from different places. The languages were cousins, which helped Annette learn bits and pieces of the other one, but they weren't close cousins.

A guard strode towards Annette and Emishtar. They both

started weeding and pruning harder. The guard tramped on past them. They breathed sighs of relief.

One of the blond women was weeding not far away. She'd been out in the sun too long. Even though it was autumn, she'd got burned. One of Annette's friends back in Ohio had what she called phosphorescent Irish skin. This woman was like that— she would burn if the sun looked at her sideways.

She must have sensed Annette's eye on her. She looked across the onions and leeks and garlic and managed a weary smile. She brushed her filthy hair back from her face with a dirty hand. Sweat ran down her cheek. She said something in her musical language.

However musical it was, it didn't mean anything to Annette. "I'm sorry, but I don't understand," she said in Arabic.

The blond woman made a face. She said something else. Annette also couldn't follow that. It was probably something like, *I don't know what you're talking about, either*. The blond woman tried to smooth back her hair again. With a wry shrug, she gave up—it was hopeless.

She spoke again. It must have made her feel better, even if Annette and Emishtar didn't understand. She was halfway between the two of them in age, which put her at the end of her twenties. Annette thought the master had summoned her once or twice. If he had, it didn't seem to have ruined her, the way it had some women. People were all different, and took things differently ways.

She's one of the lucky ones, Annette thought. Then she laughed at herself. Had the blond woman been lucky, she would still have been living in her own alternate. She wouldn't have been a slave—or maybe she would have. Maybe the slavers from the home timeline bought her the same way they'd bought Annette.

Annette wondered if she would ever know. To find out, either she would have to learn some of that language that sounded like Erse or she would have to teach the blond woman some Arabic, or maybe some French. She tried not to groan. *Another* new language to learn without an implant? How would she keep this one and Emishtar's from bumping together in her head?

"Work!" a guard shouted—luckily, not at her. She worked faster anyway. She had more than languages to worry about.

"Oh, them," Jacques said. "Yes, I think they were slaves before. I'm pretty sure, in fact."

For the first time ever, he thought he'd really impressed Khadija. "How do you know?" she demanded.

"Well, it sounds like that's what Dumnorix is saying," Jacques answered.

Her eyes widened. "You can understand him?"

He held his thumb and forefinger close together. "About that much. The language he speaks, it's kind of like Breton. If I knew more Breton, I'd be in good shape, but mostly I just cuss in it a little." He said something.

"What's that?" Khadija asked.

"Well, in French it'd be *sacrée merde*," he said.

She giggled. "Oh. All right. I understand that. But you can talk with this what's-his-name a little bit? Breton!" She shook her head in amazement. "I suppose I shouldn't be that surprised. I thought it reminded me of the Irish language, but I don't speak Erse."

"You mean there are things you can't do?" Jacques wasn't sure whether he was being sarcastic or he really meant it. "Who would have imagined such a thing?"

Khadija turned away from him, there in the courtyard. He

thought she was joking till he saw her shoulders shake. "That's not funny," she said in a strange, muffled voice.

Was she crying? That wasn't what he'd meant to do. He set a hand on her shoulder. "I'm sorry," he said.

Angrily, she shook off the hand. He remembered how the raiders who'd captured them said she'd thrown men around till somebody knocked her cold. If even a quarter of that was true, he was lucky not to go flying himself. She said, "If I could do everything the way you think I can, would I be *here*?"

He had no answer for that. He didn't think anyone would have. He did his best: "I said I was sorry." Now—would she believe him or would she stay angry?

"All right," she said, but it didn't sound all right. Sure enough, she went on, "I must be in worse shape than I thought if what you say matters so much to me."

"What you say matters to me, too," Jacques said. "We're the only two people who speak French." He paused to think. "Do they even speak French in the Kingdom of Versailles here?"

"I wouldn't bet on it," Khadija answered. "I wouldn't bet there *is* a Kingdom of Versailles here."

Jacques nodded. The idea made sense to him, however much he wished it didn't. "That makes you my oldest friend," he said seriously. "That makes you my only friend who remembers my kingdom. I really *am* sorry, Khadija. I didn't mean to hurt your feelings. You know so much—can you wonder when I think you know everything there is to know?"

"Well, I don't." Her voice was tart. "I didn't know this place was here, for instance. I didn't know my own people were running it. And I can't figure out how to get away, either. They watch the way to the chamber down below too well for anybody to sneak by." She stared down at the ground. "Knowing all the things I can't do is one of the reasons I got so mad at you."

"I know. I feel bad. I shouldn't have said that." Jacques paused, listening to her words over again. "One of the reasons? There are others?"

"There are others," Khadija agreed. "You're my oldest friend here, too, you know. It's easy for somebody like that to hurt your feelings, even if he doesn't mean to."

"Yes, I suppose so." Jacques knew Khadija could hurt his feelings. She hadn't tried, but then, he hadn't been trying with her, either. "Here. Maybe this will make things better." He kissed her on the cheek.

She looked so surprised, he wondered again if he was going to go flying. Then she managed a sort of a smile, even if only one corner of her mouth twisted up. "Maybe it makes things better. Maybe it makes them worse, too."

"I—" Jacques began.

Khadija held up a hand and cut him off. "Whatever you're going to say, you'd probably be smarter not to. Maybe the time will come when we can talk about things like that. If it does, we'll both know it, I think. It's not here yet."

Jacques thought it was. But if Khadija didn't, who cared what he thought? Things like that, as she'd put it, took two. If only one was ready, what did you have? A disappointment, that was all. "Well, you know how I feel," he said.

This time, she managed a real smile. "Thank you. It's always a compliment. But . . . here? It's not a good idea, Jacques. If we knew we could never get away—then, maybe, we'd have to make the best of things."

"I never thought I'd find a reason to want to go on being a slave," Jacques said.

Khadija turned away from him again. "Don't be stupid," she snapped. "No reason in the world is good enough to make you want to stay a slave."

Looked at one way, she was right. Looked at another . . . But if he looked at things like that, he *would* make her angry at him, which was the last thing he wanted. And he did want to get away. If he stayed here too long, he was liable to try to get a guard's musket away from him. But even if he did, so what? Even if he killed all the guards and set himself up as king here, so what? He'd be King of Nowhere.

Seeing that made him nod. "Well, when you're right, you're right."

"Oh, good." Khadija sounded relieved. "I'm glad you can be sensible."

"I can be tired, is what I can be," Jacques answered.

She yawned. "So can I. They work us hard. It's how they have part of their fun." She walked back toward the women's barracks, leaving Jacques scratching his head. He'd never thought much about people who had fun being cruel to other people. But if you had a good time shooting enemies who didn't have muskets of their own, why wouldn't you have fun working your slaves hard and watching them sweat?

On that cheerful note, Jacques headed for bed himself.

Emishtar had trouble saying Jacques' name, but not keeping her eyes open. They sparkled as she said, "He kiss you." She smacked her lips together so Annette wouldn't doubt what she meant. "Last night, he kiss you."

"Not like that," Annette said.

"No?" Her older friend sounded disappointed. "Too bad."

"Just a little one." Annette held her thumb and first finger so they almost touched. "Little."

"Too bad," Emishtar said again. She pulled up a weed by the roots. "What you got better to do?"

Get out of here, Annette thought. But Emishtar wouldn't believe that. Emishtar thought they were stuck in this alternate forever. Given what she knew, how could she think anything else? Annette didn't think so, but none of what she knew would make sense to Emishtar. Most of it didn't make sense to Jacques, and he came from a much higher-tech alternate than Emishtar did.

"It wouldn't be a good idea," was all Annette could come up with.

Emishtar rolled her eyes and went back to pulling weeds. She didn't say what she thought, but every line of her body shouted, *Fool!* at Annette. Had Annette come from her alternate, or from Jacques', Emishtar would have been right. A little happiness mixed in with the misery of being a slave would have been the most she could hope for.

But she was what she was, and she still had real hope. Sometimes she wondered why. This operation was slick, no two ways about it. The people who ran things here didn't slip up.

The blond woman who'd tried to talk with Annette was working not far away. Annette had found out the woman's name was Birigida, or something like that. She'd managed to get across that her own name was Khadija, which the blond woman had a devil of a time pronouncing. They hadn't gone much past that. The languages they used were too different from each other.

A guard yelled at Birigida. She was one of those people who did as little as they could to get by. All slaves did as little as they could, but Birigida did as little as she could even for a slave. She sped up a little when he shouted, but only a tiny bit. And she slowed down again as soon as he turned his back.

That was too soon. The guard might have been a jackass, but he wasn't a stupid jackass. He spun around to see if he could catch her goofing off. When he did, he pulled out his billy club and whacked her across the backside.

She yelped and jerked. The guard did some more shouting. He shook the billy club in her face. *If you don't work harder, you'll get more!* Annette didn't need to understand a word of the language to know what was going on.

Did Birigida get it? Annette wouldn't have bet a dollar on it, and the little aluminum coins were as near worthless as made no difference. Some people just wouldn't make an effort, even if they got in trouble for not making one. Annette had no idea why that was so, but she'd seen it was. She'd known half a dozen smart people in high school who either weren't going to college at all or weren't going to the one they wanted because they hadn't cared about their grades.

Some of them would find something that interested them and do all right anyway. Some . . . wouldn't. Birigida didn't have the choice. Nothing could make gardening and weeding interesting. But not getting whacked in the fanny should have been reason enough for her to keep her mind on her work.

The women around Birigida worked harder and faster—the guard would be keeping an eye on them, too. Annette knew she did more than she would have otherwise. She scowled at the blond woman for making her speed up.

No, Birigida didn't get it. Nothing under the sun could make her work harder than she felt like working. The guard yelled at her again. That didn't do much. Then he hit her again. She yelped louder this time—he must have hit harder. She started to cry. He shouted again, and waved his hands. *What do you expect? Didn't I warn you?* Again, Annette could follow along.

"That one trouble for everybody." Emishtar nodded toward Birigida.

"Well—yes," Annette agreed.

"One of her people should make her work," Emishtar said.

"Yes," Annette said again. "But they do not talk with her

much." She'd noticed that before. Birigida spoke the same language as the other blondes and redheads, but she didn't seem to have a lot to do with them.

"Different clan," Emishtar guessed.

"Maybe," Annette said. "But how much difference does it make here?"

Emishtar shrugged. "How much? As much as anybody wants it to make."

She was bound to be right about that. If Birigida's clan or tribe was enemy to the one the rest of the new women came from, they might not want anything to do with her. But why—why!—couldn't she work enough to stay out of trouble?

Nine

Dumnorix looked at the musket in one guard's hands. "Strong magic," he said. "Strong, strong, strong." He bent his arm and made his biceps stand up to show what he meant. "It goes *bang!* here. Over there, a man falls dead." Like most men who'd been in battle, he could do a good impression of a dead man.

"Not magic." Jacques fumbled for words, using the bits of Breton he knew and the even smaller bits of the language that sounded like it he'd learned from the redhead. "*Not* magic," he repeated. "Knowing how. Like sword. Like shovel." He hefted the one he was carrying.

Dumnorix tapped the side of his head with a forefinger. He spun the finger by his ear. He said, "You're crazy," just in case Jacques missed the point.

Jacques made the sign of the wheel over his own breast. "By Jesus and Henri, I swear this is true," he said. Dumnorix only shrugged. He knew nothing of Jesus and Henri. The other slaves who'd come here with Jacques knew who God's Sons were, but they didn't follow them. Jacques had heard the guards use Jesus' name, but never Henri's. *I'm the only true Christian here*, he thought.

"Knowing how? Art? Skill?" As Dumnorix spoke, his pick dug into the ground. He'd wasted no time learning to do enough to keep the guards from giving him too hard a time. Did that

mean his people kept slaves, so he knew from the other end how
much work he needed to do and how little he could get away
with? Jacques wouldn't have been surprised. Dumnorix asked,
"How?"

Before Jacques answered, he loaded a couple of shovelfuls
of dirt into a basket by his feet. A guard walking along next to the
trench kept on walking. Jacques had learned how much he could
get away with, too. Once the guard was gone, he stooped and
picked up a little clod of dirt and ground it to powder between
his thumb and forefinger. He pointed to the powder with his
other forefinger and said, "Word is?"

"Powder," Dumnorix answered in his language. Jacques
hoped that was what the answer meant, anyhow. He'd guessed
wrong a couple of times. Sooner or later, though, you sorted
things out.

"Powder," he echoed now. Dumnorix corrected his pronun-
ciation. He tried again. The older man nodded. "Is special powder in muskets," Jacques went on. *Muskets* was a word Dumnorix
had had to learn, because his language had no term for firearms.
"Powder burns. Burning pushes out bullet." That was another
French word. "Bullet flies fast, like arrow. Hits, kills."

"Huh," Dumnorix said. That might have meant anything.
The redheaded man did some more work—another guard's eye
was on him. Jacques shoveled some dirt. The slave with the
basket—a man who spoke the sneezing language Jacques
couldn't understand at all—heaved it up out of the trench at the
end of the roadway.

The guard nodded. As long as the slaves looked busy
enough, the men in the mottled clothes didn't give them too hard
a time. More often than not, they weren't mean to the slaves just
for the sake of being mean. They saved a lot of that for the locals.

Jacques remembered the horseman coming back with his necklace of ears.

Once the guard turned away, Dumnorix and Jacques and the slave with the basket slacked off again. "Powder, eh?" Dumnorix said. "What kind of powder?"

Jacques knew: sulfur and charcoal and saltpeter. He didn't know how to say any of them, except in French. He thought he might have been able to get the idea of charcoal across in Arabic, but that didn't do Dumnorix any good. "Not enough words," he answered—a phrase he used more often than he wanted to.

Dumnorix scowled. "Maybe you don't know enough words," he said. "But maybe you're making this up, too."

"Liar? You say liar?" Jacques let his shovel fall to the dirt. "You say liar?" He set himself and waited to see what happened next.

The blond and redheaded men who spoke Dumnorix's language understood what was going on. The rest of the road gang needed a little longer to figure it out, but not much. They'd all been around fights and the things that led up to fights. People started to gather around Jacques and Dumnorix. The guards gathered to watch, too. The men with the muskets didn't mind if slaves fought, as long as they didn't damage each other too badly. Sometimes the guards bet on who would win. It was fun for them. Why not? They weren't getting hit.

Dumnorix let his pick fall, too. But he didn't wade into Jacques. He was smaller, but had broad shoulders and thick arms. Scars on those arms said he'd done his share of fighting, maybe more than his share.

He waited to see if Jacques would charge him once they'd both put down the tools that could turn a fight into a killing match in a hurry. When Jacques didn't, Dumnorix nodded to himself. "No, I do not say you are a liar," he answered. "Maybe you don't know enough words. I said that, too. All right?" His posture said they would fight if it wasn't all right.

But Jacques also nodded. "Good enough." He held out his hand. Dumnorix didn't clasp it the way a man from the Kingdom of Versailles would have. Instead, his hand closed on Jacques' wrist. Jacques' hand took the redhead's wrist the same way. They let go of each other and stepped back.

The rest of the slaves returned to work. The guards drifted away. One of them snapped his fingers. Jacques had seen they sometimes did that when they were disappointed. If they'd wanted a fight so badly, they could have got one. If they'd shouted, *Cowards!* . . . Jacques didn't see how he and Dumnorix could have done anything but go at each other. Neither would have been able to hold up his head if they hadn't.

Guards in the Kingdom of Versailles would have done that. Jacques might have done it himself if he were a guard. The men who carried muskets were strange. It was as if they had to remember how to be mean, and weren't always good at it. Maybe Khadija knew why that was so. Jacques knew he didn't.

"Get back to work! Show's over!" one of the guards yelled in Arabic. He shouted in the language that sounded a little like it, in the sneezing tongue, and in Dumnorix's language. The guards had no trouble giving the slaves plenty of work. If they'd been more practiced at nastiness, though, they would have kept them hungry and thirsty, too.

Why didn't they? Jacques might have, if he were a master. Food cost money. But the guards and the man who told them what to do didn't worry about money. They just did what they pleased—they bossed the manor and the slaves who worked on it. Sometimes the bossing seemed to matter more to them than what the slaves actually did.

Khadija had said they were criminals. By the way she said it, having slaves was enough to make them criminals all by itself. Jacques didn't understand that. He didn't like being a slave—who did like getting the dirty end of the stick? But somebody had to do the work. Some work was hard enough or nasty enough that you couldn't pay people to do it. That didn't mean it didn't need doing. So what were you supposed to do? You made people take care of it, one way or another.

In the Kingdom of Versailles, peasants had to work on the roads in their lord's domain so many days a year. They didn't get paid for doing it, either. That wasn't slavery, not quite—nobody could buy and sell them. But it wasn't more than a long step away, either.

And real slaves, slaves of the king, worked in mines and rowed galleys. Few free men would grub for iron and lead and coal under the ground. It used them up too fast. But the kingdom couldn't get along without iron and lead and coal. So . . . slaves.

Jesus had never preached against slavery. Neither had Henri. It was part of the way things worked. It always had been. Jacques had believed it always would be. If not for some of the things Khadija said, he still would. Even now, a lot of him still did.

A lot of him—but not all of him, not any more. Whatever strange place Khadija came from had transposition chambers. It had lights that shone without smoke or flame. It had muskets that fired bullet after bullet without reloading. What other marvels did it have, marvels Jacques hadn't seen yet? Things with clock-work and gears that could do the work of slaves? He wouldn't have been surprised.

In that case, though, why would anybody there want ordinary slaves at all? Jacques scratched his head. Not everything Khadija said made sense to him. He started to decide that that meant she didn't always make sense, period. He started to, yes, but then he remembered he couldn't explain gunpowder to Dumnorix, either.

He was very thoughtful the rest of the day.

Gunfire in the night woke Annette a couple of times. She wondered if the locals were trying to attack the manor. If they were, a lot of them would get killed and they wouldn't break in. The guards here were murderous thugs, but they knew their business.

Annette didn't stay awake more than five minutes either time. No matter what was happening to the poor natives, she was exhausted. She didn't think the crack of doom could have kept her awake for long. Gunfire? Gunfire wasn't anything much, not when she was this tired.

More gunfire rang out as she went to the refectory for breakfast. The guards on the outer wall were yelling in several languages. "Goats?" Emishtar said. "They shout about goats?"

"I think so," Annette answered. "Why are they getting all excited about them, though?"

Emishtar looked sly. "Olive trees—small. Almond trees—small, too. Goats eat shoots. Goats eat everything."

"Oh!" Suddenly, Annette grinned. Maybe the locals had found a way to fight back without getting shot themselves. If their goats ate up the slavers' crops, they could say it was an accident.

The first thing the guards did was send some cooks' helpers to bring in the dead goats. That probably meant goat stew for the next few days. Annette didn't mind—it would be something different. She'd eaten goat in the home timeline, at Mexican and Korean restaurants. It wasn't bad, as long as you cooked it long enough to take away the toughness and gaminess.

But the guards didn't stop there. They didn't think the goats had visited by accident, any more than Annette or Emishtar did.

Had the manor really depended on those growing groves, it would have been badly hurt. Annette knew it didn't, but she couldn't expect the locals to.

A troop of mounted guards larger than the one that had ridden out the last time left the manor before noon. Annette wouldn't have wanted to get in the horsemen's way. She especially wouldn't have wanted to get in their way if she could only fight back with bow and arrow.

Some of the women who spoke the sneezing language that might have been related to Basque began to wail and keen. That only made Annette more certain they were enslaved locals. They knew what the guards could do to their kinsfolk—and they knew the guards were going out to do it.

Emishtar also saw that. "Too bad for them," she said.

"Too bad for everyone," Annette said. Emishtar nodded. After a moment, Annette realized it wasn't necessarily so. It wasn't too bad for the guards. They would have a happy time shooting at people who couldn't shoot back.

"I like goat stew," Emishtar said—she'd been watching the cooks' helpers, too, then.

"So do I," Annette said. "But when I eat goat now, I'll think of dead men, not just dead animals."

"Pray for the dead men's spirits, then eat the goat." Emishtar was superstitious and practical at the same time.

"Work!" a guard shouted in one language after another. Not all the men with assault rifles had gone off to punish the locals. Enough stayed close to the manor to make sure the slaves didn't get out of line. The guard walked over to Birigida and yelled at her in particular. Again, Annette didn't know exactly what he was saying, but she could make a pretty good guess.

When I say work, I mean you! I'll have my eye on you. If I catch you goofing off, you'll end up envying those goats!

If that wasn't what the guard meant, it had to come close. Birigida nodded and smiled nervously. She said something, too. *I'll be good, Mr. Guard, honest I will.*

One more strongly held opinion from the guard. Was that *You'd better be!* or *Yeah, right!*? By the way Birigida flinched, Annette would have bet on *Yeah, right!*

The blond woman really did work at a steady clip for a while. Annette hadn't thought Birigida had it in her. Maybe the guard's warning put the fear of her gods in her. Annette hoped so, for her sake.

Seeing Birigida busy at her job, the guard didn't watch her so closely. She began looking around to see if he still had his eye on her. When Annette saw that, her heart sank. Trouble was on the way. She could feel it coming, like lightning before a strike.

She wanted to go over to Birigida and shake some sense into her, the way she might have with a five-year-old. She'd never imagined having that feeling toward somebody ten or twelve years older than she was, but she did. Two things held her back—knowing *she'd* get in trouble with the guards and knowing it wouldn't do any good anyhow. She and Birigida didn't have enough words in common for her to tell the blond woman what was wrong. And Birigida probably wouldn't listen anyway.

Emishtar had the same thought, or its first cousin. Nodding toward Birigida, she said, "That woman wants trouble. She is not happy without trouble."

"That's—" Annette started to say it was crazy. She thought it was, too, which didn't mean Emishtar was wrong. People did crazy things sometimes—keeping slaves when they had no earthly need to, for instance. Maybe Birigida needed to be the center of attention, even if it was the wrong kind of attention. If she did, she was liable to pay a high price for getting what she needed.

What did the people who ran this place need? What did the guards need? Power over other people? The chance to be the boss, without anyone to tell them no? Annette couldn't think of anything else. Computer games that let you do such things had been popular for a hundred years. Why couldn't these people have stuck with those?

Maybe the games weren't enough for them. Maybe they needed the kick of the real thing. If you were the master, Annette supposed you could enjoy yourself a lot at a place like this. But if you were a slave . . .

They didn't think about the slaves, though, except as their toys. If they tried the other side of the coin, they wouldn't like it so much.

Working all that through couldn't have taken more than a few seconds. Annette nodded, too. "I'm afraid you're right."

"Some people are fools," Emishtar said. "All different kinds of fools." She looked toward Birigida again. "Here, that is wrong kind of fool to be."

"Yes, I know." Annette bent to her own work, but kept watching Birigida out of the corner of her eye. She might have been watching a film with two trains rushing toward each other along the same track. Birigida and . . . what? Her own stupidity. That seemed to be plenty.

And it was. Birigida got behind the other women working their way down the rows. That would have made her stick out to the guards. She didn't seem to want to be so obvious. She caught up with her fellow slaves by scooting along and leaving weeds behind.

Then a guard came down the row. To no one's surprise except perhaps Birigida's (and Annette wondered if even the blond woman was very surprised), he saw what she'd been doing—or rather, what she hadn't been doing. He shouted at her and yanked out his billy club.

Was that real fear on Birigida's face, or was she playacting? If she was, the play didn't last long. The guard gave her a more thorough thumping than she'd ever had before. Her squeaks of fright turned into squeals of pain. In his own way, the guard was a professional. He knew how to make her hurt without doing much real harm—without leaving her too sore to work.

When he finished, he shouted at her in her musical language. She was crying too hard to answer right away. He shouted again. Still crying and sniffling, Birigida nodded. The guard said something else. She nodded once more. He stomped away. This time, Annette wasn't sure what he'd meant. Too many possibilities. It might have been, *You'll get more of the same the next time I catch you.* It might have been, *We'll feed you to the pigs the next time I catch you.* Or it might have been, *We'll beat you and whip you and use red-hot pincers on you and then feed you to the pigs the next time I catch you.*

Whatever it was, it worked, at least for the rest of the day. Birigida kept sobbing every so often, but she worked as hard as any of the other women. Annette didn't think she'd ever done that before, not for such a long time. "Maybe she sees it's not a game," she said.

"Maybe." But Emishtar didn't sound as if she believed it. She added, "Does that kind ever really learn?"

Annette wished she weren't thinking the same thing. "Well, we can hope," she said. The way Emishtar nodded said she might hope, too, but what was hope worth?

Another day done. Jacques started back toward the manor with the rest of the roadbuilding gang. A cool breeze blew from the northwest. Thick gray clouds rolled in. The air held the wet-dust smell of rain. It wasn't here yet, but it would be soon. Jacques eyed the clouds and smiled. "They can't make us work if it's pouring rain," he said to Dumnorix.

The redhead shrugged. "They can't make us work on the road," he said. "They can always make us do something."

He and Jacques didn't really talk so smoothly. Dumnorix spoke his own language, plus bits of French he'd learned from Jacques and Arabic he'd picked up from Jacques and other slaves. Jacques had his shreds of Breton, along with French and Arabic and what Dumnorix had taught him of his language. They both gestured a lot and made silly faces. It wasn't pretty or neat or quick. After a while, though, each could figure out what the other meant—most of the time.

"Bath soon," Dumnorix said.

"Yes." Jacques was bathing more and more often the longer he stayed here. He bathed more as a slave than he ever had when he was free. They had more hot water at the manor than they knew what to do with. Finding he could like baths was a surprise. The hot water helped unkink sore muscles. And the soap wasn't harsh like the stuff he'd known in the Kingdom of Versailles—it didn't want to eat away his hide along with the dirt.

His boots thumped on the paving stones other roadbuilders had already laid. A shout came from behind him. He looked back over his shoulder. Here came the guards who'd ridden out to punish the locals after the goats went for the olives and almonds. More shouts, these from the guards. The slaves hurried off the road onto the shoulder to let the horsemen ride past.

As usual when the men in the splotchy clothes returned from a fight, they were in a fine mood. They laughed and joked and sang. Why not? Jacques would have been in a fine mood, too, fighting foes who could hardly hit back. How would the guards have done against men who also had muskets that could shoot again and again?

Are they soldiers, or just bandits? He realized that was the question he was asking. He wasn't sure. They had good discipline for bandits, but would it hold up in real battle?

He laughed at himself, not that it was really funny. When would the guards need to fight a real battle? Who could hope to stand against them? Maybe other fighting men from the strange place Khadija had described. But from everything she'd said, they didn't even know the manor was here.

A drop of rain hit Jacques in the nose when he walked into the courtyard. By the time he sat down in the refectory to eat supper, the skies had opened up. Whatever he would be doing in the morning, he wouldn't be digging out the roadbed. He didn't mind that. He didn't think the master and the guards could set him to much harder work here.

He glanced over to where Khadija ate among the women. They wouldn't be able to walk in the courtyard and talk, not in this rain. Khadija was chatting with a friend she'd made, an older woman with crooked front teeth. They both kept looking towards a blond woman about halfway between them in years. She sat by herself, which was unusual. She didn't look very happy with the world. Something must have gone wrong for her during the day. Jacques wondered what.

After supper, Jacques went up to Khadija. Her older friend smiled knowingly at him. The way she acted reminded Jacques of how Khadija's aunt might have behaved in the world from which they'd both been stolen. It amused him.

Khadija noticed it, too. It annoyed her. In French, she said, "Pay no attention to her. She thinks she knows everything."

"Who doesn't?" Jacques said, which made Khadija smile. He went on, "We could stand under the eaves, if you want to." The roofs projected out some little distance from the buildings inside the wall—far enough to need columns for support. That gave shade in the summer and, Jacques was finding, kept away the rain in the winter.

"All right," Khadija said after a moment's hesitation. As they walked out there, she added, "We have to be a little more careful about what we say, though. Easier for them to listen."

"Listen how?" Jacques asked. "There's nobody close by."

"They have ways." Khadija sounded as if she knew what she was talking about.

Jacques couldn't very well argue with her. Oh, he could, but it wouldn't do him any good. He changed the subject instead, asking, "What's wrong with that blond woman? I saw you watching her in the refectory."

Khadija rolled her eyes. "Birigida, you mean?"

"If that's her name."

"She doesn't want to work, that's what's wrong with her." Khadija didn't seem to mind talking about the other slave. "What's worse is, she's too dumb to hide it. The guards watch her all the time now. When they catch her, they give her lumps. And they keep catching her, too."

"Oh," Jacques said. "No wonder she looks like her puppy just died. At that, she's lucky. If she were a man, they'd probably kill her."

"Some luck," Khadija said. "They could do things to her they likely wouldn't do to a man, you know. They haven't—yet—but they could."

Jacques nodded. Those things happened in the Kingdom of Versailles, too. He said, "Why won't she work enough to get by? As long as you do what you have to and look busy, the guards don't bother you too much. Can't she see that?"

"I think she can. I don't think she cares," Khadija said unhappily.

"What? How can she not care, if they're beating her up? Es-

pecially if they're liable to do worse than that? Is she crazy?"
Jacques said.

"Not the way you mean, or I don't think so," Khadija answered. "She doesn't think she's a king or a tree or an angel."
Jacques laughed—that *was* what he'd meant. Khadija went on,
"But there are people who always have to have other people notice them so they know they're real. Do you know what I'm saying? They can be noticed for good or bad, but they can't stand it
when other people ignore them."

For a moment, Jacques didn't understand. Then, all at once,
he did. "Oh, yes," he said. "I once knew a fellow who kept doing
stupid things so the drill sergeant would thump him."

"That's it!" Khadija said. "That's just what I mean."

"It ended badly," Jacques said. "Finally the drill sergeant
got sick of this fool and clouted him with a musket butt. He
broke the fellow's jaw and knocked out about six teeth. The re-
cruit had to go home. I don't know what happened to him after
that, but I don't think it was anything good."

"I'm afraid something like that will happen to Birigida,"
Khadija said. "I don't know what I can do to stop it."

"Sometimes you can't do anything," Jacques said. "If people
are going to be fools, how can you stop them? You wish they
wouldn't, but. . . ."

Khadija bit her lip. "I know. I know. I keep telling myself
that. But she'd be all right if they hadn't grabbed her and brought
her here and made her a slave. It isn't fair."

Jacques put his hand on her shoulder. She started to pull
away, but then stood still. Gently, he said, "You can't even talk to
her, can you?"

"No." Khadija looked out at the rain. "What's that got to do
with anything? She's still a person, isn't she?"

"Some people wouldn't worry as much about their friends as you do about her," Jacques said.

"My friends have the sense to take care of themselves—like you, for instance," Khadija said. "Birigida needs somebody to worry about her."

"When you're home, you probably take in lost puppies and kittens, too," Jacques said. She stirred under his hand. He guessed that meant he was right. "Puppies and kittens don't know any better than to get lost. This Birigida does, or she ought to. Worrying about her won't get you anywhere—unless you land in trouble along with her."

Khadija's sigh held more winter than the weather. "That makes more sense than I wish it did."

"All right, then. You're a sensible person. You're the most sensible person I've ever met, I think. So listen to me, all right?" Khadija didn't tell him no. He knew she heard him. Listen to him? That, he feared, was another story.

When the weather was bad, the guards didn't make people stay busy for the sake of staying busy. Annette had wondered if they would. Busywork fit the way the late twenty-first century thought. But there was only so much of it to do. And the house slaves didn't want the garden slaves helping.

Annette needed a little while to figure out why. The house slaves feared the garden slaves would steal their jobs. They didn't want to leave the manor. They thought they would have to do harder, less comfortable work outside—and they were probably right.

Even if they were, seeing how they acted made her sad. All the slaves should have pulled together against the people who ordered them around. They should have, but they didn't. They had factions, too, and the masters and the guards used those factions to keep them divided among themselves. Annette began to understand how masters in the home timeline had stayed on top for so long, even in places where slaves outnumbered them.

She tried to talk about that with Emishtar. By the look the older woman gave her, Emishtar had always understood it. "Masters are masters," she said—she might have been talking about the weather. "Some not so bad, some bad, some worse. But always masters—oh, yes."

"There shouldn't be any," Annette said fiercely. "Not anywhere. Keeping slaves is a great wickedness." In the home timeline, she didn't think she'd ever needed that word. But she didn't know another one that fit.

"Being a slave is a great sorrow," Emishtar said. "If I had silver, though, if I had gold, would I buy slaves for myself? Of course I would. Why should I work like a donkey when someone else can work for me?"

I can't blame her, not really, Annette thought. *She's from a low-tech alternate. She doesn't know about machines. Slaves are the only labor-saving devices she does know. But slaves don't save labor, not really. They just put it on someone else's shoulders.*

Birigida worked harder when she had nothing to do than she did out in the garden plot. Everything she did was aimed at getting a house slave's job. She could see house slaves didn't have to do so much, too.

Nothing she tried did any good. The house slaves either ignored her or screamed at her. None of them spoke her language, but that didn't matter. A shout and a scowl and a clenched fist meant the same thing to everybody. And the guards only laughed at her. They spoke her tongue, but that didn't help her. They wouldn't do anything for her. They'd seen she didn't want to work, so they wanted to make sure she did. One of them pointed in the direction of the garden, said something Annette couldn't follow, and laughed. *You'll stay there till you rot*, Annette guessed.

Could looks have killed, the guard would have started rotting right then.

The next day, Birigida hatched another scheme that didn't work and got her yelled at. "She'd better be careful," Annette said to Emishtar. "If she doesn't watch it, they'll put her on the roadbuilding gang."

She meant it for a joke, but Emishtar took it seriously. "Serve her right, too," she said. Emishtar made a good friend— Annette had seen that. If she wasn't your friend, though, you weren't much more than a beast to her. Birigida was not her friend. To Emishtar, Birigida was a beast you couldn't count on, nothing more.

After the storm finally blew off to the east, the guards took the women out to the garden plots. The roadbuilders got to stay in for another day. Some of the women grumbled. Annette wasn't overjoyed herself, but she understood. You couldn't make a roadbed from soupy mud. You could pull a lot of weeds, though. They came out of soft dirt more easily than from hard.

The ground was still wet when they went out to the gardens. Annette's shoes squelched in the mud. When she got down on her hands and knees and started weeding, she got her dress filthy. That would have been more annoying to a slave in the home timeline than it was here. Here, at least, the slaves could get plenty of clean clothes.

Some of the women had been surprised they didn't have to spin and weave, especially while it was raining. Annette wasn't, or not very. Her long cotton skirt came from Wal-Mart.

What it meant to Annette was that the slaveowners found it

easier or cheaper to buy clothes in the home timeline than to have their slaves make them. Or maybe they just hadn't thought of that. Maybe they would one of these days. Maybe listening to their own slaves would give them ideas. Annette hoped not. They'd already had too many ideas, and too many bad ones.

As the women started to work, a guard came over and stood in front of Birigida. She looked up at him the way a kid who'd got caught doing something he wasn't supposed to at school looked at the principal. He growled at her. She nodded. He growled again. She nodded again. It went on for quite a while. At last, the guard turned his back and stomped away. He didn't kick mud in her face, but he might as well have. She bent down and started weeding as if her life depended on it.

Maybe it did.

Watching her, Annette worried. She couldn't keep that pace up for long. Nobody could. And when she slowed down, how much would she slow down? To what the rest of the slaves were doing? That would be enough to keep her out of trouble, anyway. Or would she slow down the way she usually did, doing so little she got noticed?

Annette knew which way she'd guess. She wished she didn't.

Emishtar also watched Birigida working. The woman with the crooked front teeth wasn't impressed, either. "Soon she will see a bird, or a leaf going by. That will be interesting. She will stop and watch. And she will forget what she is supposed to do."

"She shouldn't," Annette said with a sigh. "I wish she wouldn't."

Emishtar only shrugged. "They watch her all the time now. They don't watch us so much. So we don't have to do so much. We ought to thank her."

That was more cold-blooded than Annette could make herself be. She'd seen hard living in the alternate Jacques came from. She'd lived hard herself, but she'd always known she was playacting. Till those raiders caught her, the home timeline had never been far away. Emishtar, by contrast, had never had it easy. She probably ate better and worked less as a slave than she had when she was free. That didn't leave a whole lot of room inside her for compassion.

A blackbird hopped in the field. He caught worm after worm. He liked rain fine—it made the worms come up. She could watch the blackbird and work at the same time. Could Birigida? Annette kept sneaking glances over at her. The blond woman had slowed down some from her frantic opening burst, but she was still going pretty well. Annette nodded to herself in relief. She hadn't thought Birigida had it in her.

Emishtar must not have, either. "Maybe the guard really say he will kill her if she does not work," she said. "Maybe she believe him, too." She paused to murder a weed. "Me, I would have knocked her over the head a long time ago." Yes, the milk of human kindness ran thin in Emishtar.

"She's——" Annette started to say Birigida wasn't a bad person. People in the home timeline always said that. Annette couldn't do it here, not with a straight face. Birigida was out for Birigida, first, last, and always. She didn't care who knew it, either. That made her less likely to get what she wanted, of course. If she were a little smarter, she would have figured that out for herself. If she were a little smarter, she wouldn't have had a lot of her problems. Annette tried again: "She's doing fine right now." There. She'd told the truth without even being insulting. *They said it couldn't be done*, she thought.

"Right now, yes," Emishtar said. "Can she keep it up?"

The guards wondered, too. They circled Birigida like vultures over roadkill. If she gave them any kind of excuse, they would pounce. What happened then wouldn't be pretty. Annette could see as much. Could the blond woman? She sure hadn't been able to up till now. But she kept working away, and did enough so the guards let her alone. She wasn't the best worker in the garden plot, but for once she wasn't the worst, either.

She got through the whole day without more than a warning or two. Annette wouldn't have believed it if she hadn't seen it with her own eyes.

As the sun sank in the southwest, the women trooped back toward the manor. Birigida let out a long, weary sigh. Well, for once she'd earned the right. Then, with Annette only two or three meters away, the blond woman muttered, "Lord, am I beat," to herself. Annette took two more steps, then tripped and almost fell. Birigida had spoken in English.

Ten

Jacques had never seen Khadija so excited. She was doing her best not to show it, which was like asking a house not to show it was on fire. She all but dragged Jacques out into the courtyard after supper. The older woman with the crooked teeth who was her friend smiled out at both of them.

No matter what Emishtar thought, Khadija wasn't excited about Jacques himself. He wished she would be, but no. In a ferocious whisper, Khadija said, "You know Birigida?"

"The one who won't work?" Jacques said, and Khadija nodded. Jacques went on, "I can't help knowing *of* her. You've hardly talked about anybody else lately. What now?"

"She speaks my language."

"Arabic?" Jacques scratched his head. They were using French now, but she was from Muslim Marseille, so Arabic would be her first language. "Lots of people here speak Arabic. I didn't know this Birigida did, but so what?"

Khadija gave him an impatient look. "No, no, no—not Arabic. *My* language, the language I use every day in the world I come from." She said a couple of soft sentences in it.

He felt like thumping his head with his hand to let some light in on his brains. He'd known for a while now that she wasn't exactly a Muslim trader's daughter from Marseille. He'd known and he'd forgotten, because it didn't seem to matter. Now he tried to find something to say that wasn't stupid. The best he could do was, "If I didn't know better, I'd say that sounded like English."

Khadija laughed and laughed. She laughed so hard, other slaves and guards stared at her—and at Jacques. Jacques didn't even know what he'd said that was funny. Khadija laughed till she got the hiccups. "Oh, dear," she said in between them. "Oh, dear."

When the hiccups wouldn't stop, Jacques pounded her on the back. It didn't do much good. Nothing did much good when somebody had the hiccups—you just had to wait for them to stop. "Are you all right?" he asked crossly.

"I—*hic!*—think so," she said, and then, "Oh, dear," again.

"Is she all right?" a guard called to Jacques. "She acts like she's having a fit."

"She says she thinks she is," Jacques told him. The guard waved and nodded, as if to say, *That's good.* Jacques understood why he wondered—slaves were worth a lot of money. What he didn't understand was why Khadija had the fit in the first place. "Will you please tell me where the joke is?" he grumbled.

Little by little, she won back control of herself. "Oh, dear," she said one more time. Then, at last, she managed something that made a little sense: "I'm sorry." She took a deep breath and held it. She was still hiccuping, but not so often. After she breathed out, she went on, "The joke is, I really do speak English." She kept her voice low, so no one but Jacques could hear. "It's not quite the same English as the one you know about, but it's pretty close."

"Oh." He scratched his head. "I guess that's funny." He liked Khadija too much to come right out and say, *It's not that funny.*

Even if he didn't say it, she must have understood what he was thinking. "I *am* sorry," she repeated. One of the reasons he liked her so much was that she had such a good idea of what was going on inside his head.

"Why does it matter so much that she speaks English?" he asked. Most of what was in his head right now was confusion. "Maybe some people in her, uh, world use it, too." He thought French would make a better language for them to use, but that seemed beside the point.

"No." Khadija shook her head. "She doesn't speak some other dialect, the way people in your England do. She speaks the same kind of English as I do—the same kind as the guards and the masters, too. She's just pretending to be one of those people like Dumnorix."

"Who would want to do something like that?" Jacques thought it was the craziest thing he'd ever heard. "She makes a lousy slave. They beat her. They kick her. They could take her into a back room and—well, never mind. Henri on the wheel, they could kill her. We've talked about that. So if she's one of those people, why doesn't she say so? Then all those horrible things would stop happening to her."

"I don't know. I wish I did," Khadija said. "I know what I hope, though. I hope she's here as a, a spy for our government. If she is, and if she can get back, they'll come and rescue everybody."

"That would be good." Jacques would have got more excited if he thought it was likely. "If she was a spy, wouldn't she want them not to notice her at all?"

Khadija bit her lip. "You'd think so, wouldn't you? But what else could she be? She's not an ordinary slave—I'm sure of that."

"No, she's a stupid slave. She's a lazy slave," Jacques said. "So how will you find out about her?"

He watched Khadija. She started to charge right into that,

but stopped before she said anything. It wasn't as easy a question as it looked at first. That she saw as much made Jacques think even more of her good sense than he did already. At last, she said, "I'll have to find a chance to talk to her in English. I don't see what else I can do."

"I guess so." Jacques had been looking for some other answer. He hadn't found one, either. He knew why that one bothered him: "Then she'll know you aren't just a trader's daughter, too."

"You're right. That's what worries me." Khadija looked as unhappy as he felt.

And if she wasn't just a trader's daughter . . . "What *are* you, anyway?" Jacques asked.

"In one way, I *am* a trader's daughter, but not from Marseille in your world," Khadija answered. "In another way, I'm your friend, or I hope I am." She took hold of his hands.

He squeezed hers, not too hard. "Yes," he said. "Oh, yes."

Annette watched Birigida with different eyes. Her first hope had been that the blond woman was investigating the slavers and getting ready to lower the boom on them. She tried to make herself believe it. Try as she would, she couldn't. Jacques had hit that nail right on the head—he might not be educated, but he wasn't dumb. If Birigida was a cop or a detective, she wouldn't want the guards to pay her any special attention. And she couldn't have got any more notice from them if she dyed her hair purple and painted her face green.

But if she wasn't a spy, what was she? Did she work for Crosstime Traffic the way Annette and her folks did? Had she got captured in a slave raid? That made some sense, but only some. Annette didn't think Crosstime Traffic let anyone as bad at what she did as Birigida go out to the alternates. You were too likely to get in trouble and give yourself away—maybe give away the Crosstime Traffic secret, too. Annette supposed that risk was smaller in a low-tech alternate. Even so . . .

If Birigida wasn't a spy or a cop, if she wasn't somebody from Crosstime Traffic, what *was* she? Annette couldn't think of anything else, try as she would. That worried her. It made her angry, too. Birigida was some kind of key—that seemed plain. But what would happen if you turned her in the lock? What would she open up?

Because Annette spent so much time wondering about Birigida, she didn't pay enough attention to what she was supposed to be doing herself. "Have you fallen asleep out here?" a guard yelled at her in Arabic. "Pick it up, or you'll be sorry! I thought you were a good worker, not a lazy, useless fool like some I could name."

Like Birigida, he meant. Annette had enough sense not to get in trouble that way. Why couldn't the blond woman from the home timeline do the same? "I am sorry, sir," Annette said, and she worked faster.

The guard watched her for a little while. Then he nodded. "That's more like it." He went off to bother somebody else.

"May the demons gnaw at him, that son of a jackal," Emishtar said in her own language. "May he eat dust and live in shadow in the underworld forever after he dies. And may he die soon."

"May it be so," Annette answered in Arabic. When she said something like that, she meant she was annoyed at the guard. When Emishtar said something like that, she was really cursing him. To her, demons and the underworld were as real as the world in which she walked.

When Birigida fell behind the other women near her in the garden plot, a guard slapped her. He would have spoken to Annette or Emishtar. They'd shown they were reliable. Birigida had shown she was anything but. She yelped. That only made the guard laugh. One day's worth of real work hadn't changed her, and hadn't made the men with the assault rifles stop watching her for signs of weakness like so many vultures.

It hadn't made her stop showing weakness, either. Couldn't she see she paid for it whenever she did? Annette sighed. As far as she could tell, Birigida couldn't see anything.

But she spoke English, American English from the late twenty-first century. That had to mean she came from the home timeline. It also had to mean the home timeline raised just as many jerks as any alternate did. Annette had already realized that—it only stood to reason. But realizing it and getting your nose rubbed in it were two different things.

Winter days were short. The sun scurried across the southern sky. Even so, Annette felt a couple of years went by before the guards finally shouted, "That's enough!" in all the languages the slave women used.

As the women walked back toward the manor, Annette fell in beside Birigida. The blond woman had got swatted and spanked a couple of more times as the afternoon wore along. For her, that didn't make it too bad a day. She gave Annette a curious look—most of the time, Annette and Emishtar walked and talked together.

Birigida said something in the musical language the other blond and redheaded women spoke. Something like Erse, something like Breton—Celtic, sure enough. That fit their looks. What she said sounded like a question, but Annette didn't understand a word of it. She looked around. None of the guards was close by, or paying much attention to Birigida. Maybe they wanted to forget about her once the day's work was over, too.

Annette took a deep breath. "How you doing?" she asked—in English.

"I'm tired. I'm sore. Those—" Birigida automatically started to answer in the same tongue. Then she broke off. Her blue eyes opened wide, wider, widest. What showed up in them surprised Annette—it couldn't be anything but fear. And fear sharpened Birigida's voice, too, when she asked, "Who are you? *What* are you? Are you a guard? Are you a spy?"

"I wish!" Annette answered, which startled a laugh out of the older woman. Annette went on, "No, I'm a slave, just like you."

"Oh." Birigida thought about it, then nodded. "Okay. They didn't tell me anybody else was doing this, too. Hi."

"Hi." Annette tried to figure out what to ask next. *Who didn't tell you?* rose to the top of the list. But she couldn't ask that, either, because she already ought to know who *they* were. She tried a different question instead: "Why don't you let the guards know you're from the home timeline? They'd go easier on you then, I bet."

"I can't," Birigida said. "Didn't they give you a hypnotic compulsion, too? If I thought you were a guard, I wouldn't be able to talk about it with you, either."

"No, no compulsions," Annette said. There *they* were again.

Birigida said several harsh things in low-voiced English, then several more that sounded harsh in that Celtic language. It didn't sound so musical when it was loud and angry. The blond woman dropped back into English—and started speaking softly again: "I might have known. They told me they gave it to everybody, but I halfway figured they wouldn't if you paid 'em enough not to."

"I paid plenty," Annette said. That was true, even if it had nothing to do with benjamins. She still got headaches every so often. If that slave raider had hit her any harder, he might have caved in her skull. And she still didn't know whether her parents were all right. All right or not, they didn't know about her, either. She went on, "Can I ask you something?"

"Sure. Go ahead. A dollar for your thoughts." Birigida seemed happy to be speaking English.

"How come you get in so much trouble all the time? Don't you see they wouldn't treat you so bad if you did even a little more?"

They might have been using the same words, but they weren't speaking the same language. Annette had also had that feeling when she talked with Jacques, and with Emishtar. Birigida looked at her the way a teacher would if she asked a really dumb question in school—as if she should have known better. "Isn't it boring if you're a good little slave all the time?" the older woman said. "Getting in trouble is part of the fun."

"I guess," Annette said. That seemed unlikely to land her in trouble. She bent and tried to brush some of the mud off her skirt. She didn't want Birigida—or whatever the woman's real name was—to see her face.

She'd run into all kinds of horrors since she got sold to the man who called himself Marwan al-Baghdadi. Seeing people from the home timeline, people from Crosstime Traffic, in the slave trade was bad enough. Even if she thought it was disgusting, though, she could at least understand why one person might want to lord it over another one. Crosstime Traffic made the rules against having anything to do with slavery as strong as it could because the people who ran the company understood that others might be tempted.

But, while Annette could see how some people might want to be masters, she'd never dreamt others got the same sort of kick from being slaves. She supposed they talked about people like that in some of the psychology courses she wasn't taking at Ohio State. Talking about them in college was one thing. Meeting somebody like that was something else again.

She couldn't show any of what she was thinking. If anybody was the key to getting her back to the home timeline, Birigida was. As casually as Annette could, she asked, "When does your compulsion wear off?"

Her heart pounded while she waited for the answer. The compulsion *would* have to wear off, wouldn't it? Maybe some people from the home timeline wanted to be slaves all the time. But the people who ran this outfit wouldn't go for that. If men and women from the home timeline disappeared for good, others would wonder why. That could be dangerous.

"Two weeks," Birigida said. "How about you? You were here when I came."

"I've got another month to go," Annette answered.

"Wow." Birigida eyed her. "No compulsion, and you're staying a long time. You're so lucky." She might have been saying, *You're so rich.* Sure enough, she went on, "That must have cost you an arm and a leg."

Annette shrugged. "Getting away for so long was the hard part," she said, and Birigida nodded wisely. Annette asked, "So how do you like . . . your time here?" That was the safest way she could think of to put it.

"It's wonderful!" Birigida's eyes glowed. Did she understand what could have happened to her? Did she understand it nearly *had* happened to her? Maybe she did, for she continued, "Back in the home timeline, I'm a bigwig. I tell people what to do all the time. They do it, too, or they get in trouble. Here"—she laughed—"well, that's one thing I don't have to worry about, anyhow."

"No, not hardly," Annette said, and then she shut up, because a guard was getting close. The next thing Birigida said was in the Celtic language Annette didn't understand. Maybe she couldn't speak English around a guard till the hypnotic compulsion went away.

But the compulsion didn't seem to apply to other slaves. Maybe the people who'd given it to her hadn't thought any other slaves from the home timeline would be here. If their man in that other Madrid hadn't bought her by mistake, none would have been.

Emishtar walked over to Annette after Birigida went off on her own. "What was that about?" Emishtar asked. "You found a language you both know?"

"So we did," Annette said.

Emishtar wasn't very tall—she was shorter than Annette, and twelve to fifteen centimeters shorter than Birigida. She managed to look down her nose at the blond woman even so. "Does she make any sense when you do talk to her?" she asked.

"Not much," Annette said. One of Emishtar's eyebrows rose, as if to say, *Why am I not surprised?*

After Annette gave the answer, she thought about it. Why anybody would pay for the privilege of being a slave was beyond her. It seemed to make sense to Birigida, though. She wanted to get as far away from what she normally was as she could.

Before the French Revolution, Marie Antoinette and her court ladies had played at being milkmaids. Annette supposed that was part of the same impulse that made Birigida do what she was doing. But a queen's notion of what being a milkmaid was like would be different from the real thing. Birigida really was a slave.

Birigida really was a slave . . . for a while. When the hypnotic compulsion set her free, she would go back to the home timeline and pick up her real life where she'd left off. She wouldn't have to worry about beatings any more. She wouldn't have to worry about hard physical work. She wouldn't have to worry about being made into someone else's toy.

She wouldn't, no. For her, slavery was a thrill, a vacation. Annette's stomach twisted. For the rest of the slaves on the manor, this was no vacation. This was their life. *If I hadn't heard Birigida just then, it would have been* my *life, probably for as long as I lived*, Annette thought.

And it still might be. She understood that. Now she had a chance. But a chance was all she had. If she didn't make the most of it, she'd still be stuck here.

She found herself eyeing all the other slaves who worked in the garden plots. When she got back to the manor and ate supper, she knew she would look over the house slaves and the men from the roadbuilding gang the same way. Were any of them from the home timeline? Were they just pretending to come from a low-tech alternate? Were they getting their jollies by being ordered around? Would they go home with happy memories of being abused—and then fit right back into the ordinary world of the late twenty-first century?

What did you do on your summer vacation, George? someone would ask. And George would answer, *Oh, I went off to be a slave for a while. It was great!*

Annette giggled. Put that way, it sounded stupid. But that was probably how word about this place spread. You couldn't talk about it in chat rooms or by e-mail or even by telephone. Your chances of getting hacked were much too good. She wondered if temporary slaves from the home timeline got more compulsions than they knew about. Maybe they couldn't give it away in e-mail or chat rooms even if they wanted to. That made sense to Annette. It would be a good insurance policy for the folks who ran this outfit.

There was the manor. Were other people not what they seemed? *Don't act too curious*, Annette told herself. *You'll get in trouble*. That made sense, too. But she was so curious, she wondered how she could stand it.

Before, Jacques had seen Khadija excited enough to burst. He thought she was even more excited now than she had been then. Now, though, she'd pushed it down so it didn't show as much. Her being able to do that impressed him. She could use the excitement for fuel without wearing it on her sleeve. People who were able to do things like that often made big names for themselves.

The guards only smiled when Jacques and Khadija went walking in the courtyard. The two of them had been doing it for a while. The guards—and the other slaves, too—took it for granted. In the ordinary way of things, it might have led to a wedding—if the masters here let slaves marry.

Jacques wouldn't have minded if things happened in the ordinary way, not even a little. But when he went walking with Khadija now, he got something even more exciting than love. He got hope.

"Well, what did you find out?" he asked her. He didn't name Birigida. He didn't want to make things easy for anyone who might be spying on them.

"She really is from the place I come from," Khadija answered. "There's no doubt."

"What was she doing with Dumnorix and his people, then?" Jacques said. "Was she pretending to belong to them, the way you pretend to be a trader's daughter? Is that how she got caught?"

"That's what I thought at first, too." Like Jacques, Khadija spoke French. It might help keep people from snooping on them—or it might not. She went on, "But no, it isn't true. She

came here because she *wanted* to be a slave. It's a game for her."
Khadija's nostrils flared, as if at a bad smell.

"A game?" Even though her French was as good as his,
Jacques wondered if he'd heard right. "Why would anyone play
at being a slave if he didn't have to? Henri on the wheel, why
would anyone play at being a slave if *she* didn't have to?
That's—mad." He found the politest name for it he could.

Khadija nodded. "Well, my friend, I think so, too." Even
then, amazed at what she'd said about Birigida, Jacques smiled
to hear her call him a friend. She went on, "But Birigida has
more money than sense. I can see that. At home, she's rich and
important. That doesn't make her happy."

"It would make *me* happy!" Jacques exclaimed.

"That's because you have more sense than money," Khadija
said.

"Of course I do. Slaves here haven't got any money," Jacques
said.

She sent him a severe look. "Before you were a slave, too,"
she said, and looked ready to flip him over her shoulder if he argued any more. She could do it, too. She thought for a little
while. "It's not just that she hasn't got much sense. Part of her
needs to do this, too."

"Needs to?" Now Jacques frowned. "What do you mean?"

She thought again. *Looking for an example*, he realized. And
she found one: "Did you ever know, or know about, somebody
who couldn't keep from, uh, bothering little girls?"

"Bothering? Oh—like that," Jacques said, and Khadija nodded. A moment later, so did he. "Yes, one of those beasts plagued
Paris a few years ago. The father of a girl he outraged finally
tracked him down and killed him, and that was the end of it. Nobody misses him a bit—he's bound to be roasting in hell."

"Maybe. Where I come from, we think something like that is a sickness, and we cure it if we can," Khadija said.

"What can a doctor do if a man is an animal inside?" Jacques asked.

"More than you'd imagine, sometimes. We have drugs and medicines that work better than the ones you know," Khadija answered. "But they don't always work, and sometimes we have to lock up people like that to keep them from hurting others."

To Jacques, locking them up wasn't punishment enough. That was beside the point now, though. "You think Birigida is one of those people who can't help it?" he said. Khadija nodded. He asked, "Why not give her these fancy medicines, then? Why not lock her up?"

"If I can get back to where I belong, they probably will," Khadija said. "Till now . . . Well, think about it. The man who goes after little girls hurts other people. He makes other people notice him. When Birigida plays these games, the only one she hurts is herself. That makes her harder to spot."

"You have the answer for everything!" Jacques said.

She laughed a bitter laugh. "If I'm so smart, what am I doing here? I don't get a thrill out of it, even if Birigida does. Sometimes a clout in the head is worth more than a whole pile of fancy answers—and *that's* what I'm doing here."

"But the answers give you a chance to get away," Jacques said.

"Maybe." No, Khadija didn't want to show how hopeful she was. "Just maybe."

Two weeks—the slowest two weeks of Annette's life. She watched Birigida like a hawk all that time. The last thing she wanted—absolutely the last thing—was for the blond woman to do something so stupid, it would get her killed. Maybe Birigida was ready to go back to her real life, too. She didn't act quite so lazy or quite so foolish as she had before.

The guards gave her a bad time anyway. They'd got used to it by then. They punished her for things they would have ignored from other women. When she yelped, they laughed at her. *But she does stuff like that so they* will *come down on her*, Annette thought.

If she'd read about people like Birigida in an abnormal-psychology text, she would have figured she would never meet one for real. She would also have figured running into one for real would make her sick. And, in a way, it did. The idea that anyone would want to be a slave, even if not forever, still bewildered her. She didn't pretend to understand it.

But she didn't despise Birigida the way she despised the people who ran the manor. If the blond woman craved being a slave, craved being shouted at and punished, whom did that hurt? Only herself.

It was a different story for the masters and guards. They took men and women who just wanted to go on about their own business and turned them into slaves. If those men and women got out of line, the people who ran the manor hurt them or killed them. Even if those men and women didn't get out of line, the masters and guards still kept them enslaved and used and abused them for their own pleasure. That was a different wrong from Birigida's, and a worse one.

And it didn't even start to talk about what the masters and guards were doing to the people who lived in this alternate. The manor looked to be the seed of a much larger conquest. Crosstime Traffic wasn't supposed to work like this. It was supposed to be about quiet trade, about interfering in other alternates as little as it could.

A lot of history in the home timeline said that was a good idea.

Colonial conquests in the Americas and Africa hadn't been pretty. Plainly, the people with the assault rifles here didn't care.

Did Crosstime Traffic proper even know about this alternate? Annette doubted it. Word of what was going on here in Spain would spread across the world. It would get distorted by the time it reached somebody a couple of thousand kilometers away, but it would go that far. If anyone from the home timeline heard it and got curious . . .

But if no one from the home timeline was here *to* get curious, the masters and guards had it made. Exploring and exploiting alternates on your own was as illegal as illegal could be. This whole setup showed why, too.

"Tomorrow," Birigida murmured to Annette as they came back from the garden plots one chilly evening. "I can feel things getting ready inside me." She sighed. "Most of me doesn't want to go back, but I guess I have to."

"I'm afraid so." Annette was really afraid her face would give her away. It must not have, which only proved she was a better actress than she thought.

She stepped out at sick call the next morning, complaining of a sore shoulder. If she were someone like Birigida, she wouldn't have got away with it. But nobody thought she was faking, because she had a reputation as a hard worker. She stayed behind when the other women went to work.

Birigida stayed behind, too. Annette saw and heard exactly how she managed that. The blond woman went up to a guard and spoke in English: "My stretch is up." She might have been talking about getting out of jail, except she'd volunteered for this. She went on, "Time for me to go back to the home timeline."

The guard looked at her. "Oh. You're one of those. I might have known." He looked and sounded disgusted. Annette wondered if he would keep her here even if she was one of those. The joke would be on her if he did. Annette almost thought she deserved it. But keeping someone from the home timeline here might make people back there ask questions they shouldn't. Still scowling, the guard went on, "Go over there and wait while we call up the transposition chamber." He pointed to the door from which new slaves came up into the manor.

Birigida had a newfound spring in her step when she went over to stand by the armed guard who waited there. He growled at her and gestured with his rifle for her to keep her distance. Like his pal, he didn't soften up much when she spoke to him in English. She'd really made herself beloved while she was here.

She had to wait about fifteen minutes before the guard used a card from his wallet to open the lock on the door. Annette thought that was clever. People from a low-tech alternate would never figure it out, where they might if the lock used an old-fashioned key.

Down the stairs Birigida went. The guard locked the door behind her again. He yawned. Annette looked off in another direction before his eye fell on her. Birigida didn't come out again. Maybe some of the house slaves wondered what was happening to her. Maybe some of them thought she was getting killed down there. Maybe some of them thought she had it coming, too.

Annette knew what was going on. She was glad when Birigida didn't come out. That meant the blond woman was on her way back to the home timeline. *With a little luck, I can get back there, too.* Hope was supposed to feel wonderful, and it did. But it also hurt. If something went wrong, Annette would never get another chance. She really would be a slave here forever—or else she'd just get killed.

When Jacques mentioned Birigida's name, Dumnorix spat into the chewed-up dirt at his feet. "*That* one!" he said. "I don't know what happened to her, and I don't care. Gods be praised, she's not from my clan. I wouldn't have wanted such a fool among us."

Practice helped Jacques follow his words much better than when he first started trying to talk with the other man. "My friend said she was nothing but trouble at work."

"Your friend? The dark one with the nice teeth? She's pretty." Dumnorix grinned at him, then swung his pick. Jacques shoveled up the dirt the other man loosened. A guard, seeing them busy, nodded and went on walking. Dumnorix scratched, then said, "Some people are fools. They can't help being fools, any more than they can help having blue eyes. Birigida, she was like that. Do you know what's happened to her?"

"Not me," Jacques said. Khadija knew, or said she did. That box or room or transposition chamber or whatever it was would take Birigida back to where she really came from. Wherever it was, Khadija came from there, too. Jacques wondered what it was like.

That wasn't his worry. Looking busy enough to keep the guards happy was. He and Dumnorix had the rhythm they wanted. They weren't going fast enough to wear themselves out, or slow enough to get in trouble. The work seemed more real to Jacques than Birigida's disappearance did. It seemed much more real to him than Khadija's talk about other worlds. He believed her. With all the strange things that had happened to him since the slave raiders caught him, he couldn't help believing her. But believing in your head and believing in your belly were two different things.

The guards always carried those little boxes that talked. One of the boxes chirped now. The guard snatched the box off his belt

and spoke in the language that sounded like English—that
Khadija said *was* English. The box answered him. Jacques supposed Khadija would tell him that wasn't magic. It sure seemed
like magic, no matter what she'd tell him.

That guard called out to his comrades. He pointed east, into
the country where the fancy road was going. Four or five guards
trotted that way, with the businesslike lope of soldiers moving
into action.

"Don't get cute," one of the men who'd stayed behind said in
Arabic. "We're still watching you." He repeated himself in the
several languages the slaves used. Nobody got cute. The men
had seen what those repeating muskets could do.

Jacques wouldn't have thought an ant could hide on the open
ground there to the east. He would have been wrong, though. An
ambush party of locals had sneaked to within a quarter of a mile.
He wondered how whoever was on the other end of the words
coming out of the box knew. The locals weren't too far from getting in range with their bows.

When they realized the guards had spotted them in spite of
everything, they popped up and started shooting. It did them exactly no good. The guards sprayed bullets out in front of them.
They might have been farmers sowing seed, but they sowed
death instead. Archers had some kind of chance against ordinary musketeers, because they could shoot so much faster. Not
against these pitiless men. *Rat-a-tat-tat! Rat-a-tat-tat!* The
guards didn't care how many bullets they used, as long as they
flushed out the locals and then killed them.

And they did. The last couple of raiders tried to run when
they saw fighting was hopeless. Running didn't help, either. The
guards laughed as they shot them down from behind. One of the
men in mottled clothes paused and bent over a body. *Oh, yes,*
Jacques thought. *He's the one with the necklace of ears.*

"How can you fight them?" Dumnorix asked bitterly. "They have the thunder weapons, and they have the armor that keeps out arrows. I am a man. I am a warrior. Against them, I am not even a woman. I am a little girl."

"I know something about thunder weapons, and I feel the way you do," Jacques said. "They . . . are very strong."

"Someone should treat them the way they treat others," Dumnorix said. "They deserve it."

That was Jesus' Golden Rule, turned on its head. Jacques nodded. He felt the same way. "But can anyone do it?" he said. Dumnorix gave back a gloomy shrug, as if to say he doubted it. Jacques doubted it, too. But Khadija had hope. He made himself remember that. Khadija had hope.

Eleven

People talked about having a poker face. Annette didn't play poker—she didn't know anybody her age who did. But she knew what the phrase meant. She kept her face as still as she could, not wanting any of the guards to see what lay behind it. She wasn't just playing for money here. Money was nothing, or might as well have been. She was playing for her life.

If anything went wrong this morning, she would stay a slave for the rest of her life. And the rest of her life might not last long, either. They might knock her over the head or shoot her to make sure she never had another chance to get away.

Do I really want to do this? Fear made her heart pound and left the palms of her hands cold and wet with sweat. But if she didn't try now, when would she have a better chance? And if she didn't try, what did she have to look forward to? *Life?* the scared part of her suggested. The rest of her shouted it down. Life as a slave on a low-tech manor in some unregistered alternate wasn't worth living.

The breakfast mush sat like a boulder in her stomach as she went out to morning roll call. Emishtar said something. Annette answered her. She hardly noticed what the older woman said, let alone what she said herself. It must have been all right, because Emishtar nodded.

They lined up in rows of ten, to make them easier for the

guards to count. When a man in camouflage gear walked by, Annette took a couple of steps toward him. He frowned. "What do you want?" he asked in Arabic. He didn't sound angry or suspicious, the way he would have with Birigida. But he didn't sound what you'd call friendly, either.

Here we go. All or nothing. Annette answered him in English, with the same words Birigida had used: "My stretch is up. Time for me to go back to the home timeline."

His eyes widened. He wasn't bad-looking, which made Annette sorry to despise him. "You?" he said, also in English.

"Yes, me," he said. She didn't want him thinking she'd memorized the one phrase.

"How about that?" He shook his head. "I tell you, I wouldn't have guessed. Most of the the visitors"—a nice, bloodless name—"you have an idea who they are, even if you can't be sure. They're—goofy is the nicest thing I can say. But I have to hand it to you. You fit right in, didn't get in trouble, didn't make trouble or anything. My hat's off to you." He really did tip his splotched cap.

"Thanks." Annette had never got a compliment she wanted less. *You made a good slave.* Oh, boy! "How do I leave? They didn't talk a whole lot about that."

Whatever she said could get her in trouble. To her relief, the guard answered, "Yeah, they never do." He made a sour face. "Some of those people don't have it all in one bag, you know?" He pointed to the guard in front of the doorway that led down to the transposition chamber. "Go talk to Paul over there. He'll call your cab."

Annette smiled to let him think she liked the joke. She walked over to Paul. With that name, he could have grown up speaking English or French or German. With the implant you'd never know, not by listening to him. "What is it?" he asked, also in Arabic. That was the language everybody here thought she spoke.

"A transposition chamber back to the home timeline," she said in crisp English.

"*You?*" Paul said, as the first guard had. "Son of a gun!" There was that same unwanted compliment again. "Okay. I'll fix you up." He took from his belt what looked like an ordinary cell phone and thumbed a few buttons. After waiting for a moment looking at the gadget's little screen, he nodded. "Chamber's on its way."

"Thanks. Um, if I'm going to get aboard, you'll have to let me go down the stairs," Annette said.

"Coming up." Paul used the card on the lock, as he had for Birigida. He even opened the door for Annette. "Maybe we'll see you again one of these days." He meant doing another turn **as a** slave.

"Maybe you will." Annette meant coming along with Crosstime Traffic people and as many policemen or soldiers as they needed to put this place out of business for good. She had to fight to keep anticipation out of her voice.

Down the stairs she went, before Paul could find anything else awkward to say—and before he could start wondering if the manor really had a paying slave scheduled to go home right then.

The transposition chamber was already waiting in the subbasement. Traveling from the home timeline to an alternate or from one alternate to another didn't take any time. You *felt* time when you traveled inside it, depending on how far apart two alternates were. But that wasn't really time—it was only duration. That was how they explained it in training, anyhow. The math of going crosstime made quantum mechanics and genetic physics seem simple by comparison. Without massive computing power, it never could have happened.

All Annette cared about was that the chamber was there. The door sensed her and opened. She jumped in—literally. The door closed behind her. "Please take your seat and fasten your safety belt," a recorded voice said. "Transposition is about to begin."

Annette clicked the belt shut. She'd never figured out what good it would do in case of trouble, but habit died hard. She couldn't tell just when the chamber left the room under the manor, but she knew she'd got away. She let out a fierce, exultant whoop that would have made Jacques wonder which of them was the warrior.

She felt like a warrior. She'd escaped the enemy—well, at least some of the enemy. After doing that, she at least had a chance of getting away from the others. And then . . . she'd be back. With reinforcements.

Jacques watched Khadija vanish down the guarded stairway just before the roadbuilding gang left the manor. She really could talk to the guards, then. And she really did know some of the things they knew. It wasn't that he hadn't believed her. She'd sounded so sure of herself in the transposition chamber—and afterwards, too.

But there was a difference between sounding sure and knowing what you were talking about. Since Jacques didn't know what Khadija was talking about, he couldn't be sure she did. She must have, though, or the guard wouldn't have let her by.

"Your friend, she goes the same way Birigida went," Dumnorix said as they tramped along the already-paved part of the road.

"Yes," Jacques said—he could hardly say no.

"I hope it will be well for her," the redhead said.

"So do I," Jacques agreed.

"Birigida was no loss to anyone," Dumnorix said. "But losing a friend is hard."

"That's true." The more Jacques thought about it, the truer it felt—and the more painful. Khadija was the one person here with whom he could talk freely. And she was a pretty girl, or maybe a more than pretty girl. And he liked her, or maybe more than liked her. He thought she liked him back, too. More than liked him back? He didn't know about that. He wanted the chance to find out, though.

All the guards carried talking boxes on their belts. All those little boxes started chirping and chiming at the same time. Jacques had never seen that happen before. As if in one motion, all the guards grabbed the boxes and brought them up to their ears.

If the slaves had been waiting for that moment, they might have jumped the guards and wrestled their muskets away from them. But they weren't. The men in the mottled clothes quickly grew alert again. A few of them swung their muskets to cover the roadbuilders even as they listened and talked. And with those amazing weapons, they needed only a few.

By the way they shouted at the talking boxes, they didn't like what they were hearing. One of them took Jesus' name in vain. Jacques could recognize it even in another tongue. It was a funny way to swear. Jacques would have used Henri's name instead. God's Second Son, after all, was more important than His First. The Final Testament said so.

Another guard said, "Jesus!" and then several things that didn't sound holy at all. They might never have heard of Henri, or of the Final Testament. To Jacques, that made them strange, halfhearted Christians.

After a few more hot phrases, that guard held up a hand.

"Everybody stop!" he yelled in the several different languages the slaves spoke. He sounded disgusted in every one of them. "We've got to go back to the manor," he went on. "All the savages hereabouts are rising up. They need another lesson. We'll give it to them, too—will we ever. But till we do, maybe they can cause a little trouble. So you get the day off. You ought to thank them. They'll pay for it, though. Oh, yes. They'll pay."

Jacques had heard soldiers use that tone of voice before. He wouldn't have wanted to be on the receiving end of it. He especially wouldn't have wanted to be there if he had only a bow to use against weapons like the ones the guards carried.

If the countryside had really risen . . . How many hundreds, how many thousands, of archers were moving against the manor? Couldn't even a squad of men with these repeating muskets get rid of all of them? The locals were brave to try to fight back. Weren't they also crazy?

"They'll feed me, and I don't have to break my back today," Dumnorix said as they turned around. "I don't mind that."

"Can anyone fight these people?" Jacques asked.

The redheaded man shrugged broad shoulders. "I wouldn't want to try, not unless I had one of those sticks that go boom myself."

A stick that went boom was one thing. A stick that went boomboomboomboomboom was something else again. These muskets would slaughter any force the Kingdom of Versailles could raise. Jacques didn't like to think that, but he couldn't doubt it, either.

Back inside the manor, the guards had to stay in the courtyard. The guards got up on the walls. Jacques heard yelling outside, but it was off in the distance. The locals knew better than to charge the place. They would be asking to get killed in gruesome numbers. The guards took a few shots, but only a few. Their muskets couldn't shoot out as far as the eye could see, then. That was good to know.

The guards yelled back and forth to one another. They sounded furious. Jacques knew what he would have done if he were a local and the dangerous strangers withdrew to their fortress. He would have torn up everything he could that was out of range of their muskets. By the noises the guards were making, that was just what the people who lived here *were* doing.

But the locals had underestimated the guards and masters. One of the men in mottled clothes carried a long tube up onto the wall. He aimed it out where the noise was loudest. *Something* shot from it, leaving a trail of fire behind. An explosion followed a few heartbeats later. The shouts outside the walls changed pitch.

Two more guards set up a shorter tube on the ground down in the courtyard. A pair of metal legs supported it. The guards fiddled with screws. Then one of them dropped a pointed metal object with fins on the other end down the tube. An instant later, after a surprisingly soft *bang!*, the metal object shot out of the mouth of the tube again, ever so much faster than it had gone in. Another one of the finned things went in and went out, and another, and another.

Only after Jacques heard more booms outside did he realize what was going on. *It's a mortar*, he realized. It was much lighter and less clumsy than the ones his people and the Muslims used to shoot at enemies inside forts, but it couldn't be anything else.

One of the guards looked up and saw him watching what they were doing. Maybe Jacques' face showed he admired the gadget, if not the people using it. The guard grinned at him and spoke in Arabic: "They don't know everything we can do. Now they'll find out, the unclean sons of dogs."

More fire-spurting weapons—they looked something like

long, fat arrows—shot from the tube on the wall. The guards up there started laughing and cheering. They yelled something. "What do they say?" Jacques asked the mortar crew.

"The savages are running," answered the man who'd spoken before. He got to his feet. "Now we chase them. Now we really punish them." He sounded as if he looked forward to it.

"Arriving soon," the recorded voice said.

You could never tell when a transposition chamber got where it was going. Annette always tried. She always failed. She knew plenty of other people who tried, too. Knowing where across the timestream you were took instruments subtler than mere human senses.

"We are here," the voice said, and the door slid open.

Annette left the chamber. Now for the other hard part. If somebody here had a list of who was supposed to come back from the manor and when . . . That would be very bad. She glanced around. She was in what looked like an underground parking garage. As far as she could tell, she was the only person in it.

There'd be stairs somewhere, or an elevator, or an escalator. Somewhere—there, in fact. She followed the arrows and the signs under them in the six languages of the European Union: French, Spanish, German, Italian, English, and Polish. They took her to a stairway. Up she went, and up, and up. At last, the multilingual signs announced the ground floor. She opened the door.

There ahead was the door to the street. One more hurdle to leap: a man at a desk. He nodded to her and said something in Spanish. She gulped. "I'm sorry," she said in English. "I haven't had an implant for your language. Do you speak mine?"

"Yes, I do," he said in perfect British English, the kind the EU used. "I asked if you enjoyed yourself on your, ah, holiday."

While you were a slave, he meant. Annette made herself nod and started for the door. "Got to get back to the real world," she said. She was even with the desk . . . past it. She could run now and have a chance—or she could fling this guy into the middle of next week if she had to.

And she might. He rose, a frown on his face. "Won't you get your everyday clothes from the storage locker?" he asked.

She looked down at herself. Her blouse and long skirt were the only clothes she had. They weren't impossible to wear out on the street, not when the slavers had brought them to the manor from the home timeline. But they were kilometers away from the height of fashion. Well, too bad.

She had to answer him. "At the hotel," she said, and walked faster. Let him worry about what she meant.

His frown got deeper. He glanced toward the monitor on his desk. "What is your name?" he asked, holding up a hand. "When did you begin your holiday?"

"Gwyneth Paltrow," she said—the first old-time actress whose name popped into her head. "I began my vacation tomorrow." If she could just keep him confused until . . . the door slid open for her. She hurried out onto the sidewalk.

And then she realized she had a problem she hadn't counted on. Without even a dollar or a euro to her name, without a credit card in her pocket (she didn't even have a purse), she couldn't take the subway or a bus. But she could flag a cab. There was one, a little gold Honda. She waved frantically.

The driver cut across two lanes of traffic to get to the curb. Angry horns blared. Traffic here seemed as berserk as it was in Rome. She didn't know anything worse to say about it. "You speak English?" she asked the cabby.

"You bet, lady," he answered—his implanted language was pure American, or maybe he was. "Hop in. Where to?"

"Crosstime Traffic main offices," Annette said as she jumped into the back seat.

"You got it." The driver zoomed away while she was still fastening her seat belt.

Just in time, too. She looked back over her shoulder to see the man behind the desk come running out onto the sidewalk. He stared at the taxi, clapped a hand to his forehead, and dashed back into the building.

"That guy bothering you?" The driver must have seen him through the rear-view mirror.

"Not now," Annette said. Then she found something brand new to worry about. The slave ring had to be full of Crosstime Traffic people. How did she know she wouldn't run into one here? How did she know the local office wasn't full of slavers? She didn't know, and that was all there was to it. But she had to start somewhere, and that seemed a better place than the police. The police would need too many explanations.

She didn't even know where in Madrid the Crosstime Traffic offices were. They turned out to be near the train station, and near the memorial to the people killed in the terrorist bombings of 2004. That was a long time ago now—back when Gwyneth Paltrow was acting, in fact—and a lot of even worse things had happened since. Pigeons perched on the monument. People walked past without looking at the inscription. Like any old memorial, it was just part of the landscape.

Annette faced her own crisis when the cab stopped. "That'll be twelve and a half big ones," the driver said. A big one was a hundred euros, the same way a benjamin was a hundred dollars. Inflation had added enough zeros to the old currencies to make them clumsy to use.

"Please come in the office with me," Annette said. "They'll pay you in there—I promise they will."

Why do these things happen to me? the cabby's face shouted. "I didn't think you were a deadbeat," he said reproachfully.

"I'm not," Annette answered. "I don't have any money, that's all." It made perfect sense to her. The cab driver didn't look any happier. He got out of the Honda, muttering to himself in Spanish—the English did come through the implant, then.

"If they give me a ticket for parking here, that's yours, too," he said. Annette nodded. She would have promised to pay for the whole car just then.

Into the Crosstime Traffic offices they went. A receptionist spoke to them in lisping Spanish. "Do you understand English?" Annette asked.

"Of course," the woman replied. Her accent was British. After the man in the building with the outlaw transposition chamber, that made Annette antsy. The receptionist went on, "What can I do for you, Miss . . . ?" She waited for a name.

"I'm Annette Klein," Annette said, wondering what would happen next.

The receptionist's eyes widened. She called up an image on her monitor and looked from it to Annette and back again. "You *are* Annette Klein!" she exclaimed. "What are you doing here?"

"Trying to pay this nice man his cab fare, only I haven't got a euro or a dollar or anything," Annette said. "Could you please give him fifteen big ones?"

"Of course," the receptionist said again. She handed the driver a thousand-euro bill and a five hundred. He gave Annette a nod that was almost a bow, then hurried out to his car. The receptionist started to ask questions.

Annette beat her to it: "Are my mother and father all right?" That was the most important thing in her mind just then.

"Yes," the woman said. She looked back at the monitor to get her facts straight. "They were taken to, uh, Marseille, and some of our other people bought them there. They're in the USA now." She checked the monitor again. "The report was that you were taken to Madrid in that alternate, but nobody could find you there. You might have fallen off the face of the earth."

"I did," Annette said grimly.

"I'm sorry, but I don't understand," the receptionist said.

"I'm sorry, too, for a whole lot of things." Annette's mind was racing a million kilometers a minute, working out what she needed to do. Knowing her mother and father had come back to the home timeline made it easier. "Please take me to your chief administrator here. And I need to talk to the head of security. And please call my parents—here are their numbers." She wrote them down. "Set up a conference call in the administrator's office, please. That way, I can tell everybody everything at once." *And somebody outside the office will be listening when I do, too.*

The receptionist nodded. "I will take care of it." She got on the phone, where she spoke in Spanish. When she hung up, she smiled at Annette. "Mr. Olivo's secretary will arrange the call for you. And a messenger will take you to his office." A young man—only a couple of years older than Annette—hurried up. "Here's Jorge now."

"Hello," Jorge said. "Come with me, why don't you?"

"Okay." Annette wished she could clean up beforehand, but maybe looking—and smelling—the way she did would help persuade the officials that something inside Crosstime Traffic had gone dreadfully wrong.

People stared at her as she went by. She heard her name mixed in with a lot of Spanish. A man clapped his hands. A woman walked over and kissed her on the cheek. They were glad she'd made it to the home timeline. That was good. If their bosses had anything to do with the slavery ring, they would have a harder time fixing up an accident for her.

PEDRO OLIVO, said a sign on a door. Below the name was CHIEF ADMINISTRATOR in the six EU languages, Spanish first and bigger than the others. The man at the desk in front of the door grinned at Annette and spoke in English: "I have the conference call set up, *Señorita* Klein. Your parents will be glad to hear from you."

It would still be in the wee small hours back in Ohio. Phone calls at that time of day were rarely good news. Dad and Mom must have had their hearts in their throats till they found out she was all right. "Thank you," Annette whispered.

"My pleasure." The secretary opened the door to Pedro Olivo's office. "Go right on in. The head of security is already in there with Mr. Olivo. Her name is Luisa Javier."

"Luisa Javier," Annette repeated so she'd remember. "Thanks."

Pedro Olivo looked like a man who ran things. He was in his fifties, with gray hair, a neatly trimmed mustache, and an expensive suit. Luisa Javier put Annette in mind of a schoolteacher. She was thin and dark and looked clever. Annette gave them only a glance apiece, though. Staring out of a big monitor were her parents. Sure enough, they looked as if they'd just got out of bed.

"Annette!" Dad exclaimed when the camera in Mr. Olivo's office picked her up. "Are you all right, sweetheart?"

"I'm not too bad," Annette answered. "I'm awful glad to be back in the home timeline again, I'll tell you that."

"What happened, darling?" Mom asked.

"Yes—what *did* happen?" Pedro Olivo sounded like a man who ran things, too. His voice had a let's-get-to-the-bottom-of-this tone to it. He leaned forward behind his desk.

Annette spoke to her parents: "Mom, Dad, I hope you're recording this."

They looked at each other, there on the screen. Mom reached out and flicked a switch. "Now we are," Dad said. Annette eyed the Spanish Crosstime Traffic officials. Neither of them flinched. The phone connection with the USA didn't suddenly and mysteriously break, either. She took those things as good signs.

"What happened?" she said. "You know I got caught when my folks did, right? And you know I got taken to Madrid instead of Marseille." She waited for everyone to nod. "I got sold there," she said, "and when I did. . . ."

After using their deadly toys against the locals, the guards went out to clean them up. Some of the men in mottled clothes were on foot, others on horseback. Jacques wouldn't have wanted to try to stand against them, and his countrymen knew a lot more—a *lot* more—about the art of war than these people did.

Because the fighting was going on, he needed a while to realize the guards and the masters had other worries, too. He found out the hard way. A guard came up to him, pointed a musket at his belly, and said, "You—come along with me."

"I didn't do anything!" Jacques squeaked—a slave's automatic protest when he got in trouble with the people in charge.

"Ha!" the guard said, and then, "You were friends with that Khadija, weren't you?"

That told Jacques what kind of trouble he was in. He wished it told him how to get out of trouble, too. No such luck there. "What if I was?" he said—he couldn't very well deny it, not when they knew better.

"That's what we're going to find out." The guard's words held a grim promise Jacques didn't like. He couldn't do anything about it, though. The guard gestured with the musket. "Come on. Get moving." Jacques went. He was sure the guard would shoot him if he tried anything else.

The man took him to a room near the masters' quarters. He'd

never been there before. It had no windows, which worried him.
One of the lamps that gave light without fire or smoke glowed in
the ceiling. Three other guards waited there. They didn't have any
torturer's tools that he could see, but he didn't think they'd invited
him over to share a roast chicken and a pitcher of wine.

"Tell me everything you know about Khadija," said the
guard who'd brought him there.

He told everything he knew about Khadija as a merchant's
daughter from Marseille. She'd made it plain she didn't want the
guards knowing she was from wherever they came from. In the
telling, Jacques also told a good deal about himself.

"So you're not even a Muslim, then?" a guard said.

"Jesus and Henri, no!" Jacques said indignantly. He made
the sign of the wheel. "I am a good Christian, or I try to be."

They went back and forth in the language that sounded like
English—the language Khadija said *was* English. One of them
returned to Arabic: "So how did she get away, then?"

"Why ask me?" So she *had* got away, then! Jacques didn't
laugh in the guards' faces. Heaven only knew what they would
have done to him if he had. He did add, "If she got away, I didn't
have anything to do with it. You know where I was all the time.
You must be the ones who let her go."

Sometimes the worst thing you could do to somebody was
tell him the truth. The guards all started shouting. A couple of
them shouted at Jacques. The rest yelled at one another. Then
one of them outshouted the others. He told Jacques, "I am going
to poke you in the arm with a needle. It won't hurt much, so
hold still while I do it. If you try anything stupid, you'll be
sorry. Understand?"

"Yes," Jacques said, though he didn't really. If they wanted to
torture him, they could do much worse than that. He'd seen worse
done when men from his kingdom captured Muslim prisoners. The

Muslims weren't gentle to Christians they caught, either. Were the guards trying to see how brave he was? He'd show them!

The man in mottled clothes wasn't even lying. Jacques had known fleabites that troubled him more than the needle. He sat there as if carved from stone. Then the strangest thing happened. Within a few minutes, he began to feel woozy, almost dizzy. It reminded him of the way he felt when he drank too much wine. But he hadn't drunk anything at all. He didn't understand it. Before long, he was too woozy even to want to try to understand it.

"What is Khadija's real name?" a guard asked him.

"It's Khadija, as far as I know," he answered. The guard swore, first in Arabic—which sounded like ripping cloth—then in what Jacques supposed was English, and then in a language that sounded like German. How many tongues did the guards speak? Jacques was too woozy to worry about that, too.

"Have you ever heard of a transposition chamber?" another guard asked.

He wanted to say no, but what came out of his mouth was, "Yes."

"Ha!" the guard said. "Now we're getting somewhere. Who told you about one?"

"Khadija did." Again, Jacques wanted to lie, but found he couldn't. Did it have something to do with the needle? He didn't see how it could, but he didn't see what else could make him stick to the truth, either.

"What did she tell you about transposition chambers?"

"That they were how we got from Madrid to this place. That funny room that didn't move, but when it opened we were somewhere else."

"How did Khadija know about transposition chambers?"

"She said she was from the same place you people were, wherever that is."

"She *told* you that? Somebody fouled up somewhere."

"She told me." Jacques answered the question. He ignored the comment. He couldn't do anything else, not the way he felt.

"How could she? Wasn't she a slave like Birigida?"

"No. She thought Birigida was disgusting for wanting to be a slave. She came here because she got caught and made a slave, just like I did."

They didn't ask him any more questions after that. They started shouting at one another again, in languages he didn't understand. He was too woozy to care. Later on, when he could think straight, that made him sad.

"—and that's how I got back," Annette finished. She'd been talking for hours, telling as much as she could remember about the manor and everything that went on there. Several cans of Coke stood in front of her. The Crosstime Traffic people had wet her whistle while she talked. Since she hadn't had any caffeine for months, the soda hit her much harder than it would have if she'd been drinking it every day.

Pedro Olivo's face showed nothing as he turned to Luisa Javier. "What do you think?" he asked.

"I think this office has a big problem," the head of security answered. "I think Crosstime Traffic has a big problem."

Were they going to try to sweep it under the rug? They couldn't get away with that, not when Dad and Mom had a recording of everything she said. A couple of commands and it would be on the way to every news outfit in the United States. If that wasn't a recipe for stirring up a scandal, Annette couldn't think what would be.

But she'd underestimated the Spaniards. "I think you're right," Olivo said. "And I think we'd better get to the bottom of it as fast as we can, before it gets worse."

"Where exactly was the building you left, the building with the transposition chamber?" Luisa Javier asked.

"It was on Calle Rodas," Annette answered. "That's all I can tell you. I've never been in Madrid—*this* Madrid before. No, wait. The building across the street belonged to Petrokhem." The Russian company had offices all over Europe—and several in the eastern states in America, too.

"That's enough to go on." Luisa Javier pulled out her cell phone and made a call. As she dialed, she told Annette, "The chief of police." Then she started talking into the phone: "Antonio? Luisa. We have some troubles here. . . . Yes, I'm using English so the person who ran into the trouble can follow me. . . . No, worse than smuggling. . . . No, worse than terrorism, too. . . . Slaves, that's what could be worse."

Annette heard the howl the police chief let out. She would have felt the same way even if she hadn't just escaped herself. Since she had . . .

"On Calle Rodas, across from the Petrokhem building," the Crosstime Traffic security head was saying. "Yes, an outlaw chamber . . . No, I don't know how they got it. That's one of the things we'll have to run down. . . . A lot of time, a lot of computing power . . . We'll get to the bottom of it. . . . *Gracias. Hasta luego.*"

"Thank you," Annette said.

"Don't thank us yet. We haven't done anything," Pedro Olivo said. "But we will. You can count on that. We will."

"You may want to monitor your computers for people dumping data," Dad said. "You may want to do that as soon as you can, too."

"Yes." Luisa Javier nodded. "A lot of people will be scrubbing their systems, won't they? Well, they can try." There was a never-ending race between programs that erased and overwrote data and ones that read what had been erased and written over. Annette didn't know which side was ahead right now. Someone like Luisa Javier would have to.

"Some of the people involved in this—this filth will be in high places." Pedro Olivo looked as if he wanted to spit. "To try to save themselves, they will say you are lying."

"If you move fast enough, you can catch them," Annette said. "They have a base in Madrid in the alternate where my family was working. You should be able to get evidence there. And they've got the manor in that other alternate. I don't think there are any proper Crosstime Traffic people in that world. If you go there, though, take lots of people, and take guns."

Pedro Olivo spoke harshly in Spanish. Luisa Javier answered in the same language. Then she sighed and turned back to Annette. "This is going to cause Crosstime Traffic a lot of trouble, you know," she said in English.

"I thought of that," Annette said. TV and the Net and newspapers liked nothing better than blowing the lid off corporate shenanigans. She couldn't imagine anything much juicier than this. Exploiting the natives from who could say how many low-tech alternates, masters—and slaves—from the home timeline, murders . . . "But those people caused me a lot of trouble. I'm just lucky I wasn't stuck there for good."

"Yes, I understand that," the head of security said. "I wanted to make sure you knew what you were getting into, that's all." Her cell phone rang. She listened, then went, "Thanks," and put it away. She looked at Annette. "They're at that building. The chamber isn't there, but they've got evidence it stops there. And they've arrested somebody who I think is the man you got past before you came here."

"Didn't he run?" Annette said in amazement.

"Sometimes people are stupid," Luisa Javier said. "Sometimes they're smart—for a while. Not smart enough, usually, though, and not for long enough. Now it's payback time." That sounded more vengeful than Annette felt most of the time. Today? Today she liked it fine.

Twelve

After Khadija disappeared, the people who ran the manor tried to act as if everything were normal. Maybe they even made most of the slaves think so. Not Jacques. Maybe the way they'd grilled him made him notice changes in routine more than he would have otherwise. Or maybe the guards just weren't so good at hiding how worried they really were.

They kept going up and down the stairs to the subbasement room where the transposition chamber came and went. They hadn't done that very much when things were running smoothly. They didn't look happy when they came up, either. Something down there was wrong, badly wrong.

Jacques was tempted to ask the guards what it was. He fought the temptation. Fighting temptation was supposed to be a virtue. Jesus and Henri would have approved of it. That wasn't why he did it, though. He didn't want to make the guards pay special attention to him again. The last time they did, he'd got away with one needle stuck in his arm. He had the feeling he wouldn't be so lucky if they glanced his way again.

Going out to work on the road seemed a relief. The guards swaggered and strutted. "Let's see the savages bother us now," one of them said. "This time, we taught them a lesson they'll remember for years."

No doubt he was right. But the locals had done damage here,

too. The almonds and the olives and the vines and the rest of the crops would be a long time getting over their raid. If this were an ordinary farm, one that depended on what it grew, Jacques would have worried about going hungry. But it got food from elsewhere, as it got people from elsewhere.

Or it had. Jacques wasn't so sure it did any more. By the way the guards kept going down those stairs, maybe things had stopped coming. Did that mean just food? How much ammunition for their repeating muskets did they have? If the locals tried attacking again, could the guards rout them so easily? If they couldn't, what would happen then? Nothing pretty—Jacques was sure of that.

But he was also sure the locals wouldn't be back right away. For all he knew, they were still running. The copper-skinned tribes across the Atlantic couldn't face the muskets and cavalry the Muslims and his own people were using against them. The fight here was even more unfair.

For all the guards' bluster, Jacques wasn't the only slave who saw things had changed. "Why are they frightened?" Dumnorix asked him when none of the men in mottled clothes stood close by. "They took you in. They did things to you. What did you learn?"

He wanted to rise up against the guards. Jacques saw that right away. Dumnorix was a warrior, first, last, and always. If he saw a chance, he would fight—and he was looking for that chance.

"You know how you came here?" Jacques said. Dumnorix nodded. Jacques thought hard before he spoke again. He and Dumnorix didn't have enough words in common to make talking about the transposition chamber easy. "They, uh, bring things here in that box."

"Yes, yes." Dumnorix sounded impatient. "And so?"

"If that box is, uh, broken, then they cannot bring things," Jacques said. "Cannot bring . . ." He broke down. Dumnorix didn't understand about bullets. In a lot of ways, he was a savage himself. Jacques tried again: "Cannot bring arrows for thundersticks. Cannot bring food."

Dumnorix's eyes were the blue of a lake under a summer sky. They flashed fire now. "We can take them!" he said. His hands tightened on the handle of his shovel till his knuckles whitened. It might have been the neck of the guard he hated most.

"Jesus and Henri, be careful!" Jacques whispered. "They still have, uh, arrows." He hoped Dumnorix was following him. The redhead would get himself killed if he didn't watch out. He'd get a lot of other people killed, too. "For all I know, more will start coming tomorrow, too."

"Maybe." But Dumnorix didn't believe it. Jacques could see that. Those fiery blue eyes flicked towards a guard. "They don't think they can get more. Otherwise they wouldn't be so worried."

He might have been right. Even if he was, what difference did it make? "They aren't worried about us," Jacques said. "They're worried about enemies from their own people."

"So much the better." No, Dumnorix wasn't listening. All he could think of were battles—battles with him as a hero, as *the* hero. "We can take them by surprise."

"How?" Jacques asked. Dumnorix waved that aside. It didn't bother him a bit. Jacques wanted to take his own pick and bash the redheaded man over the head. He wondered if even that would help. He wondered if anything would.

When Annette got back to the United States, all she wanted to do was pick up the pieces of her life. She knew she would have to start at Ohio State a year later than she'd planned. Mom and Dad had made sure she could do that. It wasn't her fault she'd missed the start of the semester. She'd learned some things at the manor she never would have at the university. Whether they were things she wanted to know . . .

She wondered what she would do with herself till fall semester rolled around again. That turned out not to be a problem. Wondering, in fact, turned out to be foolish. Every police agency in the country seemed to want to talk to her.

It had been snowing in Ohio. When her plane landed in Seattle, it was raining instead. *Variety*, she thought. A cop met her in the baggage-claim area. She would have recognized him as a cop even if he weren't holding a sign with her name printed on it. He was built like a slightly undersized linebacker. He wore a suit that would have been almost stylish five years earlier. He looked like a man who'd seen too many nasty things, and who knew he would be seeing more.

"Miss Klein?" he said as she came up. She nodded. He held out his hand. "I'm Kwame Daniels."

"Pleased to meet you," Annette said.

"And you." He smiled, his teeth very white against his dark skin. The baggage carousel started going round and round. "Now we see if your suitcase ended up in San Francisco or Singapore."

"You know what? I don't care," Annette said. "As long as I'm back where I belong, I'm not going to jump up and down about the luggage."

"You're smart," Detective Daniels said. "Knowing what's important, that helps a lot. Too many people get all hot and bothered over stuff that doesn't matter." Annette plucked her bag off the carousel and pulled up the handle. He asked, "Shall I take you to your hotel first, or do you want to get right to it?"

"I'd like to get it over with, if that's all right," Annette said.

"My captain told me, however you want it, that's how we do it," Daniels said. "You're doing us a favor being here."

"No, I don't think so," Annette said as they started for the parking structure. "What I went through, what those other poor people are going through . . . That *needs* smashing. How could I look at myself if I didn't do everything I could to set it right?"

"You get no arguments from me." Daniels popped open a big umbrella to keep them dry while they crossed the street.

The police station to which he drove Annette looked like a fortress. Inside, though, it might have been almost any office building. Men and women sat at desks. They talked on the telephone. They sent and read e-mail. They typed or dictated reports. In most offices, though, very few of the workers would have been armed.

Most office buildings had conference rooms. So did this one, but they were called interrogation rooms instead. Kwame Daniels opened the door to one of them. Annette went in. In a loud, formal voice—everything that happened in there went onto video—he said, "Miss Klein, I would like to ask you if you recognize any of the persons seated here."

She'd cleaned up. She wore stylish business clothes instead of the outfit the manor had given to its slaves. Her blond hair didn't hang limp alongside her head any more. It rose in fancy curls. She had makeup on now. Without a doubt, though, she was Birigida, or whatever her real name was.

And, without a doubt, the man sitting beside her was a lawyer.

Annette sighed. "Yes, I recognize the woman."

"Thank you," the detective said. "And where did you last see Bridget Mallory?"

"Is that her name? I never knew what it was," Annette said.

"The last place I saw her was a manor that used slaves. It was in Madrid, or what's Madrid here. I don't know what alternate it's in. I don't think it's one that Crosstime Traffic visits, but I can't prove that."

"This is all a put-up job," the lawyer said. "If this person was a slave at this place, and if my client was a slave there— which she does not admit, not at all—what's the difference between them? That this person has bought immunity from prosecution by testifying against my client? That won't play well with a jury. We've seen it too often."

Kwame Daniels smiled a most unpleasant smile. "There is another difference, Mr. Nguyen." He turned to Annette. "Do you want to tell him, Miss Klein, or shall I?"

"I'll do it," Annette said. "I was a slave there because I got captured and kidnapped while I was working for Crosstime Traffic. The raiders didn't know I was from the home timeline. They took me to Madrid in that alternate, and the man who bought me took me to the manor I talked about. Miss, uh, Mallory was a slave there because she, uh, volunteered."

Bridget Mallory turned white, or possibly green. Under the harsh fluorescents in the ceiling, it was hard to tell. Detective Daniels threw back his head and laughed. "How do you think a jury'll like that, Sam?"

It didn't faze Sam Nguyen. Lawyers got paid for not letting things faze them. "What you say here and what you say in court under oath may be two different things," he said. "Besides, while it is illegal to make other people into slaves, it is not illegal to be made into a slave."

Annette had wondered about that. Wanting to be a slave might be sick and twisted and disgusting. Was it against the law? She had no idea. Up till a few months ago, she'd never imagined she would need to worry about it.

"Nobody's talking about charging her with being a slave, Mr. Nguyen," Daniels said. Annette wondered what *he* thought of this. His ancestors hadn't wanted to be slaves, but they got brought to America anyway. He went on, "But she dealt with people who took slaves. She paid money to people who took slaves. She worked with people who were slaves and didn't pay for the privilege. She knew they were forced into slavery, too. And she didn't say a word about any of it till we found out about it from Miss Klein here. How many different conspiracy charges do you think will stick?"

"You can bring conspiracy charges. Whether you can convict . . . You don't know how a jury will decide any more than I do." Nguyen was a cool customer. Whatever Bridget Mallory paid him, he earned his money.

But she turned and spoke to him in a low voice. Annette couldn't make out what she said, but he shook his head. She spoke again, more insistently. This time, Annette could hear her: "What will my name be worth after the reporters and the Net ghouls get their hands on this? Let's make the best deal we can. She was—"

Her lawyer held up a hand. "Whatever she was, you don't say it with the recorders running. You don't do anything with the recorders running till we have a deal. Got that?"

Bridget Mallory nodded. Annette hadn't dreamt she could sympathize with the blond woman, but she did. Her folks had had to sneak her to the airport in the wee small hours so she could go to Seattle. Too many stories had already said too much about what happened to her while she was a slave. Too much of what those stories said wasn't even slightly true. She'd had her picture splashed all over the Net, TV, and the papers. She didn't like being recognized wherever she went.

Maybe it was just as well she wouldn't be starting college for a while. By the time she did, maybe some of the fuss would die down. She didn't want people staring at her all the time. It would make her feel like a freak.

She sighed. It was probably too late to worry about that. People *were* going to recognize her. *Aren't you the one who . . . ?* She wondered if she'd be hearing that for the rest of her life. Maybe she would, because she *was* the one who. . . .

"You will be cooperating with us, then, Ms. Mallory?" Daniels asked.

Sam Nguyen started to say something, but she gestured for him to stop. She nodded. "Yes," she said. She sounded tired.

"All right, then," the detective said. "If you are, you'll need to talk to the people above me. We'll get that started now, if you don't mind." Bridget Mallory nodded again. Her lawyer looked unhappy. Annette understood why. Daniels wasn't giving her a chance for second thoughts. Once she started talking, turning back would be next to impossible.

"Please come with me, then," Kwame Daniels said. The blond woman and the lawyer got up. Before the detective led them away, he turned to Annette. "Wait right here, please. I'll be back in a few minutes."

"Okay," Annette said. The door closed behind the others. She didn't like being alone in the interrogation room. It felt almost as lonely as waking up in slavery every morning. This wouldn't last long, though. That . . . That might have lasted forever.

When Detective Daniels came back, he was grinning. "I hoped putting her face-to-face with you would crack her," he said. "We get her testimony, we get your testimony, we get all the electronic evidence . . . They've recycled a lot of files, but they couldn't get rid of everything."

"It'll be an open-and-shut case as soon as they find the alternate where the manor is," Annette said.

Daniels shrugged. "You'd know more about that than I do. Not my line of work."

"Well, I didn't want this to be my line of work, either," Annette said. "You don't always get what you want, do you? Sometimes you just get what you get, and you have to make the best of it."

"Welcome to the world of grownups, Miss Klein," Daniels said soberly. "You'd be amazed how many people never figure that out. I deal with folks like that every day."

The slavers had thought they could get what they wanted and not have to pay for it. If they hadn't bought somebody from the home timeline, they would have been right. Oh, sooner or later they probably would have made another mistake—how could they help it? But it might not have happened for years.

Or it might not have happened at all. To this day, nobody knew who nuked Damascus in 2033. The Israelis? The Iraqis? The Turks? Rebels inside Syria? Some people even said the USA did it, though the bomb didn't come in on a missile. No one had ever claimed responsibility. If there were any survivors from the people who did it, they'd be old men and women now. Hard to imagine keeping quiet for more than sixty years, but they had— unless they were all radioactive dust.

Detective Daniels broke in on her thoughts. "I'll take you to your hotel now, if you want me to."

"Yes, please," she said.

"If I were you, I'd order room service and disconnect the phone," he said. "You've got to figure the reporters will work out who you are and where you're staying."

"I was hoping they didn't know I was here," Annette said in dismay.

"Well, it's a free country. You can hope whatever you want to," Daniels answered. "That doesn't mean you'll get it."

She found out how right he was as soon as she left the station. News vans had pulled up in front of it. Reporters shouted questions at her. She didn't answer any of them. That didn't keep them from shouting more. It didn't keep them from trying to follow Kwame Daniels' car, either. But four cars with black drivers and young woman passengers left the police-station parking lot at the same time.

"I think we shook 'em." Kwame Daniels sounded pleased with himself.

But three news crews waited in the hotel lobby. Annette went right on not answering questions. Detective Daniels tried to stand between her and the cameras while she registered. He didn't have much luck.

Hotel security people did keep reporters from going up in the elevator with her or right after her. And two hard-faced men and a hard-faced woman in business clothes stalked the hallway on her floor. One of the men said, "We'll check your food before it gets to you, Miss Klein. Wouldn't want any unfortunate incidents."

Wouldn't want anyone poisoning you, he meant. Plenty of people would benefit if the star witness against them came down with a sudden case of loss of life. Some of them were bound to be rich and influential. Annette sighed. Next to worries like that, even reporters didn't seem so bad.

The jumpier the guards got, the more careful Jacques acted around them. The men in mottled clothes knew the slaves knew something was wrong. They knew they might have to deal with trouble. And they were ready to slap it down in a hurry, and hard, if it cropped up. Jacques didn't want to get shot for no reason at all, especially when he hoped Khadija would lead rescuers back here.

Dumnorix didn't believe that that chance was real. "We can take them," he said. "And when we do . . ." He knew what he wanted to do to the guards. He must have been thinking about it ever since he became a slave. Some of the torturers in the Kingdom of Versailles could have taken lessons from him.

"This is not a good time," Jacques said. "They're ready. They have muskets. We have shovels. Bad odds." He hefted his own shovel to remind the older man what he meant.

"We have spirit. We have bravery." Dumnorix sounded like a wolf on the prowl. "They have nothing. You can see it in their faces."

Were he a wolf talking about pulling down sheep, or even talking about pulling down elk, Jacques wouldn't have argued with him. But the prey he hungered for had sharper teeth than he did. "They will fight for their lives," Jacques said. "They know they all die if they lose. That makes them fight hard."

Dumnorix looked at him as if he'd crawled out from under a flat rock. "Where is *your* spirit?"

"I have spirit," Jacques answered. "I have sense, too, or I hope I do. Even if we win, even if we kill them, so what?"

Now the redheaded man just plain stared. "We have revenge, by the gods! What else do we need?"

"The guards beat the people who live here. They beat them over and over, whenever they fought. The people who live here want revenge, too," Jacques said. "The guards know how to fight them. They know how to use all their tools of war. Do you? What will the people who live here do to us? How will they tell us from the guards?"

"You worry too much," Dumnorix said.

"You don't worry enough," Jacques said, and worried more than ever himself. The only way he could stop Dumnorix from rising up was by warning the guards. He couldn't bring himself to do that. If he did, it would make him feel filthy. But if Dumnorix and however many men he would bring with him did rebel, what would happen then? Even if they won by some miracle—and winning would take a miracle—they would still lose. They still had to face the locals afterwards, and they had no idea how to work the machines or the magic or whatever it was that kept lamps burning without fire and did all the other amazing things that happened in the manor.

Dumnorix didn't care about any of that. He only cared about striking. His being a pagan didn't bother Jacques so much. The guards were enemies, and yet they swore by Jesus, if not by Henri. Some of the Muslims among the slaves had become Jacques' friends, and he thought Muslims were as wrong as pagans. No, the problem was that Dumnorix was a hotheaded fool. He saw only what he wanted to do right now. What might spring from that . . . He didn't care. It wasn't real to him till it hit him in the nose.

Wherever Khadija had gone, if she'd really gone anywhere, Jacques hoped she'd come back soon. He prayed to Henri that she would. He was the only person here who believed in God's Second Son. He hoped that would persuade Henri to listen to him.

He wasn't the only slave here who worried about Khadija, though. One evening after supper, the woman with the crooked teeth who'd been her friend said, "I want to talk to you." Her Arabic was almost as bad as the bits of Breton and Dumnorix's language that Jacques used.

He understood her, though. "Go ahead," he answered, also in Arabic. "You're Emishtar, yes?"

"Yes," she said. "You know where is Khadija?"

None of the guards seemed to be paying special attention to them. He knew he had to be careful anyway. "I'm not sure," he answered. "I hope I do."

"She is all right?" Emishtar asked.

Jacques only shrugged. "I don't know. I hope so."

Emishtar eyed him. "She go into danger, yes?" Unhappily, he nodded. She wagged a finger at him. He almost laughed— when she did that, she reminded him of his mother. But she sounded angry as she asked, "Why you not stop her?"

He did laugh then. The idea that he could stop Khadija from doing anything she aimed to do . . . The idea that *anybody* could stop Khadija from doing anything she wanted to do . . . He spread his hands. "How?" he asked.

That made Emishtar smile, too. Jacques found himself liking her smile even if she had bad teeth. Plenty of people did. And she understood what his laugh and his one-word question meant, too. "She is like bull, yes," Emishtar said, and pawed the ground to make sure he understood what she was talking about. She added, "But she like you. Maybe she listen to you."

"No," Jacques said, and let it go at that. Khadija really did like him? This older woman was her friend. She would know if anybody did. Jacques felt like grinning like a fool.

Emishtar smiled at him. "You are a good boy," she said, and walked away.

Jacques was happy and angry at the same time. A boy? He wasn't a boy! He was about to turn eighteen. If that didn't make him a man, what would?

Back in Madrid. This time, Annette came by hypersonic shuttle, not by scamming her way aboard a transposition chamber. She went through customs instead of escaping from a man who might have stopped her if he'd thought a little faster. And the reporters in Spain were just as annoying as the ones in the United States. She couldn't even tell them she didn't speak Spanish, because they all spoke English.

She'd had to make a fuss to get back to Spain. Higher-ups in Crosstime Traffic didn't care that she'd promised some of the slaves at the manor she'd come back. Several higher-ups were under arrest as the scandal widened. Others plainly wished it was never uncovered. They would rather have gone on doing business as usual. Slaves? As long as nobody knew about them, they might as well not have existed.

But Crosstime Traffic couldn't afford any more bad publicity. The company would have got it by the carload lot after trying to keep Annette from returning to where she'd been enslaved. No matter what the higher-ups might have been thinking to themselves, they weren't dumb. They could see that. And so here she was, at Crosstime Traffic's expense.

CT technicians were setting up an enormous transposition chamber in a park several kilometers from the building that was in the same spot here as the manor was in that other alternate. Next to the cost of doing that, flying Annette over from the USA was small change. Thanks to endless computer work, the techs sounded sure they could find that other alternate. Annette hoped they were right.

One of the things that moved into the transposition chamber under cover of darkness was an armored car. A couple of squads of Spanish soldiers boarded the chamber, too. So did a man who looked like a lawyer. "You say they're loaded for bear," he told Annette. "Are they loaded for dinosaur?"

"I hope not," was all Annette said, because she wasn't sure. Her helmet and body armor were made to fit women in the Spanish Army. The releases she'd signed were made to fit the toughest court of law. Without signing them, she wouldn't have been able to get into the chamber.

Her parents had made it very plain they wished she were staying home. If it were up to them, they never would have signed the releases. But she was over eighteen, so they couldn't stop her. Her father's comment was, "Yes, you're of legal age. You know what that means? It means you're old enough to be stupid all by yourself."

"Instead of someone else being stupid for me?" Annette had thought that was the perfect comeback. Her father just rolled his eyes, so he must have been less impressed than she was.

"Are you ready, Miss Klein?" asked the man who looked like a lawyer. He *was* a lawyer, and worked for Crosstime Traffic. Even if she'd signed his releases, he didn't look happy to have her along. He went on, "Remember, you've agreed to follow the military commander's orders. If you become a casualty"—a nice, polite way to say *get killed or maimed*—"the publicity would be very bad." That mattered to him. Her health? She wouldn't have bet a dollar on it. But he was coming along, too. Whatever risks she took, he took them with her.

That made her answer him politely: "I remember, Mr. Guerrero. I'll play by the rules." *Unless things go really wrong. But if they do, nobody else will be playing by the rules, either.*

Somebody closed the door, sealing the transposition chamber off from the outside world. Like most chambers, it had a human along to back up the computer. Most of the time, the human couldn't do much if the electronics went haywire. From what Annette had heard, it wasn't like that here. They were feeling for the alternate that held the manor. They had a good notion of where it lay among so many others. Its world sprang from one where Rome lost the Samnite Wars in the fourth century BCE. No one dominated the Mediterranean in that sheaf of alternates. Spain was split between people like Basques and the descendants of colonists from Carthage. Just where in the sheaf the right alternate lay . . . the human operator would, with luck, be able to tell.

The operator looked up from the monitor she'd plugged into

the chamber's electronics. "We're on the way," she said in English, after what was probably the same thing in Spanish.

If she hadn't said so, Annette wouldn't have known. The transposition chamber didn't feel as if it was going anywhere. It was, but you couldn't tell till you got there.

The Spanish lieutenant colonel in charge of things military came over to remind Annette of what she'd promised. She promised all over again. Why not? It took up some duration—time didn't really exist while the chamber was traveling, but it felt as if it did.

As they got close, the operator used the manual controls. Except in training videos, Annette had never seen anybody do that. She wondered if anybody else had who'd lived through it. Not many people had—she was sure of that.

Frowning, the operator twisted a knob ever so slightly. "We're just about there," she said. "I'm going to drop us into reality. If it's the wrong alternate, we'll try again."

"If it's the right one, they're liable to start shooting at us," the Spanish officer said. On that cheerful note, the chamber returned to the timelines.

One of the soldiers wore headphones along with the rest of his gear. He said something excited in Spanish. *I should have got a course through the implant*, Annette thought. *Then I'd know what was going on.* But she hadn't had time. Since escaping, she'd barely had time to breathe. The lieutenant colonel translated for her: "He says he is picking up wireless phone signals."

"This is the right alternate, then." Excitement of her own tingled through Annette. "In this sheaf, they wouldn't have invented them on their own."

"*Sí,*" the Spanish officer said. He called orders in his own language. The transposition chamber's door slid open. Soldiers scrambled out and ... what was the military word? They deployed, that was what they did. The armored car rolled out. The lieutenant colonel gave Annette what was almost a bow. "If you will be so kind as to come with me, Miss Klein . . ."

Stay with me. I'll make sure you don't get into mischief. That was what he meant. Annette didn't know what she could do about it, though. She nodded to him. "Let's go."

Her body armor made her top-heavy. She almost fell when she went down the ramp. The officer steadied her. He had to be used to wearing the stuff. The soldiers and the armored car were already heading toward where the manor would be. The distant skyline looked the same as it did when she set out from the home timeline. Someone had taken Madrid away, though.

Someone took away my freedom, she thought angrily. Now she had the chance to help make sure that wouldn't happen to anybody else. She hurried along with the lieutenant colonel.

Jacques was digging out the roadbed when one of the men who spoke Dumnorix's language screamed. He hadn't hurt himself—it wasn't that kind of scream. He stared off to the east, his blue eyes open wider than any eyes Jacques had ever seen. "A monster!" he shrieked, and ran back towards the manor.

He wasn't the only one who ran. Jacques felt like running himself. The monster looked something like what he imagined an elephant would look like. At least, that long snout reminded him of an elephant's trunk, even if it was at the top middle of the thing and not at the front. But shouldn't a trunk be wiggly? This was stiff and still, almost like . . . the barrel of a cannon?

When that thought occurred to him, he also noticed the thing had wheels, not legs. But it moved by itself, without horses or mules or oxen to pull it. And it moved faster than animals could have hauled it. How was that possible?

He glanced over to the guards. They could do all kinds of things he hadn't thought possible. What did they make of this— mechanical?—monster? It wasn't strange to them. He saw that right away. He also saw all of them looking as if they'd just been kicked in the belly. They didn't think the monster was good news, not even a little bit.

Their horrified expressions made hope blossom inside Jacques. Khadija had said her own people would think the guards and the masters were criminals. She'd said her own people could take care of them, too. She'd sounded as if she knew what she was talking about. And maybe she did. Maybe she did!

Men came forward along with the monster. For a bad moment, Jacques feared they were more guards, for they wore mottled clothing, too. Did the elephant with wheels belong to the people who ran the manor, then? The guards didn't think so. That was plain. And then he saw that the newcomers didn't use quite the same kind of mottling. Theirs was a little browner than the guards', with smaller, more jagged splotches. Did that mean they served a different lord?

It evidently did. One of the guards raised his musket to his shoulder and fired several shots in the direction of the wheeled elephant. The soldiers coming up with it all threw themselves to the ground. When they lay flat, they almost disappeared against the dirt and bushes.

A couple of those bullets made sparks clang off the horseless cart. *So it's armored in iron, is it?* Jacques thought. That was clever. And it spat fire at the guards—not from the cannon, but from a smaller gun next to it that Jacques hadn't even noticed.

He ducked down when bullets started cracking past. At least he'd been under gunfire before. A lot of the slaves hadn't, and had no idea what to do. When the shooting stopped, Jacques cautiously looked up. Sure as the devil, one of the slaves was hurt. He lay on the ground clutching his leg and howling. The wound didn't look too bad. Jacques was glad to see that, anyhow.

Two guards were also down. One had a wound not much different from the slave's. He was swearing in French, which surprised Jacques. He hadn't thought anybody here but Khadija spoke his language. This was a funny dialect, much more nasal than the one Jacques used, but it was French.

The other guard was the one who'd fired at the strangers. He'd taken a bullet in the face, and was dead as an old boot.

What might have been the voice of God—if God were a woman—came from the armored cart. It shouted in several different languages. One of them was a French that sounded like the dialect the guard used. She called on the guards to surrender if they knew what was good for them. As if to underline that, the cannon roared. Its shell went wide, but it went wide on purpose, as if to say it didn't have to.

Jacques would have surrendered after that. And so did the guards. They lay down their muskets and put up their hands. The strangers in jagged mottling hurried up to take charge of them. Several of those soldiers were women. Jacques didn't realize it till they spoke—the armor hid their shape, and most of the men were clean-shaven. The women seemed as tough and capable as their male counterparts. That was one more boulder of amazement piled on a mountainside of wonders.

Then one of the newcomers called Jacques' name. He stared. In that splotched set of trousers and tunic, under that helmet was . . . "Khadija!"

He ran over to her and gave her a hug. She didn't feel like a girl. She had armor on under the clothes. He didn't care. He kissed her on the cheek. He'd never kissed anybody in a helmet before. "You see?" she said in his dialect of French. "I made it!"

"You sure did," Jacques answered. "And you brought your friends." She nodded. He asked, "What happens next?"

"We give all these people what they deserve." She looked at the dead guard without flinching. "And we free the slaves. How does that sound?"

"Wonderful!" Jacques said.

Thirteen

Annette was getting sick and tired of hotels. To her, the one in Madrid wasn't much different from those where she'd stayed in the USA. Her room was a little smaller than she would have had back home. The light switches were low and flat—they didn't stick up so much. The bathroom held an extra piece of equipment. But a bed was a bed, a TV was a TV, a computer hookup was a computer hookup all over the world. Just another room. To her.

To Jacques, whose room was right across the hall, it was more like a miracle, or a series of miracles. Crosstime Traffic had decided they weren't going to send him back to his old alternate. He knew too much for that. They hadn't decided what they *would* do with him. Maybe let him settle in the home timeline. Right now, though, he didn't know nearly enough for that.

Everything here seemed strange to him. Annette found herself being his tutor. She had to show him how to make the running water work. She had to explain—gently—that it was customary to bathe every day, or something close to it, even if he wasn't doing hard work.

"Why?" Jacques asked in honest bewilderment. "You people don't stink. I'm in the middle of a great big city, and it doesn't stink."

"We don't stink *because* we bathe," she said. There were other reasons, too, of course. She'd also had to explain how to use the toilet. The hotel had to throw away a wastebasket, but she couldn't blame Jacques for that. It was the closest thing to a chamber pot he could find.

And she'd had to show him how to use a fork. He thought that was funny. "Some of the snooty nobles in the Kingdom of Versailles use them," he said. "They want to make like they're as fancy as the Muslims down south. I never thought the likes of me would need to worry about such foolishness."

"It's our custom here. People would talk if you used your fingers," Annette said. "I'm not telling you it's better or worse. I'm just saying it's how you fit in." He nodded. He could see that. He was pretty sharp. And she knew he took it more seriously because she was the one telling him.

There were other complications. Before long, Jacques found out her real name was Annette, not Khadija. He could understand why she used a false one in his alternate. But he jumped to the wrong conclusion. "Then you're really a Christian after all!" he said happily.

"Well, no," Annette told him. "I'm really a Jew." She waited to see what would happen next. People in the Kingdom of Versailles took anti-Semitism as much for granted as people in this Kingdom of Spain took eating with a fork.

He stared at her. "You're joking," he said.

"No. I'm not. It's important for you to understand that I'm not," Annette said. "People here can believe anything they want, most places. We find that works better. We still have quarrels about religion, but fewer than we used to."

"But this Spain is a Christian country, isn't it? I've seen the cathedrals, even if you don't know about Henri." Jacques sounded sad. He'd seen that nobody in the home timeline knew about God's Second Son, but he didn't like it.

"This Spain is mostly a Christian country, yes. But it's not against the law to be a Jew or a Muslim or anything else here. You don't even have to pay a special tax or anything. As long as you don't cause trouble, you can believe whatever you please."

"Oh," he said. She watched him weighing that. She watched him not caring for it very much. He put what troubled him into words: "I didn't mind so much when I thought you were a Muslim. Muslims are wrong, but they're strong, too. Jews aren't just wrong—they're weak."

Part of Annette wanted to take a vase off the end table and bash him over the head with it. She understood he didn't know any better. Even so . . . As patiently as she could, she said, "You're judging things by your own alternate. The only reason Jews aren't strong there is that it doesn't have very many of them." That was also partly true here, but she didn't want to complicate things.

She watched Jacques wrestle with it. "I never thought I could like a Jew," he said at last. "All I ever wanted to do was throw rocks at them. That's what they're for."

"Oh?" Annette raised an eyebrow. "How do you suppose they feel about that?"

He blinked. Plainly, wondering how Jews felt had never once occurred to him. Maybe he wouldn't care even after it did. There were still people who didn't care about those who weren't like them, even here in the home timeline. There were way too many of them, as a matter of fact. But Annette knew she couldn't stay friends with anybody like that.

"I don't suppose they'd like it very much, would they?" Jacques said after a long pause.

"No, I don't think so," Annette agreed, glad he'd seen that much. Maybe he could get beyond the prejudices he'd grown up with after all. She went on, "Most places here in the home timeline, it's against the law to discriminate because of religion or race or sex. We think those are good laws—they give everybody a fair chance."

"Race? What do you mean by race?" Jacques asked.

"What color you are." Annette smiled. The Kingdom of Versailles didn't have much racial trouble. How could it? Just about everybody in it was white.

"That's silly," Jacques said. "I didn't mind those Moors because they were black. They couldn't do anything about that. I didn't like it that they were Muslims, though. They could choose there, and they chose wrong."

One step forward, one step back, Annette thought. "Sometimes things that are different are just different, not right or wrong," she said again. "You can't *prove* anything about religions till after you're dead, and then you can't tell anybody else. We even have people who don't believe in God at all."

Jacques made the sign of the wheel. "Jesus and Henri! What do you do with them? Do you burn them or hang them or put them on the wheel or the cross or—?"

"We don't do anything to them," Annette broke in. "Nothing. As long as they don't hurt other people, they can believe—or not believe—whatever they want. They don't seem to be any worse, or any better, than Christians or Muslims or Jews, taken as a group. We think freedom to believe includes freedom not to believe."

"That's . . . very strange," Jacques said. "If you don't believe in God, how can you be good? If you don't think Anyone can punish you, why not cheat and rob and kill?"

Philosophers still wrestled with that one. Annette knew it. She also knew she was no philosopher herself. She gave a practical answer, not a philosophical one: "Because other people will punish you if you break the law."

"It doesn't seem like enough," Jacques said.

"It's what we've got," Annette told him. "Nothing works all the time, but this seems to work most of the time. One thing you've got to remember is, most of the Christians and Jews and Muslims here in the home timeline don't worry as much about what happens to them in the next world as people in your alternate do." She didn't say *everybody*. She talked about *most people*. Some of the exceptions over the past hundred years were pretty horrible.

Jacques scratched his head. She watched him think it through. At last, he said, "You have all these wonderful things. You have your wonderful machines. You have good health. You have plenty to eat. But when it comes to things that really matter, things of the spirit, are you any better off than we are?"

That was a serious question. "Some people will worry about those things no matter what. Some people *won't* worry about them no matter what," Annette said after some thought of her own. "We feel it's better if everybody is healthy and has enough to eat. That gives people a good start. What you do with it afterwards . . . Whether you want to worry about things of the spirit or you just want to live your life in this world, well, it's up to you. You have to make up your own mind."

It's up to you. You have to make up your own mind. More than anything else, that might have been the slogan of the strange new world in which Jacques found himself. In the Kingdom of Versailles, he'd had a place. Part of it came from what his family was. Part of it came from his service with the king. But he always had a good idea of where he stood, of who could tell him what to do (most people) and whom he could boss around (the rest).

Things were different here in what Annette called the home timeline. Part of that was because he was a stranger here. He didn't know the rules. He understood as much. Part of it, though, was because the rules were so much looser.

Christians and Muslims and Jews all worshiped in the same kingdom? They didn't try to kill one another very often. The country wasn't officially Christian or Muslim or—strange thought!—Jewish. Even the King of this Spain was nothing but a figurehead? The people chose their leaders? It struck him as one short step up from what went on in a peasant revolt, but it seemed to work.

Annette told him laws here didn't discriminate because of religion, and he saw it was so. She told him laws didn't discriminate because of race, and he saw that was so, too. He saw more different kinds of people in Spain and in the United States, her country, than he'd ever imagined, and they all seemed to be . . . people, treated pretty much the same. The United States didn't have a king at all. Now *that* was peculiar.

And she told him laws didn't discriminate because of sex, either. That also turned out to be so. He'd seen that some of the soldiers who shut down the manor were women. Women in the home timeline could be doctors or lawyers or artisans or whatever else they wanted to be. They got into politics. Some of them ran countries. The people under them obeyed them as if they were men.

It was all very confusing.

It was scary, too, maybe even scarier than going into battle. In battle, you had some idea of the kinds of things that could happen. Here, *everything* seemed up in the air. Jacques felt at home in only one setting in the home timeline.

When he testified before lawyers and a judge, he might almost have been back in the Kingdom of Versailles. Before he even started testifying, he had to take an oath before God to tell the truth. From some of the things Annette said, he gathered that was a formality here. It meant they could charge you with a crime if they caught you lying. Jacques really meant it. The authorities here didn't worry him so much. The idea that God was looking down and listening to what he said did.

Everything was formal in courts. Things weren't the same here as they were in the Kingdom of Versailles, but they weren't all that different. You could tell the courts were two branches growing off the same tree. If what Annette said was true, his whole world and this one were like that—and he had no reason to doubt her. But the worlds as a whole had grown much farther apart than their courts had.

Sometimes people questioned him in the French they spoke here. He could mostly understand it, and they could mostly follow him when he answered. A couple of them, though, went to the trouble of learning the French they spoke in his Kingdom of Versailles. Like Annette, they spoke it as well as he did. Maybe they spoke it better than he did, because they sounded more educated.

"Learning languages is easy for us," Annette told him during a recess at a court somewhere in the United States. "We have these implants." She touched her head behind her left ear. "They can connect our brains to a machine that puts the language in there like *that*." She snapped her fingers.

"That's how you speak French and Arabic so well," Jacques said.

"Sure it is." Her smile lifted only one corner of her mouth. "I found out how hard it is without implants when I had to learn to talk with Emishtar. Her language was related to Arabic, the way French and Spanish are related to each other, but it still wasn't easy."

"I saw her a couple of days ago," Jacques said. "The same court that was questioning me was going to ask her things, too.

Was that here or back in Spain? I have trouble remembering. I've flown back and forth too many times now."

"People who grow up in the home timeline say things like that," Annette said. "See how well you're starting to fit in?"

She was joking. He knew it, but couldn't help answering seriously: "I don't know if I'll ever fit in here. I can feel how far from home I am. Is Emishtar going to stay here, too?"

That made Annette stop joking. "Maybe she'll try," she answered slowly. "If you think this world is hard for you to get used to, though, it's a lot harder for her."

"She's older than we are," Jacques said. "She's probably older than both of us put together. That makes her more set in her ways than we are."

"That's part of it," Annette agreed, "but that's only part of it. Your alternate is different from the home timeline, Jacques—"

"I'll say it is!" he broke in.

"Yours is different, but hers is a lot more different," Annette said. "Your people know about gunpowder. You have Christians and Muslims and Jews. Her people still use bows and arrows. There was no Roman Empire in her alternate, so nobody like Jesus ever lived there. Christianity never happened. And without Christianity, Islam wouldn't happen, either."

"You don't say anything about Jews," Jacques said.

"Maybe there are Jews there. We don't know that alternate very well yet," Annette said. "Judaism got started before that world and the home timeline separated. But if there are, they'll have different ideas from ours about what being a Jew means."

"Are they really Jews, then?" Jacques asked. "Are the Christians in this home timeline really Christians? How can they be? They don't know anything about Henri."

"That's a good question," Annette told him. "It depends on how you look at things. People in the home timeline would won-

der if the Christians in your alternate are really Christians. They
would say you added Henri to your faith, not that we don't know
him here. Christians in most alternates have beliefs more like
ours than like yours, because Henri didn't become God's Second
Son in them."

"But Henri *is* the Second Son!" Jacques exclaimed. "The
way you make it sound, the only reason we have Henri and other,
uh, alternates don't is because the dice turned up with four sixes
for us and with different throws for the rest of them."

To his dismay, Annette (whom he still wanted to think of as
Khadija) nodded. "What other reason is there?"

"Because God gave Henri to us," Jacques said stubbornly.

"Well, I can't prove God didn't do that," Annette said, and
Jacques felt a little better. But then she asked, "How can you
show God did do it, though? And why did He do it that way in
your alternate but not in the others?"

He started to tell her the Final Testament proved what God
had done. He feared he knew what she would say if he did. The
Final Testament was a thing of his alternate, not a thing of all the
alternates. Unhappily, he asked, "Is this why some people in this
alternate don't believe in God?"

"Maybe some," Annette answered. "People have all kinds of
reasons for believing or not believing, though. Why they do, why
they don't—that's not simple."

"Nothing here is simple." Jacques wished Annette would
tell him he was wrong. She didn't. She just nodded again.

When Annette talked with Emishtar, they used the same mix of
Arabic and her language as they had while they were slaves. Nobody in the home timeline knew Emishtar's tongue well enough
yet to prepare a scan Annette could learn through her implant.

"When I come here, I think you people must be gods or devils," Emishtar said. "You have carts that go by themselves. You fly through the air like birds. You have pictures that talk. You make it hot when you want. You make it cold when you want. You have so much food. You have the thing that keeps the food fresh. You have the medicine to make my teeth stop hurting. I think they never stop, but you make them stop. You kill my lice, too."

"We're only people," Annette said. They had both just testified against a Crosstime Traffic official in Seattle. So had Bridget Mallory. Annette continued, "We know how to do things your people don't, that's all. It doesn't make us better or worse—only stronger." Stronger was hard enough. They could blow up the world. They hadn't for the past century and a half, but they could.

"I see it," Emishtar said. "People act like people. Not just like my people—you have different customs, different gods, uh, god—but people. Some good, some bad, some wise, some foolish. People with strength of gods or devils."

She had no idea what people in the home timeline had done to one another. Maybe she was lucky. "What do you think about living here?" Annette asked.

Her friend shrugged. "I don't know. To learn a language . . ."

With an implant, learning to speak and understand would be easy. She would have to learn to read and write, though, too, to become fully a part of the home timeline.

"I would have to learn about your strange god," Emishtar went on. "Only one? For everything? It seems foolish. And many of your customs are so strange. Maybe I just go home again."

Annette wasn't sure Emishtar could do that. The authorities might keep her away from her own alternate because she knew so much more than she should. Crosstime Traffic tried to interfere with the other alternates as little as it could while it did business with them. Those were the rules, anyhow.

Annette's mouth twisted. Quite a few Crosstime Traffic people hadn't played by the rules. Spanish authorities were still trying to figure out how they'd got an illicit transposition chamber.

All sorts of governments were looking at Crosstime Traffic more closely these days. By the nature of what it did, the company was the most multinational of all multinationals. It had to have tentacles all over the world to travel to the most interesting and profitable spots in other alternates.

Up till now, Crosstime Traffic hadn't faced a lot of regulation. It was the engine that drove the home timeline's prosperity. Nobody'd wanted even to pluck a pinfeather from the goose that brought home so many golden eggs.

But if Crosstime Traffic people went into business for themselves, if they took slaves and became masters, if they let other twisted people from the home timeline play at being slaves (Annette thought of Bridget Mallory and shivered) . . . If they did all those things—and they did—maybe (no, certainly) they needed to be watched more closely.

Emishtar tapped Annette on the arm. Even in ordinary clothes, the woman with the crooked front teeth looked out of place in the courtroom waiting room. The way she sat, the way she looked around, said she wasn't used to the furniture or to the fluorescent panels in the ceiling.

"If you have to come to my village for the rest of your days," she said, "could you do that? Would you want to do that?"

"I . . . could," Annette said. "Would I want to? No. I have to say, we have so many more things than you do, I would not be happy there."

"It is for me like the other side of a plate," Emishtar said.

"You have too many things. I do not know what to do with them. I do not see how I can ever learn."

"You are new here," Annette said. "You may change your mind when you learn more about the way we do things. You may decide you like not working as hard as you did. You may decide you like having enough to eat all the time."

"What would I do here? How would I earn my food?" Emishtar asked.

"Teaching us about your people and your alternate would make a good start, I think," Annette answered. "We have a lot of bad things to fix there. You grew up there. You know more about it than we do."

"I would rather farm," Emishtar said.

Farming here was an industry. She didn't understand that. "We use machines to farm in the home timeline," Annette said. "We don't do it the way they did where you grew up." She pictured oxen pulling, men with digging sticks, and others with hoes—an even more primitive way of doing things than they'd had at the manor.

But Emishtar was picturing what she'd known all her life till the slave raiders took her. "If I cannot go where I want to go, if I cannot do what I want to do, am I not still a slave here?" she asked bitterly.

Annette found no answer at all for her.

Jacques rubbed at the skin behind his left ear. He could feel something hard under there. It wasn't much, though—it couldn't have been the size of a grain of barley. Somehow, that little thing connected with his brain, and with the thinking machines they had here. He spoke and understood English now, just about as well as if he'd been born knowing it.

Khadija—no, he had to remember she was really Annette—
had told him getting the implant wouldn't hurt much. He'd had
trouble believing her. They were cutting his head open, after all.
But she'd been right. A sting like a fleabite from a needle—the
same sort of needle they'd used at the manor—and then he'd
gone numb. The doctors did what they did. He didn't feel it. It
did hurt a little when the numbness wore off. They gave him pills
that pushed the pain far away.

The pills made him a little woozy. "They remind me of the
way poppy juice makes you feel," he told Annette.

She gave him an odd look. "They're made from poppy juice,"
she said. "They have other things in them, but that's a big part."

He laughed, which he probably wouldn't have done if not for
the pills. "That's funny," he said. "I thought you would have your
own fancy things here."

"We have other things that fight pain," Annette said. "But
the medicines we get from poppy juice work well. Why shouldn't
we use them?"

He'd needed to heal up before they could give him their language. From what Annette said, the implant was making connec-
tions inside his head during that time. He almost wished she
hadn't told him that. He thought of it like a spider, with legs
reaching out to weave a web. . . . He didn't suppose it *was* like
that, but that was how he thought of it.

She drove him to what they called a learning center to get his
dose of English. Riding in cars fascinated him. Here he was,
smoothly gliding along faster than a horse could gallop. It was
cold outside, but the car had its own heater. And people could
buy these marvels more easily than a man bought a sword back
in the Kingdom of Versailles.

"Could I learn to drive one?" he asked as they pulled into
the open space around the learning center. It had lines painted

on the smooth blackness to show where the cars should stop. He thought that was very clever.

"Yes," she answered. "But you can't learn that through an implant. You have to learn by doing. And you have to be careful. These cars go fast. If they smash into each other, it can be very bad."

He'd seen a few accidents. They did look bad. But he liked the idea of going so fast. Well, that would have to wait for now. Into the learning center he and Annette went.

One of the people there greeted him in English. That was funny, since English was what he'd come to learn. Annette spoke to the person, a woman, who picked up a telephone. Jacques knew what it did even if he didn't understand how. A man came out of another room. He spoke to Jacques in what the home timeline used for French: "Let me see your identification, please."

"Yes, my lord." Jacques took out the little plastic rectangle. It had a picture of him, his name, and a bunch of thick and thin black lines only one of the machines here could read. From what Annette said, you weren't real in the home timeline without your identification.

"I'm not 'my lord.' I'm just a technician," the man said. That meant something like *artisan*, Jacques gathered. The man fed the card into a machine. Words came up on a screen—a *monitor*, they called it. The man studied them. He eyed Jacques. "So Crosstime Traffic is picking up the bill for this, *n'est-ce pas?*"

"That's right," Annette said in the French of the Kingdom of Versailles. The technician nodded, so he could understand her. "He's one of the people who got rescued. Without him, there might not have been any rescue."

"I see." The man eyed Jacques. "You did well there, young fellow, if that's true. What do you think of the home timeline?"

"So far, it's mostly confusing," Jacques answered. The man

and Annette both laughed, though he meant it. He went on, "I hope I'll fit in better once I understand the language."

"Well, it can't hurt," the technician said. "Come along with me. Since you're not from here, maybe your, ah, friend should come, too."

"Yes, I'll come," Annette said. "Jacques and I *are* friends." The technician smiled. Did that mean he wondered if they were more than friends? Back in the Kingdom of Versailles, it would have. Jacques wouldn't have minded. Maybe if he spoke English, Annette wouldn't think of him the way he thought of the savages in the new lands across the sea.

He was in those lands across the sea now. He hadn't seen any savages. People from Europe had known about these lands for centuries here. He supposed they'd conquered the natives and wiped them out. Winners did that to losers in his alternate. Why would it be any different here?

The technician sat him down in a chair that was halfway to being a couch. The man fiddled with a machine behind Jacques' head, and then put something that felt—cold?—above the implant. "Making the connection," he said. Jacques followed the words, but didn't know what they meant. "Are you ready?" the technician asked.

"I guess so," Jacques answered.

He heard a click. Annette spoke in a low voice: "It will be very strange for a little while. Don't worry. It's supposed to feel that way."

And then he was . . . invaded. That was the only word he could think of. He was invaded from the inside out. He could sense not just the new words but the whole shape and feel of English rushing into his head. The pieces seemed to look around and find homes alongside the French and the Arabic and the bits of Breton he already knew.

His head felt very crowded. That was the only word he could find for what was going on in there. And then, all of a sudden, it didn't matter any more. All of a sudden, everything felt the way it was supposed to again.

"How you doing?" the technician asked him.

"I'm okay," Jacques replied. "Boy, that was weird." His mouth fell open. The man in the white coat had asked the question in English. Not only did Jacques understand it, he answered in the same language. He'd felt it going in, but he hadn't imagined it could come out so easily. "Boy, that was *really* weird," he said, still in English.

Annette spoke in the French of the Kingdom of Versailles: "I felt the same way when I learned this speech. I felt filled too full too fast. Everybody does at first."

Filled too full too fast. Jacques found himself nodding. That fit what had just happened to him, all right. "It's better now," he said in English. He didn't have any trouble making the sounds. When he spoke Arabic, anyone could tell he was someone who'd grown up speaking French and then learned a new language. With English, though, he might have been raised in this Ohio province.

And he could *think* in English. He was thinking in English. When he spoke Arabic, he thought in French and translated what he wanted to say. Here, it was as if he suddenly had a new map for the land inside his head. It seemed to be a more detailed map, too. English had more words, more *ideas*, in it than his French did. It was a better language for splitting hairs. The home timeline seemed to have more hairs to split, too.

"Is everything all right?" Annette asked the technician. "Can I take him home?"

The man eyed a couple of monitors. "It all looks good," he answered. "If he has any kind of problem—anything at all—

bring him back. We'll analyze his synapses. If we have to, we'll
run the course again."

"Thanks," Annette said. "Come on, Jacques."

"Sure," he said. Synapses. He knew what the word meant:
the way signals in his brain passed from one nerve cell to another. In his French, he hadn't even known there were cells in
his brain. He had thoughts in his French. In English, he understood *how* he had them. He hadn't just learned a language. He'd
learned a different way of looking at the world.

Cold bit his nose and stung his cheeks when he walked outside. An enormous flock of starlings flew by overhead. They reminded him of the Kingdom of Versailles. When he said so,
Annette made a sour face. "The Kingdom of Versailles is welcome to them. They didn't used to live here. Two hundred years
ago, a crazy Englishman brought 120 of them across the Atlantic
and turned them loose. Millions and millions of them live here
now. They're miserable pests, is what they are."

As if to prove the point, white droppings splashed her car.
She said something in English he wouldn't have understood an
hour earlier. It made him blush now. So did another thought. "I
have been brought here, too, from a far country," he said. "I hope
I will not be a pest."

Annette squeezed his hand. "I expect you'll fit in just fine,
Jacques," she said, and winked at him. "Besides, there aren't
millions and millions of you. It only seems that way sometimes."

"Thanks a lot," he said. Laughing, he got into the car.
Laughing, Annette drove him home. And he did feel like someone who was at least starting to fit in pretty well.

Annette sat in a courtroom in Albuquerque. The man about to be
sentenced was one of the masters at the manor. He'd also been a

leading Crosstime Traffic security official. "Do you have any state-ment to make, Mr. Degrelle, before receiving your punishment?"

"Yes, your Honor." In a suit and tie, Degrelle looked like anybody else. What he'd done didn't stand out in letters of fire on his forehead. Annette thought it should have. He sounded like anyone else, too, as he went on, "I didn't mean any harm. I don't think any of us meant any harm. The people there"—he didn't call them slaves—"had better food and medicine than if they'd stayed in their own alternates."

His lawyer nodded. Degrelle's wife and children were in the courtroom. They nodded, too. They didn't want to see him going to jail for years. Annette didn't suppose she could blame them, though she didn't agree with them. From what she'd read, the of-ficers at the German death camps in World War II had families that loved them, too, in spite of what they'd done. She'd thought that was a sickness out of the past. She seemed to be wrong.

The prosecutor got to her feet. She was a little gray-haired woman who looked like somebody's grandmother. She probably was. But fury crackled in her voice as she said, "May it please the court, but 'I didn't mean any harm' from Mr. Degrelle is like a plea for mercy from a man who killed his parents on the grounds that he is an orphan. Evidence at this trial shows he and his followers killed slaves who tried to rebel, to make themselves free. It shows they treated female slaves in a way that shows they forgot about the past 250 years of our history. And it shows they bought slaves and took slaves. And they betrayed the trust Crosstime Traffic had in them. They did it for no better reason than that they enjoyed the feeling of power they got by oppressing—by *owning*—other human beings. Mr. Degrelle de-serves to be punished to the full extent of the law."

"We have one of the people most closely connected to this

case here with us today," the judge said. He found Annette with his eyes. "Miss Klein, will you please come to the microphone?"

"Yes, your Honor." Annette walked up to the lectern. Cameras followed her. She didn't like standing there in front of the whole world and talking. Who would have? But she'd done so much testifying, it didn't terrify her the way it would have a few months before.

"I am obliged to hear you before I sentence Mr. Degrelle," the judge said. "I am not obliged to take what you say into account in the sentencing. I may, but I am not obliged to. Do you understand?"

"Yes, your Honor," Annette said again. "Mr. Degrelle and the people under him didn't give me food and medicine that were better than what I would have got in my own alternate. They didn't know I was from the home timeline, of course. They probably would have killed me to keep my mouth shut if they had."

Degrelle's lawyer stirred. The judge waved him to silence. Annette could say what she thought now, not just what she knew to be true. The judge nodded to her to go on.

"They treated us like things," she said. "Like *things*. They bought us—they bought *me*. We could have been so many used cars, for all they cared. And they used us like cars. No, it was worse than that, in fact. They could have done so much more with machines, if that was what they wanted. But it wasn't. They wanted to lord it over us, to have fun being in charge of other people. I don't know much about the law, your Honor, but I know that's wrong."

A few other people spoke. Jacques and Emishtar were testifying at other trials halfway around the world. Crosstime Traffic officials agreed with Annette. Even though they did, she couldn't help wondering if they were tainted, too. Lots of people would be wondering about Crosstime Traffic officials for years to come—one more thing the slave ring had done.

Character witnesses for Degrelle said he was a very nice man when he wasn't being a slavemaster. That wasn't how they said it, but that was what it amounted to.

The judge listened to everyone. Then he sentenced the master to life in prison, with the possibility of parole after twenty-five years. Degrelle's shoulders slumped. His family burst into tears.

Annette didn't know what she felt. Part of her wished they'd thrown away the key. But he was going away for a long, long time, and he'd never have the chance to do anything like that again. It could have been worse.

It could have been worse. That was one of those adult phrases, one that meant it was as good as it was going to get and you were stuck with it. The more of those phrases she understood, the more of her childhood she left behind. She walked out of the courtroom. She still had a lot of growing in front of her.